THE WICKER LIGHT

MARY WATSON

BLOOMSBURY

LONDON OXFORD NEW YORK NEW DELHI SYDNEY

BLOOMSBURY YA
Bloomsbury Publishing Plc
50 Bedford Square, London WC1B 3DP, UK

BLOOMSBURY, BLOOMSBURY YA and the Diana logo
are trademarks of Bloomsbury Publishing Plc

First published in Great Britain in 2019 by Bloomsbury Publishing Plc

A catalogue record for this book is available from the British Library

ISBN: PB: 978-1-4088-8491-1; eBook: 978-1-4088-8492-8

2 4 6 8 10 9 7 5 3 1

Typeset by RefineCatch Limited, Bungay, Suffolk

Printed and bound in Great Britain by CPI Group (UK) Ltd, Croydon, CR0 4YY

To find out more about our authors and books visit www.bloomsbury.com
and sign up for our newsletters

THE WICKER LIGHT

For my boys. Stay free.

BEFORE THE BEGINNING
An apostrophe

Ten years earlier

David

She doesn't remember that first time we met, down our field where she played her game of sticks and stones. How she squatted on the mulched leaves, dark hair falling over her shoulders.

I'd asked the girl what she was doing. I was tired of Oisín's games, of always playing sidekick to his hero. Oisín's games that usually involved hard fists on my arms and stomach.

'Reading.'

'Leaves aren't for reading.'

I heard Dad in the mocking tone of my voice. The way Dad spoke when he wasn't sure of something. When he knew he might be wrong.

'I read them.'

She moved one of the leaves from a cracked twig as if this made everything clearer.

It was just a child's game, the muck and leaves and twigs. Just a no one girl from the village who looked like she hadn't seen a soaped-up washcloth in days. But the way she sat. Her fierce concentration.

'Tell me,' I said, crouching beside her. I was bigger, but she acted older. 'What are you reading?'

'It's a story,' she said. 'An apostrophe.'

I looked at her in confusion but she was pointing down. 'This family is broken. That's the daddy.' A mottled leaf near a twig. 'And he's destroyed. Because of greed.'

'And the mammy?'

Against my will, I was drawn in. The sticks seemed to take on form. Shadow figures planted in the earth. I could almost hear them whispering, like in the old days when trees and wind and water spoke to us. I examined the girl, curious.

'Bleeding. But not from cuts.' The girl ran a finger along a stick lying flat near a mossy rock. 'She bleeds in her heart and it will kill her quietly and slowly. The mammy will be dead a long time before she knows she is.

'The brother, also ruined.' She pointed to the broken twig, 'After being made to pay for it all.'

'And this one?' I touch the only stick standing, planted in the earth.

'That's the one who caused it all. That's the one who

destroyed them.' She looked at me from beneath her lashes. 'That's you.'

I recoiled from the girl. She brushed hair from her eyes, streaking more muck on her face.

Just a game.

But for a second it wasn't mulch on the lake shoreline and I floundered. It was more like a law where each item had real power. But this child wasn't one of us, she wasn't judge. She couldn't know the power of words or how to form a law.

I kicked at the leaves and sticks and then I stepped on them to be sure. A twig cracked beneath my shoe.

'Wait,' she said.

I turned, scrabbling away.

'I haven't told you how it all turns out.'

But she had. Ruin and destruction. All my fault.

As I ran, I could hear Dad's laughter echoing through my head. Running along the lake, I imagined the silent stares of Mamó and Oisín observing my weakness. Afraid of a little girl.

I was out of breath when I crashed through the trees between the shoreline and the Rookery. My knees were bloodied and my face scratched. My palms were grazed, with gravel embedded in the skin.

That day, I swore I would never run from a girl again.

How could I, second son of Jarlath Creagh, thirteen generations of fearsome garraíodóirí, be afraid of a skinny child playing in muck?

I ran up behind the house, too close to Mamó's cottage.

Mistake. I should have gone around, and come in through the front drive. Mamó was outside, examining the flowers on the path.

'Davey.' Mamó's voice was like skidding on small stones.

My feet were rooted to the ground. I wasn't sure which was worse: Mamó or Dad finding me like this. If I was lucky, it would have been Mammy with her soft pale hair. She would have pulled me into her arms and cooed and lied.

Mamó was a statue. A single disfigured finger crooked to summon me.

'What's wrong?'

My feet walked towards her as if compelled. Mamó always said magic, proper magic that was silver and shiny, was stuck. That we made do with grey magic, slow and plodding, or blue magic, rare and hard to come by, because silver was blocked to us.

But sometimes, and for some people, it seemed the silver magic leaked out. That some people had found, mined, stolen, hoarded silver, and for them the usual rules didn't apply. If anyone had siphoned silver it was Mamó. My father's mother.

'What happened?' she said again as I stared at her black slacks. Mamó always dressed smart, even when she was tending her flower beds. And always in black. To remind everyone that she's supposed to be descended from the Badb Catha, the Crow-Mother and goddess of battle.

'I fell.'

Her bony hand with its twisted fingers clutched my shoulder. It probably hurt her more than it did me.

'Don't lie to me.'

I felt tears pricking. But she couldn't see me cry. I swallowed hard to get rid of the wedge in my throat.

'You can lie to your soft, spoilt mammy. You can lie to your stronger, meaner brother. Lie to your daddy, if you dare. But don't even try lying to me.'

'There was a girl.' My voice was weak and choked.

'Speak up, Davey.'

'There was a girl. I think she is a witch.'

'No such thing as witches.' Mamó held on to my shoulder, leaning over me and clutching tighter than those twisted fingers could surely manage. The smell of cigarettes clung to her turtleneck jumper.

'It was just a stupid girl,' I said, fighting tears. 'Playing a game. She pretended she could read things in the mulch.'

'The mulch?' Mamó said. 'What did she say?'

'That our family was destroyed.' I shut my big mouth

5

from saying that it was me who destroyed them all. 'Every one of us dead or ruined. It was like she could tell the future through the stones.'

'Did the rooks complain?'

'No.' I sounded sullen. 'She was just a stupid girl from the village.'

Mamó let go of my shoulder. She looked out across the garden, thinking.

'Nothing to worry about,' she said eventually. 'But mind that girl.'

'Yes, Mamó.' I started walking away.

'Davey,' Mamó called me. 'Remember what I told you. How must you deal with something that threatens you?'

'Make sure it doesn't,' I said, the smell of cigarette smoke and roses making me feel sick. 'Contain the threat.'

'What else?'

'Always turn the threat back on itself.'

'That's right. Be sure that you're the threat, Davey. Never the prey.'

But how, I wanted to ask her.

'If that little girl likes games so much,' Mamó said, holding my eye, 'make sure she plays one with your rules.'

And she was done with me. Mamó turned back to her flowers, checking the roses for signs of disease.

ONE
For Laila

Last night I squeezed through the back hedge and
into the field behind.
LAS

Zara

It's evening and Dad is in the downstairs bathroom. The
scrape of his razor against skin is both familiar and strange:
it's been years since I've watched him shave. Through the
door, the edge of his arm moves in a careful downward
stroke. His eyes, dark with grief, appraise his reflection.

'Dad?' I push the door open. Rinsing, he startles slightly.

'Zara.' He speaks to the me in the mirror. The smell of
his shaving oil is thick in the small room.

'You going out?' I hate that I sound so afraid.

'There's a work thing on.' He rubs his jaw. I wait a
moment, wanting to ask more: what kind of work thing?
Who else is going? But these are not my questions to ask.

'Where's Mom?'

'Upstairs. Sorting.' Dad is cleaning up the sink, packing his things in a little bag which he stashes in the drawer. 'Tell her I had to run.' He pulls on a shirt hanging from the door.

He's halfway to the front door when I summon the nerve. 'Seriously?'

He doesn't look back as he pauses at the door. 'I'm late, Zara.'

He waits a beat, and I'm thinking: late for whom?

I'm thinking: coward, he won't even tell Mom himself.

The door slams, emphasising the quiet.

I hate this house. I hate that after ten months of living here, it still feels new. I hate its modern cookie-cutter design, replicated by the two houses next door, both abruptly empty since January. I hate how it squats like a trespasser beside the gates to a large estate, the Rookery. I hate how we have become while living in it.

I hate most that it's where Laila was last with us.

'Dad gone out?' Adam appears in the doorway to the kitchen. This is how we live now, scuttling in the shadows from one room to another, hoping we don't have to engage.

'Yeah. Work, he said.'

No girl should think about her father heading into the city like this. No girl should think of her father in a restaurant, his gaze on an unknown woman, probably with red lipstick, on the other side of a candle. Or maybe in a booth in some hip, too-young place, his hand settled on the inside of a thigh. Sheer tights and high heels.

Adam hasn't yet learned to hide what he's feeling. His fear makes him look younger than his fifteen years and I wish so hard that Laila were here with us.

'I'm heading out.' He's defiant, but it's unnecessary. There was a time someone would have stopped him. Checked on his homework. But if Mom's sorting things, she won't notice.

'Don't do anything stupid,' I warn him. 'You know she's looking for an excuse.'

He leaves and I'm alone in the passage, thinking about Dad's work thing.

The door to the room at the top of the stairs is open. Laila's room. But she's not there.

We lost Laila long before we buried her ashes. Even in those months before she died, she wasn't really with us. Laila seemed to fade out slowly, every day a little less present until one day she wasn't there.

They found her that cold March morning on the village green. I imagine her staring up to the morning sky with unseeing eyes, her cream faux fur spread beneath her.

They'd thought she'd fallen asleep, maybe taken some pills, maybe too much to drink. A fleeting mistake because they knew within seconds that she was dead: the fixed gaze, her right arm bent to touch her heart. No blood, no bruising. And later, doctors searched beneath her skin, examining her from the inside out and finding only a riddle. There is no reason why she should have died that morning. It was like someone had flipped an off switch and Laila just stopped. Then dropped down to the frost-covered grass, eyes to the sky.

Upstairs, Mom's on Laila's bed with the contents of the middle drawer dumped on the pale blue covers. But her sorting never achieves anything. Laila's clothes are still in the wardrobe, her desk stacked with textbooks.

On the wall is a giant corkboard with photographs of Laila smiling, Laila in the woods. A study plan, in bright colours, for the Leaving Cert exams she'll never sit.

Mom picks up the charm bracelet she'd bought Laila for her eighteenth birthday.

'Did Dad get the dinner on?'

'Dad's not here.'

'He went out?' Mom falters a moment.

'Work,' I beg her to play along. 'Said he was running late.'

We'll pretend that Dad is at a work thing and there isn't anything to worry about. We've done it so many times, why stop now?

I don't tell her about the shaving downstairs. I don't tell her about the pungent oil or the trendy shirt I know cost stupid money.

Mom's eyes on Laila's bracelet are wide and fixed. She touches the crow charm.

'Is this new?' It's a black, ugly thing. Two black pearl eyes. Too big for the delicate gold bracelet.

I'd not noticed it before, but then I wasn't really looking. It doesn't belong with the gold heart, star and fish. It's wrong, somehow. It unsettles me in the way of a voodoo doll stuck with pins.

'Does it matter?' I say.

I get up from the bed and touch a picture of Laila laughing. The impossibility of it all, that she was here and laughing and now she's not and never can be, hits me like a fist in the gut. More precisely: it feels like someone has punched right through me, tearing through skin, fat and muscle, to wrench out my organs in their bloodied hand.

The picture is from just before March, because her hair is still long and the trees are beginning to bud. The resemblance between us is too close. Looking at photos of Laila is like looking into a distorted mirror. Her eyes are darker, the honey gold in her brown hair more pronounced.

Behind her is a massive grey house I don't recognise. How did I miss so much of her life? How is there so much I don't know?

'Pearls are for tears,' Mom says, looking at the crow's eyes. Mom is full of weird superstitions I don't entirely understand. They're from her childhood, passed down by her mother and aunts like some kind of arcane knowledge. Theirs is a bond formed by stories, by songs and recipes handed down generations. By women with soft cloth covering their hair, and henna-stained fingernails. The early morning call to prayer chanted through the wind. Stories of slave ancestors and curses, of boys who dance with swords, that make me shiver a little when I hear them.

Mom and Dad are not from here. She's from South Africa, and Dad was too, kind of, but he grew up in Australia. They met when he was visiting relatives, and he swept her off her feet. They settled in Dublin before we were born, when Dad got a job at the university. Mom's never fully made peace with what she'd left behind. And now she wants to go back, to her real home, and I won't let that happen.

This village was supposed to be our new beginning, not a place of endings. Last June, living in the city suburbs, Adam was in a dark place. Then Laila was caught with a mind-altering drug, and Dad with Lindy from Human Resources in an underground car park. We weren't supposed to know about Dad and Lindy from HR but of course we did. Mostly because she wasn't the first Lindy.

Mom had been furious. She'd had enough. It was the line in the sand, she'd said in a cold, detached voice. We were leaving. She was taking the three of us and starting over in a place I'd only visited a handful of times. Without him.

Adam and I were dead set against it, we didn't want to be so massively uprooted in our last years of school. Laila pretended not to care, mostly because turning eighteen, she could stay if she had a mind to work.

Dad begged for a second chance, arguing that Laila and Adam needed stability more than moving away or a hellish custody battle. We all piled in, resistant.

Fearful of our family splitting up, Mom was defeated and agreed to start over. One last chance. With an ironclad condition: that we move. Away from the city and its temptations. Her practice partner would buy her out, Dad would negotiate remote office days and we would focus on rebuilding our family.

We sold up and moved to this new build in a sweet village at the far edge of the commuter belt. Kilshamble. When Mom had said quiet, I hadn't realised that she meant the village at the end of world.

We barely see Dad, who commutes to the city with no remote office days. Mom tried doctoring part-time and baking bread in the afternoons. After two weeks of hard, tasteless loaves she was clamouring for more hours at Dr Kelly's practice.

And I'm half left behind, pining for my friends and a boy called Nathan. We moved to Kilshamble for a new beginning. Now Laila is dead, and Mom is hell-bent on finding proof that she died because of drugs. Mom blames herself. That if she hadn't given Dad another chance, we'd be far away and Laila would be alive.

'Leave this,' I say. Mom's hunched over the bright plastic accessories, utterly miserable.

She wraps Laila's charm bracelet around my wrist and I recoil. I don't want it.

'Will you wear this?' She pulls the hook on the clasp. 'For Laila?'

I'm frozen. I don't want the bracelet.

'She'd want you to have it.' Mom frowns at the crow as she clasps the bracelet around my wrist. 'Remove that one. I don't like it.'

Which makes me decide to keep the crow. I will wear the bracelet the way Laila did.

Looking down at Mom, her red-rimmed eyes and quiet desperation, I understand. She needs to know it's not her fault. That she didn't let Laila down.

You can't say sorry to ashes.

'I'm going to Cape Town.' She doesn't look at me as she puts Laila's things away. 'Next month. For a week. I need to do this alone.'

Which means she's going to investigate. To see how she could move us there.

If Mom keeps blaming herself, I'll be made to move far away no matter how much I resist.

It's not Mom's fault that Laila died. And it's not Mom who Laila reached out to that night. Who let Laila down.

It's not Mom who should be trying to atone, to fix things with Laila.

It's me.

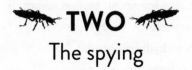

TWO

The spying

David

There are monsters in these woods. Dangerous creatures wait
and watch. The villagers warn of fearsome tree people, with
bark-covered skin and thick roping muscle. Beautiful and
deadly, they lure boys and girls into the deepest parts of the
forest. The victims fall in love with these exquisite monsters,
and this is what destroys them. Every kiss is a feed, every touch
a drain, until they are nothing more than shells. Or dead.

I'd rather be dead than a shell.

But these are stories. There are no tree people haunting
the woods. Real monsters have ordinary faces.

You wouldn't know if you see them in the supermarket.
You wouldn't know that this one, with his gang of friends,
hurt an older woman and tried to force her into his van. Or
that one betrayed his granddaughter in the most brutal way.

Here's the thing about the monsters in my world: they're
normal people living at a knife's edge, poised between
decent and depraved.

Raising my binoculars, I peer through the bifurcated trunk. Beyond the low hedge, thick with growth, is a bungalow with a small backyard.

This is the house where my favourite monsters live.

The yard is bare and barren. Just crumbled cement where barely a weed survives. Inside, the woman with wild curly hair is alone in her kitchen. Maeve, the worst of them all.

She looks up, like she can sense me hiding behind the tree. She peers out, eyes hard.

For Maeve, for those like her, I am monster.

She turns away. I guess the augurs don't expect anyone out here in this isolated part of the village. Maybe they believe their magic will alert them if the enemy is close. But their magic is weak, a dull glow fading in and out. Fortune tellers reading jumbled futures in the lines of a hand, half guessing, usually wrong. Dad says however much we've lost, they're worse off. That augur magic was never as strong as ours, even in the before times.

Through the window, Maeve dries dishes. This woman is shrewd, cunning and ruthless, beneath her apple-cheeked facade.

Without warning, she hurls the pan across the room. Her hands fly up to her eyes and press against them.

She's upset.

Good.

It's been more than two months since I started my watch. Since we discovered that augurs live here in the village, even though Kilshamble is our territory.

The door opens and I sink lower. Maeve rushes outside and for a second I think she's seen me through the exuberant summer growth. Her face is turned up to the sky, furious.

I feel a little nudge in my head. There's a word that's teasing, but it stays out of reach. It's making me antsy, this word I can't get a hold on.

'Mam?' The dark-haired girl, Sibéal, appears at the kitchen door.

Maeve wipes a hard hand over her eyes before turning to her daughter. I'm irritated. I'm not here for the tender moments or old lady breakdowns.

I'm here to find out what they're planning next. Dad thinks we've nothing to worry about, that the augurs played their hand and have now retreated. He thinks that stealing or damaging the sacred places that fuel our magic, our nemeta, is the only threat the augurs pose.

I don't believe it for a minute.

The augurs are up to something. It's there in their faces. It's there in the tight way they hold themselves, tension stiffening their shoulders, hunching their backs. In the cars that pull up in their drive, the meetings with other grove members that run late into the night as they lean over charts on Maeve's kitchen table. In the way that Maeve talks to Sibéal just now, with big arm gestures, her voice carrying across the yard. There's nothing of interest, until—

'We've looked everywhere.'

'Then we look again,' Sibéal says stiffly. 'We'll find it.'

Find what?

Sibéal is angry. I can imagine her narrative: we deprived them of nemeta, making them weak. We persecuted them. When, centuries ago, it was the augurs who initiated Sunder, where augurs, bards and judges went separate ways.

They rebelled against our laws, claiming they were corrupt. They refused to share their divinations, nursing their bitterness until it became a weapon.

The augurs brought ruin on themselves. But they won't hear that.

'This time, they'll get what they deserve.' Sibéal is making a vow to the trees, to the scrappy weeds, to the sky. It feels like her words have power, and I don't like it. I lean closer to listen to the now quieter conversation, to find out what it is they're searching for.

'Mam?' she says hesitantly.

Maeve has wandered over to the edge of the yard. If she looked through the summer growth she'd see me. But she's searching the sky. Above are light wispy clouds. Her fists are clenched and her jaw locked. Her body begins to shake, a light jerking. If it were my mam, I'd be getting the pills.

'What is it?' Sibéal is unfazed.

'The girl.' Maeve's voice is a gasp. 'The girl.'

I'm trying to figure out what I'm witnessing. Is this augur magic? Trembling and gasping and muttering? Not gonna lie, I've seen better. And what girl? Could Maeve be more unspecific?

'We know that.' Sibéal is unimpressed.

'No,' Maeve says. She's bracing her hands on her knees like she's done a six-minute mile. 'Not that ...'

But her words are lost to me. I sense him before I see him, someone approaching from behind. I turn fast, hand on my knife. But it's only Cill, and I sheathe the knife, giving him a small smile. I signal to stay back, get behind a tree. Cill holds up his hands and backs up, rolling his eyes. It's time to head anyway, we're due at HH in less than an hour. Cassa is announcing the War Scythe contenders at the Rose summer party and I can't be late for that.

Only Cill knows I've been coming here, all the way to the other side of the village, and watching the augurs with a dedication that borders on obsessive. He's always laughed at my single-mindedness, my black-and-white vision of the world. But there's no room for grey, no room for uncertainty, not when you're a soldier in a world that could tip to war at any time.

Moving backwards, Cill steps on a loose stone. He teeters for a moment before catching himself, but it's too late. The stone falls, clattering down.

'What's that?'

'Who's there?'

The cries ring through the evening air as augurs stream out of the house.

'Run.' I don't have to say it. Cill is skedaddling, jumping over stones and thick roots.

My hood up, I leap up a boulder. Behind me, Sibéal is at the hedge. Their grover friend, Simon, is over it and gaining. He's slowed down by the boulder, but not enough.

Cill and I split up. I'm sprinting towards the thickest part of the forest, Simon on my heels and others trailing after him. I do take a moment to appreciate the irony of being chased through the woods by augurs.

We're deep between the trees before I lose Simon by jumping from a ridge to the riverbank below. Dad is going to be raging that I went and poked the hornet's nest. Moving along the river, slow and silent, I see the figure lumbering above. Simon.

We have our centuries-old warrior method, where battle is art. Judge boys are trained from young, then sent to

Birchwood for formal schooling in the art of battle. And augurs have grovers: heavy guys and vicious women with ski masks who'll rake concealed, rusted nails down your face while you're carrying your groceries to the car. Guys like Simon. Their attacks are small, dirty and unfortunately effective. I should know, I've experienced more of them than I care to count.

Pressed against the muddy embankment, I wait as he jogs down the slope. He's looking around, not sure which way I've gone. He doesn't see me until I grab him, going for a sleeper hold. But he's strong and fights me, and then we're hitting ground. My feet are in the river, boots soaked, but I have him, blade to skin.

'What's Maeve looking for?'

The silver of the knife at his neck. The green of the trees. Wet rocks and black boughs. My head is whooshing. That word I've been sensing hovers close. And then it's not.

'Nothing that concerns you.' If Simon's afraid, he doesn't show it.

I'm struggling. Suddenly, I can't feel any urgency to this. I can't make myself grip harder, push the blade down.

'What is Maeve looking for?' I repeat.

Simon senses my lack of conviction. That I've no heart in this. That I want it over. So I push the blade deeper. A line of red forms on his pale skin. Not blood. Not yet.

'A letter.' His words are clipped. 'Nothing important.'

I'd be daft to believe an augur. It was clear that whatever Maeve and Sibéal were looking for was very important.

'I swear,' he grits out. 'A girl who did a few jobs wrote a letter to her family telling them about the secret community living in the village. Maeve doesn't want the family asking questions about draoithe.'

'What girl?' I'm thinking about Maeve gasping, her hands to her knees. *The girl*, she'd said.

'The dead girl. The one from the village green.'

I search his face, to see if he's telling the truth. This close, I can see a light spray of freckles, the long-healed scar beside his eyebrow. And for the briefest second, I imagine an alternate universe, one without Sunder. Maybe we would have been friends, beers down at the pub, kicking the ball on a Saturday afternoon. But this is not the world we've inherited.

'Let me up, David.' Simon sees me falter. 'This is pointless. You can't kill me. Not like this.'

'Don't be so sure about that.' My voice is low. He can't know the Warrior's Oath, the words all garraíodóirí swear when leaving Birchwood. New soldiers promise to only take a life, even grover life, in battle or in defence. Never in cold blood. Whatever the augurs may think, we are not monsters.

23

And augurs would demand blood for blood. That's how it goes. A sleeping war, Dad calls it. Hostilities, with small, sometimes lethal, attacks. Here, everywhere, is our battlefield. The street, the library, the bus stop, the woods, every place is just another arena where we might fight each other. A contained horror. But this sleeping war could wake up into a full-on fucking nightmare, with the right provocation.

'C'mon, David.' Says the fella with the knife at his neck. Who somehow knows that I haven't the emotion to drive the sharp edge through skin, slicing through vein and artery.

I've hated them for so long that my hate has lost all strength and urgency. This hate has become so familiar, so ordinary, that I've begun to forget it's there. Why it's there. What I see instead is my brother, broken and haunted. All in the name of a centuries-old sleeping war.

Simon's looking at me again with that normal guy face. I think he sees it too: a recognition that things could have been different, that we could have been different. That he could have been someone I went to school with, if I hadn't trained as a soldier instead.

'Let's just forget any of this happened. The spying. This conversation.' His tone is cajoling. His facade is straining. He is anxious. Afraid. I'm known to be volatile.

And suddenly I can't take it any more. The ordinariness of this boy, my enemy. An unfamiliar discomfort settles over me, and I'm feeling wrong. My skin is too tight. I feel like I, the me that is hidden and lost inside the muscle and blood and bone, am trying to claw my way out of my body.

I lift off him, pulling up my hood as I step away, willing my body to obedience.

He's right. This is pointless.

'We'll forget this happened.' It's a warning: he can't tell the augurs it was me spying at the house.

'Never saw you.'

He's on his feet and the intensity of the exchange is receding.

Still, I feel all kinds of odd as I walk away. Reeling a little from the shock of looking into your enemy's eyes and seeing your own.

'David,' Simon calls.

'What?'

'One last thing.'

He's just behind me when I turn. I realise what's happening a second too late. His fist lands close to my mouth, my ears ring and my vision is obscured by a thin film. Something sharp sinks into my lip – the bastard has a spiked ring. I've only myself to blame, my stupid thoughts. I deserve nothing less.

I'm stumbling back when he says, 'That's because you're an arsehole.'

THREE
Stabbed

The old lady gives me the creeps.
LAS

Zara

Mom has shut herself in her bedroom. No light shines from beneath her door and I'm sure if I put my ear to the wood, I'll hear muffled crying.

I'm back in Laila's room. It's as she left it, her books on her desk, the school bag beside the wardrobe. Like she popped down to the Spar for Skittles and any minute she'll throw herself on the bed and tell me she walked through the forest and how the trees shimmered with an unnatural silver glitter and what can it all mean?

Except, she won't.

It bothers me that Laila's room is still the same. That, like her body, it bears no sign of the brokenness that's become our normal.

I don't stop to think as I grab the heavy scissors from Laila's desk.

I don't know if it's sorrow or anger or helplessness that makes me dig the sharp end into the wall, gouging it deep into the paintwork.

There. Scars show pain.

It helps, so I do it again. A large, deep fissure across the wall. And then another, until I'm attacking the plaster with short hard stabs. I catch myself then, crying and trying to hurt a wall. I step back, realising the damage I've done.

We don't do this. We don't behave like this. We never lose control. I still don't know what came over me, and I drop the scissors like they possessed my hand.

Shaking, I look at what I've done.

Jarlath Creagh, our landlord, will not be impressed. Mom and Dad are dealing with their own stuff, there's no room for my vandalism.

I take down the giant corkboard, twisting the hooks from the wall. Moving it to the left will hide the damage, barely. If Mom notices, I'll tell her a hook came loose. But as I move the board, a small card that had been tucked behind it falls.

THE SCAVENGER HUNT
Find your treasure.

A phone number beneath. The flip side is covered in Laila's untidy scrawl. She's written what looks, with some effort, like *Bad Eye is a Knot*. Beneath: *standing stones, fairy forts, dolmens, burial stones, ancient trees etc. = nemeta*. The word is circled twice. And, bottom right, *Find Meadowsweet on School. Wickerlight*.

I pull my phone from my pocket and look up 'nemeta'. Sacred grove for ancient Celts. Ritual space. Temple. Yup, sounds like Laila. I have no idea what 'Find Meadowsweet on School' means. It looks like a note to herself, a reminder. I search 'wickerlight' but that's not a thing.

Downstairs, Adam is home, cheeks flushed and grass stains on his school trousers. I would think he's been drinking, but he's not like that. For all her claims that she's not religious, Mom doesn't drink, and Adam is more like her than he'd care to be.

'What was that noise?' Adam glances up from his maths book.

'Stabbed the wall.'

He nods, his eyes holding mine briefly, and then he's back at his books.

I slip out of the house and into the fading light.

Our cookie-cutter mini-mansion is on a small private lane. On my right is a dead end. High iron gates and two large cement birds perched on pillars form the entrance to the Rookery.

I turn left, and head down the gently sloping road to the village main street. Mom's wrong, Laila wasn't into drugs. She'd experimented with jimsonweed last summer, hoping to cross the threshold to another realm, but found herself in hospital instead. She'd felt an idiot afterwards.

Something else made her go down to the village green the night she died.

I don't know how long I'm there on the green. Village folk say it used to be an open-air slaughterhouse, that animals were killed and butchered here. That's why the grass is such a deep shade of green. Because it's a place for dying. For pigs and sheep.

And now, for girls.

I've stepped into the road when I hear the noise. I turn, and see a car tearing down. It's going too fast, veering towards the edge of the kerb. My panic is paralysing. Petrifying.

The headlights are blinding and I hold out a hand to block the glare as the car speeds towards me. I'm thinking it would really suck if Mom and Dad lost both daughters right there at the village green.

The car swerves, then swings wildly, pulling to an abrupt stop. My legs are jelly, but I stand there, glaring. It pauses for a long while.

The car revs, hard and loud. The wheels spin and screech and the car takes off, careering in a circle. It's dizzying to watch, the car turning at speed, burning rubber into the tarmac. I think I hear the sound of maniacal laughter, but it's probably just the squealing tires as the car spins. It skids to a stop, and holds for a moment. Then, speeding through the smoke, it disappears into the distance.

I am rooted in the same spot, unable to move. The car is gone, leaving black rings in the faded tarmac.

FOUR

Its name is Promise

David

Oisín, pale and disengaged, leans against the wall of the white room at Harkness House. He's missing a tie and the crumpled suit jacket looks like it was pulled from the bottom of his laundry basket and then stomped on.

But he's here, at a Rose party, and that's something. My brother hasn't left the Rookery in five months, so skulking in the shadows with greasy, overlong hair and a vacant gaze is a significant improvement.

HH is swarming with judges. I'm told that in before times, when draoithe weren't Sundered, we spoke the language of trees, of smoke, water and flame. Mamó believes this absolutely; I have my doubts. One thing is true, we judges sure like to talk. Hard, loud talking where no one is doing any listening.

Oisín's eye drifts over the room. There was a time when he loved Rose parties. When he would talk and dance and flirt. But tonight he's not interested in the women with their glitter and tulle, not the men in suits, not the waiters serving blood-red wine. His gaze roams, then comes to a sudden halt on the newly erected dais.

He's staring, have to say it, with creeper eyes. A girl sits up there, quiet and alone.

Oisín has never met this girl, not even seen her until just now. I doubt he's even heard of her before this evening. But she's grabbed his attention. I look at her as if, like Oisín, I'm seeing her for the first time.

Her name is Wren and she has wavy hair and brown skin. Green eyes that seem to see more than what's there. She is our newly made Bláithín, the third in our long history. She is the Keeper of the Forest, the girl of leaf and petal. Many judges believe that the third Bláithín brings on the third golden age. And just as the first ré órga gave the judges our superior military strength, and the second brought prosperity, the third promises unfettered silver magic.

On the dais, surrounded by flowers, Wren looks younger than her eighteen years. She stares ahead, ignoring the room. A single finger worries the embroidery on her dress.

The Rose circles, sharks anticipating a feed. Smelling blood. Even Dad can't hide his interest. It's no secret that she's not exactly my favourite person, but I almost feel sorry for her up there. How grim it must be, the weight of expectation. The hunger.

Growing up an augur, Wren has hated us for most of her sorry young life. Sucks for her, because turns out, she's half judge. The distress this must have caused her is one of my go-to happy thoughts. Her judge half protected her from having her eyes pecked out on the shoreline when she played her little game in the muck ten years ago. No augur can set foot on our land without offending the rooks and because she'd come down our fields unharmed, she'd confounded me.

But as long as I've known Wren, I've known she's wished us ill. I'd always felt it, that intuitive knowing when a threat is near. A soldier's instinct for danger. But now she's one of us and I can't get my head around it. I don't think she can either.

From across the room, Dad downs his wine and runs an eye over my black formal uniform, hastily changed in the car. The stiff military jacket, the Bláithín insignia on my armband, feel like binds. If Dad notices the bruise forming on my lower jawline, my newly busted lip, he doesn't let on.

'Davey.' Mamó appears beside me, clutching a tumbler of whiskey with her gnarled fingers.

Heads turn, dresses rustle as a woman enters the white room. Silvery blonde hair swept up, a long shimmering dress, Cassa is every bit our queen. She is not only the leader of our gairdín, the Rose, but of all judges everywhere. Two of her guard, Tarc and Elliot, walk behind.

That word again. It brushes against me, a light touch of butterfly wings before lifting off.

I sometimes wonder what it must be like to be Cassa. To be so small and delicate that her enemies could snap her neck with a bare flick of the wrist, and yet the strongest person I know. Her ruthlessness is underscored by that hint of vulnerability and it makes her unpredictable. Adds to her charm.

Tonight Cassa will announce the four final contenders in the challenge for the highest honour a garraíodóir can achieve: to become War Scythe. Known also as the Raker, the Caretaker, Death's Song, or, my personal favourite, the Gyve. Which, apparently, means shackle. I've spent my whole life wanting nothing more than to be the Shackle. I am a therapist's dream.

'Your father married the wrong sister.' Mamó nods at Lucia, my mother, then dismisses her in favour of Cassa, my mother's half-sister. Though similar to look at, the two women are very different.

'Mamó,' I reproach her.

But it's what she does. Mamó compares. Lucia and Cassa. Me and Oisín. She's never forgiven my mother for not having daughters to bear the strength of our maternal ancestor, the Crow-Mother.

34

'Cassa was the better match. Your father, he is …' She pauses. 'Hungry.'

I'm thinking that Mamó is trying to tell me something. I search her face and then I see it. She looks hungry too.

'Mamó? What do you know?'

But she just smiles. Mamó is a law unto herself. She is black silk, cigarette smoke and feathers. Two crow-feather combs hold back her silver hair, making her sharp face sharper.

Pinned to her dress is a round brooch with intricate knot-work. Not an exact replica, but similar enough to the ancient Eye of the Badb. This is Mamó's way of proclaiming that even though we're broke and recently disgraced, the famous warrior disc brooch, said to belong to the Crow-Mother herself, is our family heirloom.

Cill sidles up, smirking at my split lip. He's smug, not a mark on him. He bends to Mamó, tapping his cheek. He's the only one she kisses, not me, not even Oisín before he became useless.

'So?' Cill tilts his head towards Wren, and I just shake mine. No. That's all I have and I can't even say it. I don't know where to begin.

But then he notices Oisín. I rarely see Cill at a loss, but he's floundering now as he sees my brother for the first time in months. Since Oisín shut himself from

35

the world. The greasy hair and crumpled suit. How thin he is. But worse is that look in his eyes. Damaged. Lost. Helpless.

Cill takes a deep chug of his wine.

'Haven't seen him in a while.'

I can sense the battle inside. He's been careful to not pry. But curiosity wins.

'Augurs, right?'

From the dais, Cassa addresses the room: 'Good evening and welcome.'

'Around midwinter.' I whisper this family secret. It's like by not talking about it, we pretend it didn't happen. 'Oisín found augurs on a judge farm, at a megalith.'

The augurs are constantly trying to steal or destroy our nemeta, the ancient places that fuel our rituals and feed our magic. 'They ganged up on him. Beat him. Held him for ten days.'

And whatever happened during those ten days, Oisín won't say. Says he can't remember and I'm sure this is true. But I know from the darkness in his eyes that it's not the complete truth. Because forgetting would have been easier than living with whatever haunts him.

'I know you've been waiting for the announcement of the four contenders,' Cassa continues. 'But I ask for patience. Because first, there's someone I want you to meet.'

Cassa turns and gestures for Wren to stand beside her.

'This is Wren, and she is our Bláithín who will waken silver magic.'

Cassa's voice is strong and decisive. With those words, she dismisses Wren's upbringing as an augur, that Wren came to HH to steal from us, that some judges don't even believe in the myth of the Bláithín. It may sound like an introduction, but it's really a warning.

'When?' a voice calls from the crowd. 'It's been more than two months since the changing.'

'Magic takes time,' Cassa responds. 'And, as you know, requires ritual. We will prepare and complete the necessary rituals when the time is right.'

Cassa holds up a hand to silence any more questions. She kisses Wren on both cheeks, a sign of her favour and affection. Wren looks relieved as she steps down from the dais, away from scrutiny, and stands beside Tarc.

'And now, our four contenders. These are the best of our excellent young soldiers facing a once in a lifetime opportunity …'

As Cassa does the preamble, Oisín stares at Wren. Dad stares at Cassa, gripping the stem of his glass, and Mamó smiles at me. I'd better be among that four. Not only because we're broke and badly need the money winning will bring, but because our name is mud.

Only Lucia, my mother, looks down. She's standing with a group of women, but a little outside their circle. Her face is troubled. But drawn by my gaze, she looks at me, hiding her worry with a brilliant smile.

'Elliot Galvin.' A garraíodóir from Boston goes up. Cill has the dagger eyes on Elliot. He blames the recently arrived contenders that he's no longer on Cassa's personal guard. But Cill's not garraíodóir. He was only ever a stand-in and has no business being resentful.

'Tarc Gallagher.'

No surprises here. Tarc's always been Cassa's favourite; he's like a second son to her. But what does surprise me are the disgruntled mutters from the room. They don't like that Tarc fell for the augur spy, when his duty is to protect Cassa and the Rose from augurs.

Dad's now watching me so intently I can almost read his mind: *Show us what you're made of. Are you worthy of your name? Or will you disappoint?*

Mamó places her twisted fingers on my arm. That touch says much the same as Dad's eyes.

'David Creagh.'

The relief of it. I want to sink to my knees. Instead, I push through the crowd. Cill's sister Breanna beams at me. 'You're the Raker we need, David.'

Dogged. Determined. No love for augurs. A Creagh.

38

The applause is thundering as I step up beside the others. It's obvious, despite our disgrace, the Rose has a new favourite. But oddly, it makes me uncomfortable. I catch Wren's eye as she watches from the front of the crowd, and I get it. That weight of expectation.

Lucia beams as she applauds, but I'm still seeing a shadow in her eyes.

Ian is the last garraíodóir to be called up. The four of us stand tall before the Rose gairdín as we recite the pledge. One of our oldest traditions, the contest is open to eligible garraíodóir at the onset of manhood. The title is for life, unless challenged by a usurper. No one ever quits, except Oisín. After his attack he gave it up, and since then we've been disgraced. Shunned. Even the judge families who'd lived in our rental houses moved out, escaping the taint of the failed War Scythe.

All eyes are on my brother in his creased suit as he makes his way to the dais. There are whispers, sneers, from the same people who cheered him on to victory three years ago.

Oisín carries large red velvet bag which he makes look like a sack of spuds, not some of our ancient treasures. He struggles beneath the attention of so many people. It makes me mad at him, *just pull it together for five minutes*. But also, that awful heart-sink. He wasn't like this before.

Come on, Oisín, I will him forward. The crowd watches, with more than a hint of amusement as he walks towards us.

That uncomfortable tingling flares up again, demanding I pay attention. It's a weird, indefinable feeling. An emptiness that responds to the one thing that will fill it. A hunger for something specific but I don't know what it is. It's a mosquito buzzing in the dark and you need somehow to stop that infernal noise. There is a word out there, and it's for me to find. If I don't, the word will disappear and the discomfort will diminish. But words are power, and any judge's worth is determined by how many words they've turned to law.

There's a light laugh from right beside him. Oisín falters and the word retreats. One step at a time, I'm thinking. Just one foot forward, then the next.

'… the state of him.' The sneer is casually vicious.

Oisín quails at the centre of the room. He stands motionless for endless seconds. It feels like cracked glass inching out. Broken. Irreparable.

Then he shuffles forward, slowly. Painfully. Some eyes are kind, some are pitying. He finally reaches the platform.

'Do you return the War Scythe's trove?' Cassa says.

'I do,' Oisín rasps.

'Should you win the contest –' Cassa turns to the four of us still standing to attention – 'these treasures will be yours.

You will learn the secret rituals to release their hidden magic. They will strengthen and guide you.'

Three of the four treasures release their magic through ritual. Not the Eye of Badb, which is a Knot. Knot magic requires action. The Eye is the 'oh crap' treasure, the one that's triggered only when the world has gone to hell.

With shaking hands, Oisín peels open the velvet and takes out a shield, which he hands to Cassa.

'The Shield of Donnacha.' Cassa lifts the shield, old as a museum piece. 'For protection.' She passes the shield to Elliot, who holds it up so everyone can see it.

Oisín now takes the lunula, a flat crescent-shaped gold collar with intricate inscriptions, and gives it to Cassa.

'The Seventh Lunula, for command.'

From the velvet, Oisín draws out the small jewelled dagger that belonged to the first Bláithín, the original girl of leaf and petal who made a desperate deal with the forest. The forest thrummed through her blood, gifting her with powerful magic, and judges have honoured her since.

'The Bláithín's Dagger. For bravery.'

Finally, Oisín takes out a black velvet box. Mamó is rigid with pride. In the box is the Eye of Badb, an ancient warrior disc brooch that's been passed down her family. Because of its power, the Eye is required to be part of the War Scythe's

41

trove. But it's really owned by Mamó and she won't let anyone forget it.

'And for victory,' Cassa says while Oisín releases the catches on the black box.

The Eye is said to summon the Crow-Mother, Badb, through the four offerings. It can only be used once in a hundred years. If pleased by the offerings presented, Badb will do whatever is asked of her.

'The Eye of Badb.'

The Badb Catha is a harbinger of death. She is a battle goddess, who would mess with the minds of the enemy on the battlefield, sending awful visions to distract and destroy. So, I'm guessing she's most pleased by death and destruction.

Oisín opens the velvet box. Blood drains from his already pale face. There's a problem. I can't see what it is, not from this angle.

'I don't understand,' Oisín says, passing the box to Cassa like he's looking for confirmation. As it moves, I see what's wrong: the box is empty.

The news spreads fast. The crowd is muttering, craning their necks for a better view.

'I must have forgotten to pack it.' Oisín's words are a mumble. I'm cringing, hurting, and without realising it, I've broken from position without any heed to Cassa or Dad or the proper decorum.

All I see is Oisín, bewildered. Laughed at.

'Please,' I beg Cassa. 'I'll bring him in tomorrow. Let me take him home. Please.'

For a long moment she just looks at me. I work for Cassa, here at the Harkness Foundation, on the security team supposedly guarding the many valuable artworks and antiques. But really, I'm on her personal guard, doing the two-year placement required by soldier school. And she never goes easy on me. So I'm expecting her to say no. To have the whole humiliating interrogation here tonight.

To my surprise, she gives a quick nod.

I step down from the dais, holding up my brother who was once the War Scythe, the strongest, most heroic soldier of our generation.

Passing Wren, Oisín stops. He turns to her. If I could yank him away without drawing comment, I would.

He holds out a closed fist. There's no disdain or pity on her face, and she raises her hand at his unspoken question. He presses something inside, furling her fingers over it, then gives her a bow.

'Keeper of the Forest.' The words are breathed in awe as he straightens up. He leans forward and says something too quiet for anyone else to hear.

The mutters increase. I place a hand on his arm and steer Oisín away. I feel like a cartoon character with steam blowing out my ears, but I heed my internalised instructions: back straight, face clear. Don't let them know what you're feeling. On one hand, it's exhausting having been brought up to believe that everyone is out to get you. On the other, my family have prepared me well for my life.

We leave the white room side by side, shoulders squared. We are watched, we are shamed. Taunted and jeered at. But we walk like the princes Lucia and Mamó always told us we were. The only thing they've ever agreed on.

There's often blood at Rose parties. I just hadn't realised that tonight it would be ours.

We drive home in silence.

I have so many questions. Where is the Eye? How in the name of all that's sacred could you forget to pack it? Why would it even be out of the box when there are rules for how it should be stored? But those aren't the questions I really want to ask.

What I want to know is, what happened during those missing days? What could be that bad it could break *you*?

Oisín had always been ruthless, even as a child. Not the blunt cruelty of kicking puppies, but something more subtle. Oisín knew how to salt wounds, he knew how to hurt without leaving marks. He knew intuitively that psychological damage was more lasting than physical. But I yearn to have him back, the big brother who knew how to

44

make me turn a blade to my own skin and still have me worship him.

'What did you give to Wren?' I say at last.

'A coin.'

'And what did you tell her?'

'That its name is Promise.'

I jerk my head to him, my jaw dropping. 'You gave her a word? Why?'

We never, ever give our words away. We need them to form laws because that's how our magic works.

Oisín is back to gazing out of the window, preferring the night to me.

I want to jolt him out of whatever fug has enveloped him.

'Remember how we used to race down by the quarry,' I say, picking up speed and edging too close to the kerb because Oisín doesn't like it when I do that. I want to make him angry. Or afraid. Anything but this vacant brokenness. I want to put the pedal down, to go too fast on this quiet village road.

I want to make him feel.

But then my elusive word veers up, sharp and painful, like talons grabbing my throat. It's unusually vicious. I clutch the steering wheel, trying to keep from crying out. My foot is down on the accelerator but all I know is the clutch at my throat.

'Watch out,' Oisín says. 'The girl.'

Just beside the village green, a girl suddenly appears in the headlights, one hand held out in front of her. I'm breathing heavily as the car screeches to an abrupt stop. Oisín is rigid. I know what he is thinking. That it's the dead girl, the one found right there on the village green the morning after Cassa's ritual with Wren back in March. Like some kind of weird footnote to that night.

Her picture had been all over the local rags: brown eyes, delicate features. A nice girl. One who played sport, did her homework and listened to her parents. It was a studio photograph that didn't capture the amusement that lingered at the sides of her mouth. That inclination to mischief that was written all over her face.

Tonight she's dressed all in black, like a vengeful spirit. More angular than I remember, she throws a heated glare at the car. Her hair is crazy and loose.

I shut my eyes, my hands clasping the steering wheel. When it comes, the word floods me.

Keep.

It's a strong one and I need to know where to put it. I search around the word, sensing its texture and feel. Hard? No. Not rough. There's a familiar smell that reminds me of Dad's study. Leather. I'm relieved that it's not something like paper or ash. Last year at Birchwood, in the middle of a hand-to-hand combat skills practical exam, I received a word that could only be encased in a feather. Affinity. I lost that one.

The seat or steering wheel? Again, it pushes out at me and I grip the wheel tight between two fingers and my thumb and squeeze. Focusing hard, I encase the word in the leather there. I'll have to cut out that patch from the steering wheel later.

For once I'm relieved that Oisín is so absent. We guard our words. We don't share any information about them.

When I look up, Oisín is still gazing out of the window. The dead girl stares back. The walking dead observing each other.

Oisín turns to me and yawns. 'Chicken.'

It's a challenge.

So I edge up to where the road widens, revving hard so that the wheels spin beneath us. Then we fly, going round in a circle, casting light and shadow on to the girl. And again and again until I know I've burned rings in the road.

When I come to a stop, there's an almost-smile on Oisín's face.

'Because I wanted to welcome her.' His near smile is grim in the dim light as he finally answers my earlier question. 'Wren's one of us now.'

He makes it sound like a punishment.

'She will bring on silver magic.'

I look at him curiously. 'How can you be so sure?'

He's silent a moment. 'I can see it. Smell it. That girl belongs to the woods.'

FIVE
You need to be a little Horrible

*I met a man in the village and he told me he was a
scavenger hunter. His name is John Canty.*

LAS

Zara

Once upon a time, there was a horrible little girl called
Horrible Zara and she had a horrible sister and a horrible
brother. They lived in a horrible ditch down the bottom of
the garden and ate leaf stew and boiled dirt for dinner. Filthy
rag clothes just about covered their mud-streaked skin. Their
hair was matted and mucky, their teeth crumbed with soil.

They were Horrible, not cruel or mean or hurtful, and
needed only each other. But Horrible Laila began to realise
that the world was bigger than their ditch down the bottom
of the garden. She wanted to find other ditches, she longed
for bogs and pits and swamps.

'There is such delicious nastiness out there,' Horrible
Laila would dream.

'No, Horrible sister,' Horrible Zara would cry. 'If you venture too far, the Inky Black will get you. Stay here in our damp little ditch.'

Horrible Zara spilt tears into her dirt-leaf soup because she needed Horrible Laila with her. And then one day Horrible Laila ventured too far and the Inky Black drew her into its terrible embrace.

She died. The end.

I first made up the Horribles, but it became Laila's thing. She told stories about Horrible Zara and Horrible Laila and Horrible Adam in a raspy horrible voice until we begged her to stop, unnerved by our shadow family who lived down in the ditch.

'Zara.'

I can hear Laila's horrible voice as if she were there with me: *Why did you shut me out? Why wouldn't you let me talk?*

'What are you doing?'

'What?' I register that Mom's been calling me.

She gives me a look. I know what she wants to say: don't sit there. Do something. Mom is a doer. Idleness bothers her. Get up and move. Pretend to be busy.

And there I am, just sitting at the sash window with the purple-blue skies, dank black boughs beyond. A solitary magpie on the grass. In the distance, dark clouds promise rain.

'Playing a game.' I wave my phone and lie. The summer holiday, starting next week, is going to be a blast.

'What game?'

'WordSpat.' Because WordSpat is zero points. Chess is two and Piggy Run minus two. Not that Mom still keeps score. But it is there, so deeply ingrained from my childhood, where the things we did were scored and rated. Top marks in class? Five points forward. There you go, up the ladder. A strop outside the Spar? Oops, down a snake.

I put my phone face down to hide the lie. I can't play WordSpat. Not since Laila died. Even after Laila started disappearing, living her secret life, we'd play WordSpat, her words appearing on my screen when I least expected.

'Come.' Mom touches my shoulder. 'You haven't had breakfast.'

Mom's off again, scuttling to the kitchen, then outside, doing small jobs like moving this thing here and that thing there. Pointless jobs. Mom wants to fix things. It's why she's a doctor. And she can't fix this. Worse, she doesn't even know how it all broke. It bothers her that she can't know why Laila died, just that she did. There were no signs of injury or trauma. There is no logical reason for Laila to have died. It shouldn't have happened. It's an impossible thing.

And again that twist, like someone has reached into my chest and given me a snake bite, that burn of forearm skin, but in my heart. Laila always hoped for six impossible things before breakfast.

I'm surprised to see Dad at the kitchen table with a cup of coffee in front of him. He usually leaves home before seven. An impossible thing.

'Home office?' I sound foolishly hopeful. But he's looking at his phone with a big smile. I freeze.

'Hmm?' He looks up, distracted, reaching for his mug. 'No, late start today.'

Adam is slouched over his breakfast cereal. He's a slobbery eater and it grosses me out. And then that fist to the gut: Laila was too. Those wet crunches always made me want to kill her. Ha ha.

I pour hot water into a mug with a squeeze of lemon, a habit I picked up from Laila.

'What you looking at, Dad?' Adam says, and I want to hit him.

'Dad?' Adam persists. I hold on to my water so I don't accidentally throw it at him.

'What?' Dad puts his phone beside his cup. He's still looking at the screen. 'Just Steve from work.'

Mom moves to the utility room. I don't think she needs anything.

'Your bus,' Mom calls. Through the door, she's reaching above the sink, trying to open the window. That window has never opened. It's been stuck since the day we moved here. But, teeth gritted, Mom is determined that this morning the damned window will open.

'I'm ready.' I cast an eye over Adam's pinstriped pyjama bottoms. 'Get dressed.' I chuck a dish towel at him. 'The bus won't wait for you.'

On his way out, Adam leans over Dad's shoulder. 'That looks boring.'

Dad laughs. 'It wasn't a wild night out.'

'This from last night? Where did you go?'

Mom kneels on the counter in the utility, pushing at the window. She mutters something under her breath.

'A talk on Byronic heroes in twenty-first-century popular literature.'

'Crazy times, Dad.' Adam clamps a hand on Dad's shoulder. The phone swerves on the table and I see cable-knit jumpers and grey thinning hair.

Not a Lindy then.

I turn to the sink, relieved. Dad really was at a work thing last night. Another impossible thing.

'Oh for God's sake,' I hear Mom breathe beneath a soft thud.

Dad's up, moving to the door. 'Naz?'

'Just my hand.' I hear her voice muted through the door. Dad moves to the utility room, where Mom holds her hand

53

over the sink, blood dripping. He takes her hand. Their eyes are locked on each other's. Three impossible things.

'I'll call Jarlath Creagh.' Mom's flustered, and starts blabbing about our landlord. 'There are some other things that need fixing and it's time he …'

'C'mon, Zara,' Adam sings from the hall, voice muffled as he pulls a T-shirt over his head. 'The bus won't wait for you.'

I leave quietly. Opening the hall closet, I can't see my summer raincoat among the many hanging jackets. I call to Mom, and she yells that she's put it in the wash. I grab an old parka, even though it smells musty, and step into the morning, a small hard bud of hope tight inside.

It's the last days before the long summer break, and we're mostly biding our time at school. After the final bell goes, I get on the school bus, an old Mercedes twenty-four-seater that weaves through small outlying villages before finally reaching Kilshamble. Without Laila, I sit alone near the back. Adam almost always has music or sport or goes over to his friend Patrick's.

Again, I'm lost to the pain. It's a living thing that crawls around inside my skin, moving to different parts of my body. Today it lies in a straight line on the inside of my forearm. A sharp, tingling thing. Yesterday it was curled up in the centre of my hands. Next it might be an ache in my throat, a thud in my gut, a burn in my cheekbones. My grief. Even in those brief moments when I forget that Laila is dead, it's always there, this unyielding strain in my body.

Outside, sunshine dances on leaves and grass and I avoid looking at the empty seat across from me. Grief stirs in the line of my inside forearm. I think of it as a dog. A greyhound reaching out his paws, stretching his back. Laila loved dogs.

Laila.

Back in March, I'd found her in the bathroom, the hair scissors in hand.

'You won't stop me.' She said it like she was holding the blade to a vein.

Long chunks of hair had fallen to the tiles. The burnt gold, usually hidden in the brown, was obvious that morning.

'Not here to stop you.' I leaned against the doorjamb.

I should have noticed the distress that simmered as her hair fell until only shaggy ends brushed her neck.

'Why?' I said.

'I …' she started, then broke off. 'This place.' With scissors, she gestured to the walls, and I didn't know if she meant the house or the village.

'This …' She gestured down to herself. To her neat body, shaped by years of swimming and a mildly dysfunctional relationship with food. She was breathing heavily, her eyes wide with the strength of her feeling. She was willing me to understand, that she felt something big. Something important.

'I meant why didn't you go to the hairdressers?'

Stung by my bland response, Laila turned away, dropping her chin to her chest.

I reached to her. Our old practised dance: one hurts, the other retreats, the first reaches out.

'Mom won't like your hair.' A peace offering.

Her face was grim as she replied, 'Yeah, well. Mom endures.'

She ran her fingers through the blunt ends. I waited.

'I need to be more,' she relented. 'I need to be different from who I am.' She was calm, her earlier inarticulation gone. Long honey-brown tresses lay discarded on the floor.

You already are, I wanted to tell her. I wanted to say that I hardly recognised her.

'This village,' she said. 'I think it's possible here.'

Laila had become obsessed with the village myth of the tuanacul, the beautiful tree people who lured foolish boys and girls into the woods. Laila was certain that she could sense them. That a tree man was watching, ready to step in and save her from deathly ordinariness.

'Something is … beginning.'

I usually tuned Laila out when she started on this. On her mission to become some kind of superhuman. She'd worked through witch, demon summoner, rain princess, moon dragon warrior. Laila was hungry, no, ravenous, for magic.

'... careful.' Laila was talking to herself while I checked my phone. 'Like poison in the water. There is an Inky Black, and it's here.'

I bit back the impatient words. If I annoyed her again, we'd end up fighting.

'Mind yourself, Zara.'

I didn't like how she was looking at me.

'I think to survive here,' she said, 'you need to be a little Horrible.'

But I am a little horrible.

I fold it up, like a secret written on page. I fold once, twice, ten times until it is a small tight knot.

It wasn't only the night she died that I pushed Laila away. I'd been so cold to her in the months before. Laila had been dreamy, nursing something secret. Something happy. Back in the city, I'd waited two years for Nathan to look at me as more than a friend. Our togetherness was new and fragile and fell to pieces when I was forced to move because everyone else had messed up. I was angry and jealous.

I wouldn't listen to her. I didn't want to know. I didn't want to be kind. I wanted to feel sore and horrible. So when Laila would look at me like she'd burst if she didn't tell me her secret, I'd turn away.

She needed me, and I blanked her. And now she's dead.

The bus stop is ahead and I get to my feet. I pass a girl with dark hair and darkness in her eyes who sketches in her notebook. Sue, the driver, will give out to me. She's like a bear with a sore head if we stand before she's pulled over. But the memory of Laila slashing her hair, that unbearable guilt, has me breathing in short shallow gasps. I won't cry. Not here.

As the bus lurches to a stop, I fall sideways. I catch myself, but not before I've stumbled against a girl near the front: Breanna, who's laughing with the beefy boy beside her. Was laughing, until my heavy school backpack hit her head. The buckle pulls her hair, yanking a chunk from its high ponytail.

I've nearly scalped Breanna, who is smart and clever and funny. Everyone, even the surliest teacher, loves Breanna.

'Watch it,' she growls, touching her hand to her hair.

I catch the driver's eye in the rear-view mirror. Breanna glares at me and the boy, Ryan, Dr Kelly's son, looks amused. Like I've gone and poked a dragon, and he's curious to see what happens next. When she heard he was repeating his Leaving Cert, Mom was dead keen for us to make friends with Ryan. But he's been off school a lot, and when he is there, he couldn't be less interested in my friendship. Nor is Breanna, who's perfectly nice, but doesn't make friends outside of her small circle.

'Sorry,' I mumble, and I'm not sure if it's to Breanna, the driver or Laila.

I'm off the bus when I see another boy sitting on the low wall. Cillian, I think. He's sometimes there, waiting for Breanna and Ryan. With the same long, wiry build as Breanna, I'm sure he's her brother. Behind me, Breanna, retying her hair, is still fuming.

I'm about to cross the road when I hear Breanna say, '… clumsy cow drop dead like her sister.'

I stop. The boys are laughing, and I almost envy them their careless laughter. How nice it must be, to find death funny.

I turn slowly. The dark-haired girl with the sketch pad is off the bus, smiling lazily at Breanna and her boys.

'Hey, guys.' Her voice is huskier than I expected. 'Any good garden fires lately?'

The mood changes immediately. The laughing stops, and anger radiates from them. The bus pulls off with a loud belch and the girl smirks as she passes them. She's not taken more than a few steps when they crowd her.

'You're not wanted here.' Breanna is more threatening when she speaks quietly. 'Leave.'

'It's Sibéal, right?' Cillian gets in right beside her. He tugs lightly at the ends of her long hair.

'You know who I am.' The girl is unperturbed and he is such a creeper, touching her hair.

'Unfortunately, Sibéal, we're going to exact a penalty for trespassing.'

I don't know what he means. We're on the side of the road, no one's trespassed.

'Look, if you're going to do it, hurry up,' Sibéal says with exaggerated boredom. She pulls something from her boot, black biker boots, which is not the only way she flouts the school uniform policy. She's holding a letter opener, thin and unusually sharp. The boys smile. I step forward.

'You going to take it or not?' she says to Cillian, turning it so that the blade glints in the sunlight. Then she lifts it to her hair and, holding it taut, slashes hard. In her hand, a few strands have sliced off. It's a weird rhyme to Laila's haircut, but it shocks me more.

Breanna stands rigid, her hands locked on her hips. She's so much taller than Sibéal, and with the boys behind her, it looks like a mean gang beating up on the wimpy kid.

Sibéal lets the hair flutter to the ground. 'Thought not.'

She turns and walks. She's only gone a little way when Breanna grabs her by the arm, pulling her hair so that her neck is forced back.

'I prefer to take it myself. Like this.' Breanna is pulling her hair so hard that she's ripping strands from Sibéal's scalp.

'Breanna, no,' I yell, but she only tugs harder. 'Stop her,' I shout at the boys, but Ryan just shakes his head, a small smile curving his lips.

I'm moving forward, I don't know, to pull her off, kick her shins, do something, when Sibéal twists out of the hold, her blade raised. It's level with Breanna's throat and for a second I think she's going to do it. That's she's going to jab the blade in Breanna's throat. But Cillian catches her hand and pulls it back.

'I'm not going to run from you.' Sibéal is angry too.

'You should.' It doesn't sound like an idle threat. Cillian leans into her space, the other two close behind. They're all so much bigger, so much *more*. Despite the bravado with the letter opener, they're way scarier than she is.

'Does it make you feel strong? Better?' My throat hurts from shouting. 'A gang of you picking on one girl.'

Their attention shifts to me.

'Nah,' Breanna laughs. 'But two girls might do the trick.'

'You should be ashamed,' I breathe. I sound like Mom.

I've no hidden weapons. I've nothing to take them on. Cillian releases Sibéal's hand, pushing her arm so hard that it twists in a way it shouldn't. Her hissed intake of breath is the only sign that it hurt.

Cillian turns to me and I feel a flash of panic. He's loping with a false easiness, a languid cat facing a cornered mouse, and as he reaches me, he bumps his shoulder against mine. Hard. I stumble to the side, my feet tangling with a crack in the tarmac. As I regain my footing, my hand brushes the outside of the deep parka pocket and I feel something chunky. Cillian continues to Ryan, like nothing happened. I want to lob something at his head, so I reach inside the pocket and pull out the thing there.

And then I see what it is.

It is so ugly, almost alive-looking, that I drop it, shaking out my hand. Just, ew. I'm checking if it's a dying baby demon rat when Breanna's trainer tramps down, pushing whatever it is into the crumbling road surface.

'You look like a nosy sort of girl,' she says, like we're just shooting the breeze. But it's a warning. 'Some advice.'

Her make-up is so flawless it's a mask. But looking at Breanna's perfect eyebrows, her glowing skin, I sense something hidden beneath the mask. Something that simmers beneath her nice girl veneer. I'm not sure I want to know what it is.

'Mind your own business. Keep away from us.' She lifts her foot. 'Got that?'

She starts to move away before she glances down.

We both stare at the thing for a tense moment.

'And keep away from her too.' Breanna jerks her head back at Sibéal before taking another look at the thing on the ground. Before she can, I grab it and put it behind my back.

'I'm heading,' Ryan calls. I don't move as Breanna finally turns away. She goes to him and together they walk away.

Sibéal stands between the tarmac and patchy grass. She's watching me, studying my face. Her eyes are dark and intense and it feels like they're boring into me. She turns away abruptly, and then she's gone.

Just me and the thing from my pocket.

I hold it out it between my thumb and forefinger.

It's hard to describe. Something so hideous it shouldn't be looked at. Shouldn't be carried in jacket pockets. It's made of cobweb and hair, both coiled strands and matted chunks. Laila's hair, forming a small nest of yuck.

It's like a disgusting hairball vomited up by a mangy, diseased cat. As I lift it, the smell hits my nose. How did I not notice this stink from my pocket?

Between the twine and hair are fingernail cuttings.

This must be one of Laila's spells.

Even though I don't believe in magic, it's difficult not to connect this horrible thing with the strange way she died. It feels like Laila doomed herself, accidentally cursed herself, and died.

Knowing Laila, there's probably blood and spit on the hair and twine. Earwax and snot. Because that's how she believed, by putting everything of herself in it. And I'm clearly deranged by grief, because I like that it brings me a little closer to her. That I'm touching something that was part of her once living body, a body I'd do anything to have with me again.

I feel such sadness for Laila, who wanted magic so badly. For all the spells she'd cast that achieved nothing. For all the moonlight chants around trees that didn't help her. I am unspeakably sad for the girl who believed so fiercely and in the end it all meant nothing.

But I want to know. Need to know. What this hideous thing means, what Laila thought it would bring her. I pull out the card I'd stuffed in my purse.

THE SCAVENGER HUNT
Find your treasure.

I dial the number. Nervous, I wait.

 **SIX**

I can keep a secret

David

Oisín is nowhere to be found.

I've searched the Rookery, the fields, the outbuildings and courtyard. I've even checked the dusty confines of Mamó's cottage, where no living man dares tread.

I'm bricking it as I run back down the fields behind the house to search the lake shoreline. I don't know if I'm more worried that he's done a runner, or if something unspeakable drives my panic.

And then I see him. Pensive, he leans against a tree, looking out at the water. Like it's Sunday afternoon picnic time, and not the day he gets hauled over the coals by Cassa for messing up her ceremony.

'Oisín.' I want to tear my hair out. But losing my cool will get me nowhere. 'We have to go.'

Oisín ignores me, slowly getting to his feet. Nothing to say for himself, pathetic bag of bones that he is. Never have I wanted to shake him, hug him, punch him more. He gathers his jacket, wraps himself in his large grey scarf like a granddad with his blanket, and ambles across the fields. The car is parked on the side of the house.

'You've got it, right?' I check before we get into the car.

'Got what?'

'Your knitting.' I restrain myself from giving him a slap upside the head.

But he's looking at me blankly.

'The Eye, you twit.' I can't help rolling mine.

'I don't have the Eye.' He opens the car door.

I pause. Oisín is obviously in one of his moods. I have to talk to him like I would a petulant child.

'Well, don't you think you should get it?' I nod encouragingly. 'Before we go to HH?'

He shrugs, staring down the drive.

'Get the fucking brooch, Oisín.' I get into the driver's seat, trying to control my vexation.

But Oisín sits mulishly, pulling the car door shut.

'I don't have it.'

'Yes you do,' I sigh.

'It's disappeared.'

'Can't have.'

I'm tired. Hungry. Worked an early shift at HH and overdid it with the training earlier. Running around looking for Oisín hasn't helped. But Dad is on my case. He's determined that I must win. He reminds me daily that his company is haemorrhaging money, that the Rookery is in danger of falling down on us as we sleep. He tells me again and again: winning is the only thing that can save us.

'I don't have it any more.' Oisín lays his hands flat on his lap. His jeans hang off him, and his hands are strangely large. Disproportionate. 'It's not in the safe where I kept the trove. It's not in my room or anywhere else. It's gone.'

'The Eye can't be stolen.' No one can enter the Rookery without us asking them in. Not a postman nor plumber. Anyone gets too close to the house without an invitation and the rooks will chase them off. But our best protections are saved for augurs – they can't even set foot on one of our fields without the rooks flying at them. Our birds love the taste of augur blood.

'When did you see it last?' I turn to Oisín. Three rooks swoop down in front of the car. Keen-eyed, they're watching us.

'Around three months ago.' Oisín stretches his arm through the open window, and the nearest rook lifts off and flies towards us, flapping its wings a moment before flying away. They don't even look at me. The rook is Oisín's guide, as it is Dad's and Mamó's. I am irrelevant to them. 'Beginning of March. I took it out of the box because …'

He clams up.

'Because what?'

He's not saying.

I start the engine. We're going to have to go HH without the Eye, which is not unlike wading into croc-infested waters.

If we're lucky, Cassa will understand, Oisín's been ill. It has to be somewhere in the house. With a bit of time, we'll find it. OK, a lot of time. The Rookery is old and huge, and there's a lot of clutter. Things could stay lost in that house forever.

Small stones scatter beneath the wheels as I drive out of the Rookery gates. 'Spill it, Oisín.'

'Someone wanted to see it.' Oisín unwraps his scarf. The day's turned good. Warm, bright sunshine has chased away the earlier showers.

'You showed the Eye to someone who wanted to see it?' My brother is a big walking headache. 'Who?'

'A girl?'

'A girl?' I spit the words out.

If Oisín lost the Eye trying to impress some girl he likes, I'm going to kill him. And Mamó and Dad will bring him back to life so they can kill him again. There must be some dark, ancient ritual for that.

'She was my friend. That's all.' He begins pulling the

scarf around him again, oblivious to the sunshine. 'She was nice.'

'What friend?' Oisín doesn't have friends, other than one or two garraíodóirí. And Laney, a family friend who's also Cassa's assistant.

'Laila.'

'Laila who?' The name's familiar and I'm trying to place her among the judge girls. There's no Laila in the Rose, but maybe she's from another gairdín?

'Laila is the girl who died. On the village green.' He's so wrapped up in the scarf that his words are muffled. Intentional, no doubt. 'Did you ever meet her?'

That Laila.

'Handful of times. Trespassing down our fields.'

'It's not trespassing if she asked.'

And suddenly I wonder what else Oisín has been doing while I thought him hiding beneath his bedsheets these last months.

'Let me get this straight. The last time you saw our ancient, our most treasured family heirloom was the day you took it out of the safe to show to some random village girl because she was nice?'

I can't stop the string of expletives that fall from my mouth.

'Did she know about us? What we are?' I'm thinking of

69

Simon in the woods yesterday evening. Maeve gasping about the girl. 'What were you thinking?'

'I can keep a secret.' There's bite to his words. 'I didn't tell her any of that. We talked about other things.'

'What things?'

'You wouldn't understand.'

He's quiet as we continue on the narrow road.

'What did you talk about?' I sound rougher, abrupter than I mean to. But this is the second time she's come up in two days. Can't be nothing.

'We talked about dreams, about hope, about belonging. History. The limitations of family. How she hated being called exotic, and how people treated her different because of how she looked. About how it's been drilled in me from birth that strength and ambition are more important than kindness. That feelings are something to be overcome.'

Why does he have to speak so slowly? So mumbly? Whittling on about feelings. There's a tractor ahead and I want to blast it out of my way. Cassa is waiting.

'And we got talking about family treasures. I told her how the Eye has been passed down in ours. She wanted to see it.' He folds his arms like this is perfectly reasonable.

'And then?' But Oisín ignores the heat in my voice.

'Then we went for a walk. I must have packed it away.'

'Must have?'

'Probably.'

'You need to give me better than that, Oisín.'

He doesn't answer. I speed up, passing the tractor on the narrow road.

'I don't know.' His words are nearly whispered. 'I mean, it would have been careless to not pack it away, but I haven't been …'

He hasn't been himself.

'Laila was my friend.' He shakes his head. 'She wouldn't have stolen it from me.' But he sounds unsure. Vulnerable. I don't recognise my brother in this boy who connects more with a stranger from the village than with his gairdín.

'When did you last see her?'

'That day.' Oisín swallows. 'That was the last time she came over. Three months ago. Three weeks before she died.'

Yeah, this is not looking good.

'We'll have to search the tenants' house.' There are three houses just outside the Rookery that we rent out. Only one is currently occupied, by Laila's family.

'I already did.' Oisín releases the words with a sigh.

'You did?' I take a pothole too hard and the car jolts. 'All of them?'

'I spent most of today looking. If Laila took the Eye,

it's not in their house.' For a few seconds, Oisín sounds almost like his old self. 'Nor the empty two. I'm sure of that.'

It's hard to hide a magical artefact this old and powerful. There's a slight thrum off it when in arm's reach. Like Mamó, it likes to tell you that it's important. In a house filled with ordinary things, the Eye would stand out. And Oisín may be damaged, but his new slowness makes him possibly more methodical.

'It's not there,' he repeats.

My thick lip, still tender, tells me that Simon is not to be trusted. It doesn't take a genius to figure out that the missing object Maeve and Sibéal were talking about outside the bungalow could very possibly be the missing Eye. I don't know how they're connected to Laila, if they are at all. But augurs are schemers, and this reeks of them.

'Do you think the augurs want to summon Badb?' I muse out loud. Oisín ignores me, fishing earphones out of his pocket.

'It's cheeky. Stealing our treasures to defeat us,' I continue. But stupid. They mustn't understand how it works. The Eye, with its twisted knotwork design, is a specific form of silver magic. And Knot magic demands action. The augurs can't know what action it needs. I don't even know what action the Eye needs.

'It's not like they can actually use it.' I'm talking to myself. Oisín plugs in one earphone, then the other. In fairness, this is the longest conversation we've had in months.

'Sure, they don't know the offerings,' I say. 'And they never will, unless they think they can read our minds. Which they can't. So this is a waste of time.'

'Shut up, David,' Oisín says. He's staring rigidly ahead. Tinny beats escape from his earphones.

'How many offerings do you know?' I glance at him, not really expecting him to tell me.

Knowledge of the offerings is gifted to deserving descendants of Badb. Mamó and Dad know at least three each, if not four. I remember Oisín, aged thirteen, blinking out in the courtyard the day one was revealed to him. I, apparently, am not deserving.

'You're wrecking the song.' Oisín angles away from me. He's cross, and I don't know why.

Together, my family could make the four offerings, summon Badb and make a demand. With her particular taste for death and carnage, we could cause severe damage to the augurs. If we wanted to.

But, like I said: not monsters. The Eye is for desperate times, it's the red button to be used only when the world is falling apart. Difficult as things may be, we are not at tethers' end.

If it's not in the tenants' house, and Maeve doesn't have it, then where is the Eye of Badb?

Out of the infuriating narrow lanes around Kilshamble, we make up time on the motorway. But in the network of roads around the city, the traffic moves at a snail's pace.

We're thirteen minutes late by the time I drive through the gates at HH. Resisting the urge to dash inside like a naughty schoolboy, I pull myself tall. Mamó and Lucia said to always keep up appearances.

Downstairs, to the back of the house, is the office for the Harkness Foundation, the arts and heritage organisation Cassa runs. Cassa's private rooms are upstairs, but immediately at the top of the wide, marble staircase is the enormous room where she oversees judge matters. Her court.

On the far side of the large room is an imposing table in dark wood with intricate carving. The vast area, the pressed metal ceilings and dark furniture are designed to intimidate. I've spent enough time bleeding on the floor to know it works only too well.

The silence amplifies the sound of Oisín's shoes as we cross the room. Cassa is seated at the heavy table, her bench, with Tarc and Ian standing beside her.

'Did you have a pleasant afternoon?' Cassa smiles at me. Her sweetest smile. The one she uses before she cuts me to shreds.

74

'I'm sorry,' I say, and even though I know better, I continue, 'The traffic was worse ...'

'Save the excuses, David.' She sounds weary. Like I try her. Test her.

'It was my fault.' Oisín is chatty today. 'I delayed him.'

'David took on the responsibility of bringing you here. He should have brought you here on time.'

Always my fault.

'Do you have the Eye?' Cassa says.

'The Eye appears to have been misplaced.' Oisín sounds grand and ridiculous. Inappropriate laughter threatens to rip out of me. Knowing it would piss Cassa off makes the urge worse.

'Misplaced?' One raised eyebrow.

'Unfortunately, yes,' Oisín continues. 'Misplaced. Perhaps my family can offer another piece in its place?'

Cassa gives the smallest smile. 'Your family doesn't have much to offer.'

Ouch. That knocks the laughter out of me.

'Perhaps your grandmother has it?' Cassa says. 'For safe-keeping?'

'Mamó doesn't have it,' Oisín says.

From the way she looks at him, I'm not sure Cassa believes Oisín.

'The Eye of Badb is one of our oldest treasures. We can't

afford to lose it. And negligence, especially from the former War Scythe, can't go unpunished.' Cassa marks something down in the notepad in front of her.

I'm waiting for her to offer Oisín the chance to pay in blood or coin. It's going to have to be coin, even though we don't have the money. But Oisín can't pay a blood fine.

'You will pay in blood and coin.'

'Blood and coin?' The words burst out of me. It's too much. But I'm silenced by Cassa's sharp glance.

'Twenty thousand.'

'Twenty thousand?' We're so badly in debt already.

'But I'll accept an acre.'

Another field. Dad has been selling off our land, field by field.

'And I will administer Niall's ninth row.'

'Cassa.' I swallow hard. I'm going to make things worse if I don't shut up. 'That seems excessive.'

'If the brooch is found before reparation, I will drop the blood fine.' She gives me a quick nod. 'You have until nine this evening.'

Cassa is playing chicken with Mamó. She's made the reparation particularly hard because she believes Mamó has the Eye.

'Better get going.' She nods to the door, dismissing us.

Except I know Mamó hasn't taken the brooch. She's way too proud to claim a family heirloom in such an underhanded way. More than that, Mamó likes that it's part of the War Scythe's trove, it appeals to her own predilection for death and blood. Her sense of grandeur. And she's pretty determined I will be the next War Scythe, so hiding it is counterproductive.

Oisín is going to have to pay that blood fine.

I can't let him.

Oisín isn't able for this. Niall of the Waters was a fourteenth-century War Scythe who had some pretty sick ideas. Of all the punishments, the ninth row is one that demands endurance. It's a punishment for a garraíodóir, for someone at peak strength. Oisín is so thin, so diminished. His eyes are empty and I think that the ninth could finish him. Send him so deep inside himself that there'll be no hope of getting him back. I remember finding him after the attack, lost beneath the blood and bruises, and I can't let him do this.

'Cassa,' I say again. She looks up from her notes, peeved that I'm still there.

'I'll perform the reparation,' I say. My eye twitches; I'm remembering three months ago when Cassa served me Niall's second row, which had me walking stiffly for a week.

'This is my punishment,' Oisín objects.

'Oisín has been ill for months,' I plead with Cassa. 'He's not strong enough. The old and infirm are allowed a stand-in to bear their punishments. These are our rules.'

Cassa examines Oisín and for once I'm glad he looks as awful as he does.

'Very well,' she concedes. 'David, you must return at nine tonight for reparation.'

SEVEN
Fix that too

I watched a boy take a metal box from the hollow of an oak. He unlocked it and spread these ordinary objects like they were treasures.

LAS

Zara

Laila's depressing 'spell' is on my desk.

I don't know why this hideous thing unsettles me so badly, why it gets in under my skin. Makes me feel peculiar.

Sometimes it feels like this house does that too. Today when I came home, it felt strange. Like someone had been there, touching our things. That odd feeling of the air having changed. Like the dust was disturbed, or things shifted the tiniest fraction from where they'd been before. This is the secret lives of houses: that fleeting certainty that things happen when we're not there. But I'm being fanciful. Like Laila.

I glance at the time. It's well after six. Mom's taken Adam for new strings, so there's at least an hour before they're back.

I can't focus on my reading. The spell is distracting. Laila prized her long hair. She must have wanted something really badly if she cut off her hair for it. Using a pencil, I turn it over, looking for something that will help me understand.

Mom can't find this. Laila made this Horrible thing in the weeks before she died, and Mom will think it's further proof of how she failed Laila.

I wrap it in a scarf and hide it in my grey mini backpack. I move the chest of drawers that blocks the knee-wall door and open it. Crouching, I go into the dark attic and leave it there, like I'm hiding evidence of a crime.

My crime.

Laila called me a few hours before she died. And I wouldn't help her.

We'd argued earlier: she'd lost my lipstick, she was always taking my things. When she rang, I'd coddled my anger until it had swelled from lipstick, to that dress she'd wrecked, to my life without my friends. To Nathan.

I rejected her call.

Much later, I saw she'd left a short message on my voice-mail, something she never did. I hadn't even known I had voicemail until that message.

'Zara, I need to talk to you.' She sounded upset.

I called her back, but she didn't answer. I sent a text. No reply. Going to bed, I found she'd started a WordSpat game, sending a new word. *Boot.* When I couldn't get her on the phone, I texted that we'd chat in the morning. I'll never know if she read my final message because her phone was found weeks later between the shrubs on the green, destroyed by rain.

If I'd answered her call, maybe she wouldn't have died.

In need of old comforts, I break my rules and open Instagram.

I'm still one of the gang, I tell myself. Even though I don't recognise where they are, or the people smiling beside Ciara and Hannah and Nathan. My oldest friends.

That grief, always present in my body, pulls from my arm all the way down to my hands. Sharp pricking pain on my palms reminds me how much everything hurts.

Even though we only meet up once a month. I'm still one of the gang.

I make myself look at how Nathan's arm is draped around Hannah, his fingers curling around her exposed hipbone. *I'll mind him for you*, Hannah had laughed. Slipping the phone in my school skirt pocket, I issue another temporary ban on social media.

But, what was it like in those last minutes? I'd heard of fear so overwhelming it could turn dark hair white. And I was afraid that what happened to Laila was so terrifying, so awful, that her body had just stopped.

There's a tread in the passage. I turn out of the room, thinking Dad's home early. And I collide with an intruder. Suddenly, fear in the abstract becomes this living thing that makes my heart gallop and my body go rigid. I think of the Inky Black.

'Whoa,' the stranger says, hand on my arm to steady me.

I step back, taking him in. He looks as solid as he feels. Dark hair, waxed jacket and dark jeans. Heavy boots, which aren't allowed on the pale blue carpet. He's both pretty and fierce, the wind-stirred pink on his cheeks softens the hardness and undermines the sullen, bruised jaw.

'What do you want?' I demand, hiding my fear. Even with the split lip, he doesn't look like an intruder, but then I wouldn't exactly know the current preferred garb and demeanour for breaking into houses. He's carrying a metal toolbox that could well contain torture weapons. Punishment for jealous, cowardly younger sisters.

The shake of his head is barely perceptible and then he smiles and loses that heaviness in his eyes.

'This is embarrassing,' he says with practised self-deprecation. 'I rang the bell and when no one answered, I came in. I am so sorry.' He is laying on the charm now, his smile slightly crooked.

'The door was locked,' I say, my heart still thudding. I trust charming boys least of all.

'I'm from the Rookery.' He holds up a key. 'David.'

One of the Creaghs. I can see a little of Jarlath Creagh, our surly, hulking landlord, in the boy in front of me.

'Your mam called my dad about some things that needed fixing. Said she wanted them done today.'

'The window is downstairs.'

'Yeah. Dad said some shelves in the hot press have fallen down.'

I reach for the key and grab it.

'Hey.' He frowns.

'The doorbell doesn't work.' I walk down the passage. 'You should fix that too.'

He follows as I drop the key into my pocket.

'My key,' he protests.

'No, my key.' I don't turn around. 'Next time, try knocking.'

He follows me into the dark hot press, flipping on the lights.

'This doesn't look good,' he says to the shelves. He stops to examine the wall where the shelves had been unsuccessfully attached.

David starts moving towels and bedding from beneath the fallen shelves. I help him, carrying them to the low shelf beside the boiler.

'She was your sister, right?' he says, addressing the thing

that follows me everywhere. It's weird if people don't talk about it, and it's weird if they do. 'Laila?'

I pause. Usually people say the dead girl or that poor girl dead-on-the-grass. They hardly ever use her name.

I nod and scoop up another pile of sheets, avoiding the sympathy in his eyes. He doesn't need to say it, it's so obvious, but I hear the awkward sorry anyway. Like he could have done anything to stop it. I wonder which of the village versions for dead-on-the-grass he believes. The most pervasive has Laila dying by drug overdose. I swear I've even heard a suggestion of death by foreign food. For some of our neighbours, it doesn't matter that I've lived in this country my whole damn life, for them I am still from somewhere else.

'What's your name?'

An earwig scuttles towards his foot but he doesn't move.

'Zara.' I'm curious: 'Did you know Laila?'

He's searching the toolbox but glances up. 'Seen her around.'

Lifting another stack of bedding, I glimpse Laila's Princess Jasmine bedcover and I can't believe that Mom has kept it all these years. I have a sudden vision of Laila's room, thirty years on, with thick spiderwebs covering pink lip gloss. Mom's sorting will never bring the closure she needs.

David takes down the loose bracket, frowning. I can guess what he's thinking: whoever put up these shelves did a shitty job. I've zero interest in home construction and even I can see it's a shitty job. The whole house is like that, put up quickly on the cheap. For all that it's a big fancy house with a stupid number of bathrooms, it's a knock-off. All appearances but when you look hard enough, you see the faults.

Just like us. Doctor, university professor and A-grade, sport-trophy-achieving children all put together in an attractive package. But inside we're hanging by the hinges.

David is looking at me, a pensive stare that makes my cheeks burn. It's like he can see more than he should. That he knows I'm a little Horrible. And he gives me a small smile, as if to say, *Yeah, I know what it's like.*

In the yellow, energy-efficient light, I look at this boy, his wide shoulders and dark hair. A little tight around the mouth, and I don't think kindness comes easily to him. His eyes are heavy lids over whiskey brown. I realise, as I study him, that I find him attractive. This doesn't happen often. For as long as I can remember, all I've seen is Nathan.

But, this boy. I inch a little closer, Princess Jasmine's smiling face between us. There's something disconcerting about this boy. He's a polka played slow. Something fast, hard and vital stretched out with each note strained and deliberate. And then I get it. He's sad. Like he too has been burying his dead.

Oddly embarrassed, I put down the pile of bed linen. But the stack is too high and it topples over. Lifting Princess Jasmine, I see that something has shaken loose from its folds. David leans in and picks up a red leather zip purse.

He holds it out in his work-roughened hand and I wonder who this boy in front of me really is. He has the bearing of someone who has been told that he's important, who believes that he is important. The only boy, other than Nathan, who's stirred this flare of interest in me. An interest I thought had vanished after dead-on-the-grass.

As I take the red purse, Laila's red purse, Laila's charm bracelet dangles down from my wrist. His eye catches the bracelet, lingering on the charm, on the black crow. David looks up at me, his surprise evident. He opens his mouth to speak but my phone pings and he raises his drill.

'The jammed window is in the utility,' I say, and walk away, wondering if he was Laila's secret boyfriend. He's really not her type, not otherworldly enough. Too present in his body for my sister's taste. Not enough tree bark.

On my bed, I tug the zipper on Laila's purse and it snags. Pushing my fingers in, I see the curl of notes. Tearing the zip, I pull out the bundle. Five hundred euro. Our allowance goes straight into our bank accounts and Laila always ran dry before the month end. Yet there's five hundred on my bed. I can't think of an easy explanation for this.

The Scavenger Hunt business card and the disgusting hair thing. The photograph of Laila outside the grey house. Five hundred in cash. These are fragments of a secret life.

I catch the words in Laila's scratchy writing: *Bad Eye*. Like some evil thing watching.

The walls I'd erected around Laila's secrets are flimsy. Like this house, pieces are beginning to fall.

But I'm glad. Because I'm ready. I want to know what happened to my sister.

EIGHT
Each time he is destroyed

David

Drill to the wall, I wonder how I could have mistaken Zara for Laila out at the village green last night when they are so different. Un-neighbourly creature that I am, I'd had this weird idea Laila's siblings were much younger.

I fix the broken shelf and reinforce the others. When Dad called about the repairs at the tenants' house, I was quick to agree my help. Even though Oisín's searched, doesn't hurt to have a nose around.

Tools packed, I leave the hot press. What a disaster these rental houses have been. After Oisín quit, the judge families who rented the other two huffed off in disapproval, escaping the taint of the failed War Scythe.

I peer in the bathroom, wondering about the people who live here. There are no long hairs on the tiles, no toothpaste smears. The house is clean, but uncomfortably so. The beds belong in a hotel. Nothing, not a book, not a pen is out of place, and it's making my freaky radar ping.

This house a home only in the way that it resembles one. Like a mannequin resembles a person.

I peer into Laila's room. Step inside.

But it's no good. I'd need to look in her wardrobe, open the drawers, sit on the bed, and I can't do that with Zara in the next room.

Towards the end of the passage, Zara reads on her bed.

'Shelves are fixed. I'll head downstairs for the window.'

There's a picture of Laila on the bed, the grey walls of the Rookery behind her. A fierce wave of empathy hits me: when Oisín was thought dead last year, I couldn't bear it.

'Sure,' Zara says. Again, I'm drawn by the rook on her bracelet. It doesn't fit with the delicate gold and there's something unsettling about it.

'It was Laila's.' Zara sees me looking at the charm. 'I don't know where the crow charm is from. It's kinda hideous.'

'Kinda.' Did my brother give this to Laila?

'My grandmother lost a brooch in our field.' I blurt the words out, hoping I don't sound like I'm accusing her dead sister of theft. 'I was wondering if Laila maybe found it, not knowing what it was. You haven't seen anything like that, have you?'

Zara shakes her head. 'My mom's sorted through all Laila's jewellery. C'mon, you can see for yourself.'

She swings herself off the bed. Like Laila, she's graceful. I wonder how much this composure costs her. I recognise the internalised discipline that comes from relentless parental commentary. But I'd guess theirs was gentle, a careful nudging and shaping to their best.

In my family, with Dad, it's something different.

In Laila's room, she opens drawers. I touch the desk, attentive for that familiar intensity I feel when the Eye is near.

'You see it?' Zara says, perhaps a little snippy.

'No.'

She goes around the bed and I follow. I feel a little bad, intrusive, but I'm going to feel a lot worse if Cassa gives me Niall's ninth.

'There's another box in her wardrobe.' She opens the door, flicking on the light. We step inside. All three walls are in arm's reach and I know for sure it's not among the dresses and folded shirts.

'I'm pretty sure if Laila found your granny's necklace she would have given it back straight away.' Definitely snippy.

'Brooch.'

'I don't get brooches.' She slinks by me like a cat, out of the room, and I walk with her. Going down, she pauses near the top step. 'I mean, no one wears them.'

'My grandmother does.'

'Exactly.' She raises a pointed finger. 'And they're always ugly. Let me guess. A diamanté bow? A lady's face in profile?'

'Something like that.' Nothing like that. But I'm enjoying the sudden animated tirade against brooches. She's wrong, but it's funny.

'... quite useless.' She stops abruptly. 'I've gone off, haven't I?'

She smiles and it's infectious.

'You have.'

We're still standing on the top steps. Or she is, I'm two down. It brings her face closer to mine and I'm taking in the clear skin, brown and free of make-up. Her face is angular with large brown eyes. Burnt-gold patches in dark hair.

'You're not at Anne's, right?'

She knows I'm not at the school a few villages over.

'No.'

It's impossible to explain that I've spent the last three years overseas at a school that's trained me as a dutiful soldier. That I've spent years learning to fight, maim and kill. That even from a young age, my father trained me for this life, moulded me to his shape. It's impossible, but there's something about the way she looks at me that makes me want to tell her.

Downstairs, the front door opens and her dad, holding a bundle of papers and laptop case, appears at the foot of the stairs.

'David's from the Rookery.' Zara steps by me, going down. Her dad stares suspiciously at me. 'He's come to fix things.'

'Got to run.' I check the time. 'I'll be back for the window.'

At the door, I glance at the stairs. Zara's at the bottom step and she looks sad. Like there's no fixing what's wrong here. And with her sister gone, I guess there isn't.

I'm back at HH before nine. In the upstairs room, heavy curtains have been pulled across the windows, blocking out the still bright sunlight. The room is lit only with candles.

When she heard about the reparation, Lucia tore apart the Rookery looking for the Eye. Dad, Mamó and Oisín worked together to ask the rooks to search the fields with their sharp eyes. This is not as easy as it sounds: the rooks help us, but on their terms. Anything more requires silver magic.

But the Eye is still missing. And now, Tarc, Elliot and Ian stand beside the tall, heavy wood frame near the entrance. It's old, and if you look closely, you'll see the knife marks and rust-coloured stains. Some call it the cradle, because it can make a grown man bawl like a newborn.

Only Tarc can meet my gaze. I can guess what they're thinking. The War Scythe rounds are never announced in advance. We might hear an hour, even minutes, before one because being ready is part of the assessment. If a fight is called tomorrow, I'm out of the running for sure.

Cassa unlocks the cabinet at the back of the room and my shoulders tighten in anticipation. She brings out a black leather case and lays it on a small rolling worktable.

Tarc takes my arm to lead me to the frame, and his kindness will undo me. I'd rather he was rough and aggressive but that's not his way. I do wonder how Tarc makes gentleness seem like strength.

I remove my jacket and T-shirt. Then shoes, socks and jeans until I'm in my jocks, the black more faded than it should be, and I hate how vulnerable I feel.

Tarc cuffs my wrists, while Elliot brings the chain. It's clipped on the cuffs, and the chain raised to the hook at the top of the frame. The chain pulls, and I'm half suspended from the frame, the balls of my bare feet touching the ground.

Cassa opens the clasps of the leather case. She draws out a small pruning blade. There are bigger, uglier things tucked in the silk lining. Things that can do worse damage. But the art of Niall's ninth is the symphony of wounds in strategic places.

Cassa dips the blade in a small tub and the tip is stained green with whatever poison plant concoction she uses to make hell more hellish.

The first incisions are never the worst. Cassa knows I struggle just before halfway and she saves the most delicate spots, under my fingernails, the long slices on inside skin. The poison on the blade burns as it chases through my body. Three-quarter-ways through, and my eyes are fluttering. My hands are slick against the chain, blood cooling my skin.

I should be impressed at Cassa's skill, her precision. That she knows how to cut: deep enough to hurt without inflicting lasting damage.

By the time Cassa wipes her tools, I'm held up by the chain. I'm tired, bleeding, weak. My arms hurt and I want down. Someone opens the curtains and the candles are snuffed out and then there's silence. I fall asleep or pass out but when I wake, I feel a soft touch.

'Water.' The voice comes to me in the dark. I feel a cup reached to my lips and I drink.

'I'm not sure if you're brave or stupid.' Tarc's voice, a low whisper. If Cassa catches him in here, there'll be trouble. Even for him.

'Get out of here, Gallagher,' I say, but my words are slurred. 'Before you're strung up with me.'

'Hang in there.'

'No choice.' I'm fading out. I don't know if I even say the words.

Then he's gone.

The night is long.

In the morning, Cassa comes in with Elliot and they take me down. On the ground, I'm all animal. The thinking part witnesses the boy groaning on the floor. But there can be no weakness in front of others. So I pull it together. Make myself stand up, a just-born calf on new legs. I'm sore and stiff as I pull my T-shirt over the burning wounds. But, back straight, chin up. Don't let them see you're hurting.

It's wearying trying to shape myself into the man Dad wants me to be.

'"When the soldier is vanquished",' Cassa quotes Niall of the Waters to me, '"his true strength emerges. Each time he is destroyed, he is forged into his most powerful weapon. He becomes man of iron."'

Then I must be really fucking strong.

'Take the day off.' Cassa is uncharacteristically generous. 'But the ritual of the seed remains scheduled for tonight.'

Tarc is at the security rooms when I get there. He washes

my wounds. He treats them with one of Cassa's milder plant salves to seal the cuts, apologising that he couldn't smuggle anything stronger.

And then I sleep, deep and dreamlessly, until late into the afternoon.

NINE
You'll just have to suffer

None of them see me. I'm a no one, the invisible girl.
But the invisible girl gets in where others can't.
LAS

Zara

There are days in Kilshamble when outside feels different.
The sky more purple, the trees too green. The wind has
intent. Today, it nudges into me, lifts my hair and pushes me
down the front path as I set off to the Scavenger Hunt.

A sharp gust rattles the heavy iron gates of the Rookery.
The wind rests, then rises again, and it feels like it wants me
to go to the gates. They're open, just a little, and I draw
nearer. Down the shaded drive, I see the bright green of the
trees, the curve of the road.

When I turn to leave, Jarlath Creagh is just a few feet
behind me. Not for the first time, I feel that blast of panic.
He strikes me as volatile, a man ready to drop a match after
pouring petrol. There's no friendly nod as he passes. It's like

I'm not even there. He looks past me, and I feel insignificant. Invisible. Stepping through the gates, he disappears down the drive as they swing closed behind him.

In the village, tucked away down a quiet lane near the hotel is the junk shop. It's so small and hidden, you wouldn't know it was there. After calling several times, I'd finally reached a young woman who gave me the address, explaining they were on restricted hours. Check the shop door, she'd told me.

But now the door is slightly ajar and I push it open.

Near the counter a young man, I'd guess early twenties, leans against a wall, so lost in thought that he barely glances at me.

The shop is jam-packed with an odd assortment of things: ornaments, DVD collections, musty old coats. Above the cash register, I see the sign made of salvaged scrap: THE SCAVENGER HUNT.

'Shop's closed.' He barely pays me any attention.

Then he looks at me again, properly this time, and straightens up in a slow, languid movement.

'You're Laila's sister.' He steps towards me, wearing an old, misshapen moleskin jacket. A yellow flower in the lapel.

'You knew Laila?'

'I did. Such a loss. Your sister was a rare creature.' He looks like he means it. 'I'm John Canty, but everyone calls me Canty.' He gives a small bow and takes the flower from his jacket, handing it to me. 'Poet.'

'She came in here?'

He pulls his phone from his pocket and fiddles with it. After a moment, he holds it out and there's Laila. I'm greedy for it, this picture of my sister that I've never seen before. Laila is laughing so hard her eyes are nearly shut. Her head is thrown back and she's wearing a wide grey scarf with red stripes at the bottom. Canty is beside her, a broad smile on his narrow face. The letters from the salvaged scrap sign are behind them. I don't know why he's shown me this evidence of their friendship, but I'm grateful.

'This is my mother's shop,' Canty says. 'But she's been poorly these last months, so I've helped out where I can. Laila would come in sometimes. Loved a good chat. She bought the key from me, but it wasn't right for her.'

'What key?'

He gestures to the charm bracelet. But there's no key charm.

'A bad fit, the cadence was all wrong, you know? She talked about you, asked if she could bring you here. We'd agreed, but then … well. I guess you're here now.'

Having hung out with the Drama crowd for years, I recognise the exaggeration, the voice intonations, the careful facial expressions. John Canty is one of those people, the ones who are always performing. The world is their stage, everyone their audience.

'Do you like poetry?' he says.

'Sometimes.' I don't really think about it much. 'So … you write?'

'I scavenge.' He smiles with too many teeth. 'Words are overrated. Come on. I've some new things in.'

He jiggles his keys and turns for the back of the shop.

'Do you know what makes a good poem?' He opens the door at the back of the room and I scurry to catch up.

'Um, the right words?'

'Poetry isn't limited to words,' he scoffs. 'Poetry is when human experience, emotion, impressions, moments, are exquisitely distilled and perfectly organised.'

Laila must have lapped this stuff up. I feel like I've found a piece of my missing sister here in this strange shop.

In the small office at the back, the desk is cluttered with papers. Boxes with picture frames, teacups, feather boas, lampshades spilling from them are stacked around the room. The small space is dominated by a heavy cabinet.

'Poems have power.' John Canty searches through the bunch of keys. 'The gift of the poet is to capture what's otherwise elusive and present it to his audience.'

He holds my eye, pushing meaning into his words: 'Bards are magicians. Enchanters.'

Enchanter. Okaaay.

'Was Laila alone when she came in here?'

'Laila was always alone, even when she wasn't. No, don't be sad.' He must see my face fall. 'That's a good thing. Her solitariness was her strength.'

It doesn't make me feel any better for pushing her away.

'That key on your bracelet is one of my rarer pieces. One-hundred-per-cent crow feather, all harvested from the Rookery. I told your sister I didn't think it would work for her, but she'd fallen in love with it. Not all chants suit everyone. Sure, it didn't matter, it wasn't like she was going to use it. Well, I hope she didn't. She'd be crazy to mess around at the Rookery.'

I look down at the ugly crow on the bracelet. Why is he calling it a key?

'How is it rare?'

'I'll take it back if you want. Same price, four hundred.' He doesn't answer my question.

Four hundred? Laila spent four hundred euro on this? Where was she getting the money?

Canty pulls open the cabinet door, his body blocking my view of what's inside.

'I think I'll keep it, thanks.'

Canty steps aside. In the cabinet are jars and vials and tubs. Everything labelled in a small spiky hand. On the middle shelf are boxes, a weird blank-faced doll made out of red floral cloth and leaf limbs. Creepy. I can well believe the black crow charm came from here. Key. Whatever.

'Here –' he points to vials and tubs on the top shelf; there're some objects, like a tiny wheatgrass wreath, or twigs bound together to form a star – 'are the chants I've made. Beneath are what I call my curious artefacts.'

Like Laila's spell. The one she'd cut her hair for. Did she get the idea for it here?

'Do you know why Laila cut her hair?' I say as Canty reaches for something on the top shelf.

His hand falters. And then he turns to face me.

'I didn't mean for her to do that.'

'What did you mean for her to do?' I feel like I'm on the edge of something, but it's just out of reach.

'She wanted to know if she could make found magic hers. I told her it needs to be encased in her essence. Next thing she chopped off her hair. I don't know any more than that.'

He looks guilty. And it's beginning to make sense.

John Canty is a top-notch scam artist. The poet-wizard who makes money by selling his magic 'chants' at stupid prices. Offering stupid magical advice. And Laila cut off her hair for his lies.

He pulls a small vial with a greenish oil from the top shelf. 'Can I interest you in a love chant? Any boys you want to reel in? This one is made of grass from a handfasting. The lovers would have stood right on it when they pledged to each other. Their love is strong, this is A-grade stuff.'

'Why not?' My words are tight, angry, but Canty doesn't notice. It's like I'm greedy for his lies, so they may fuel my anger. I'll buy his fake love potion, because it is evidence that he is a cheat.

'You look like a girl who's searching and I have just the thing for you. Here, ash from a burnt sacred oak to weed out the irrelevant. Just blow the ash and it will guide you.'

It's an elaborate theatre, but if he's getting four hundred for an ugly black crow, it must be worth it.

'Where do you get these?' I gesture to the wood cabinet.

'Poets are scavengers, whether they use pretty words or not.' He smiles at me with his lank hair, his ill-fitting jacket and crowded teeth. 'Magic always leaves remnants and I trawl through the leftovers hoping to find traces. It's usually only grey, or maybe blue if I'm lucky. But the rare time, I get silver.'

He eyes Laila's charm bracelet with some greed.

'But if a chant doesn't work, I don't take responsibility,' Canty continues. 'There's no money-back guarantee.'

Of course there isn't.

I cast a final glance at the cabinet before he closes the doors. On the top shelf, I see a tub with a dark smear inside it. There's a rough label with a date and a single word: *Sacrifice*.

John Canty sees me looking at the tub and hastily pulls the door shut. But it's too late, I saw it. In his cabinet of scavenged things, John Canty has a jar labelled Sacrifice and the date of Laila's death.

Laila's death chant. And that anger surges again.

How grim. How utterly vile that he uses my sister's death to flog his potions.

I have to get out of there. I knock over a box in my haste to leave. In a minute, I'll be screaming, and the whole village will know that the second daughter lost it. Mom will be humiliated as well as grieving and cheated upon.

'That's not Laila's.' He speaks softly. I don't believe him. 'Please, wait.'

I stop. Look at him over my shoulder. He reaches into his pocket and comes towards me.

'I have something for you.' And holds out a thin delicate band, a small black stone on the ring.

'Is this a chant?' He must see how rigid I am. How furious.

He shakes his head, eyes averted. 'A gift. I guess I wish I'd given it to Laila.'

'Canty,' a voice calls from the shop. 'Where the hell are you?'

'Hey, John,' I hear Breanna sing.

'Stay in here.' I can see the unease on his face as Canty moves to the door of the office. 'No. Too late, they're coming in. Quick, under the desk. You can't let them see you here.'

I pause a moment, my cheeks hot. Is this a trick? Am I going to find pictures of myself cowering beneath the desk shared at school?

'Now,' Canty bites out.

I scramble under the desk.

The office door opens and through the cable hole, I see long legs clad in denim.

'I could have made off with your mam's things.' Cillian's voice is lazy and arrogant. 'Oh yeah, no one wants that shit.'

'What can I do for you?'

'Breanna saw something yesterday. Lots of hair, a bit of twine.'

He's talking about Laila's ugly thing that fell out of my pocket. Why is he interested in that?

'And?' Canty says.

'She got a feeling off it.'

'You're telling me this because?' Canty sounds un-interested.

'Did the girl get it from you? Did you scavenge it from somewhere and sell it on?'

I press my eye to the hole to see Canty shrug.

'And why would I tell you?'

'C'mon, Canty. Small details. This is nothing important.'

'You know my currency. I deal in chants, artefacts and information. You want to know something, you give me something I can use.'

'Help a friend out here.'

'I've always stayed in the middle, Cillian. I help those who pay. Anything else muddies the waters.'

Cillian moves closer to Canty.

'How can I change your mind?' The threat is clear in Cillian's voice.

'Information. Or an object I can use.'

Cillian is silent. He obviously doesn't have what Canty wants.

Then I hear a loud crash. Pressing my eye to the hole in the desk, I see Cillian shoving Canty against the wall. He has him by the neck, wrapping his hands so tightly the man can't breathe. Breanna watches.

'Get your hands off me,' Canty breathes.

Cillian pushes harder on Canty's slim neck.

'Not mine.' Canty breathes in deep gulps of air. 'She didn't get it from me.'

Cillian drops his hands, steps back. Canty takes a few moments to catch his breath.

'You do that again, Cillian, and I won't help you, any

of you, again. That's a promise.' His eyes are furious as he steps forward to Cillian. 'You don't want to make an enemy of me.'

'Always a pleasure.' Cillian tilts his head and turns out of the room, Breanna leading the way.

I wait a moment and then emerge from the desk. Canty has smoothed down his hair, his clothes.

'Do you need anything else?' He's shaken.

'No. Who is that guy?'

In the last month or so, Cillian seems to be always around the village. Doesn't look like he's working or at school, so he's usually just hanging around.

'Do yourself a favour, give that boy and his friends a wide berth.' These are the first words Canty's said that don't feel like performance. 'They are dangerous.'

Leaving the shop, it feels like coming up from underground. I'm feeling queasy, and not only because I've just spent a two hundred on a love chant and ash from a burnt oak.

It's gone five, so passing Kelly's practice, I pop inside. If Mom is nearly done, I'll walk back with her.

A selfish part of me is glad that Mom isn't as busy as she used to be. Before we moved, she had her own practice, a large and busy place that kept her there from early in the morning until late in the evening. At one time, that had

107

been everything to her. That was before Laila and the jimsonweed, Dad and the last Lindy.

I go inside and see Mom near the reception desk.

'This is a surprise.' She's delighted and it makes me feel guilty. It's a simple thing to seek her out like this and it's cheered her up like nothing else these last awful months. It's cheered me up too.

'I thought we'd walk back together.'

'I'll be done in twenty. Take a seat.'

Behind the half-wall is a new receptionist. She's striking, almost ethereal, with her dark blonde hair and startling brown eyes.

'I'm Zara.'

She's staring at me so intently, it's a little unnerving.

'Aisling.'

'You're new here?' I say.

'I'm covering Emer's maternity over the summer.' She smiles.

I've taken a seat when I hear the door open.

'I'm sorry, we're closed.' Aisling stands up. She doesn't look at all sorry. Her body is lined with tension as she stares at the door.

I can't see who's come in, the wall is in the way, but Aisling really doesn't like whoever it is.

'I said we're closed,' she says.

When they emerge from the short passage, I see David. He's with someone, his brother by the looks of it. But the brother is a cheaper version of David. It's like whoever made David ran out of materials to finish the second and so made a dull, scrawny copy. Still beautiful, but in the way of a dying prince. Elegant, haughty with that sense of being beyond earthly things.

This is a boy Laila would have loved.

And, if I believe John Canty, Laila had a 'key' to the Rookery.

But I don't believe John Canty. Whatever the connection is, if there is one, I don't get it.

'Emer not here?' David falters as he approaches the desk.

'Do you see her?'

'I need a script.'

'Please.'

He sighs: 'Please.'

'No.' She folds her arms.

'You can't do that.' David sounds weary.

'Yes, I can.'

There's history here, and I wonder what it is. Watching them from my corner in the waiting room, I decide that it must be bad romance. Perhaps they dated and maybe he couldn't bear her chewing gum and she despised his obvious obsession with fitness and now they're barely civil with each other. But it surprises me, this tiny smear of jealousy. I don't know this boy, why would I care?

'Look, I know you can print one out for me.' David is barely holding on to his patience. 'Emer's done it before.'

'I can.' She drags out the word as if contemplating it. 'But I won't. If you want a script, I have to check with the doctor. And since your buddy Kelly's away for the weekend, you'd have to ask Dr Salie. But sorry, we're closed. So you'll just have to suffer.'

She looks at him a moment and a slow smile spreads on her face.

'Wow, someone got you bad. Who was it? I'd like to send them a gift basket.'

He turns to his brother and I see David's face. He looks pale and drawn. Like all of this takes effort. Whatever he needs a script for seems pretty serious to me.

'If it's a repeat prescription, I'm sure my mother won't mind.' As I speak, David and the other guy turn to me, surprised. I'm across the room, on the low couch. They hadn't realised I was there.

Down the passage, a door opens and I hear her heels on the tiles.

'Aisling, have you sent the …' She stops as she sees the two boys.

'What's this?' Mom looks at them. Worry crosses her face. 'Do you need an emergency appointment?'

'I need painkillers,' David speaks up. 'Dr Kelly's prescribed them for me before. I know you're closed and I'm sorry to bother, but could you please print the script?'

Mom's a sucker for good manners.

'Aisling, can you call up the record for me?' Mom steps into the reception office. 'You're Jarlath Creagh's boys, right?' Her words draw attention to how weird it is that we've not really met. But their house is set back on their land, behind paddocks and hidden by trees.

And we live in our ruts. Blinkers on, we do the same things, see the same people day after day. Until we die.

No wonder Laila longed for magic.

Mom leans over Aisling's chair and reads the computer screen. Whatever's there, she doesn't like.

'I won't prescribe these without a consultation.'

David goes rigid. 'Never mind.'

The other guy says, 'David, just do it.'

'I'll manage without,' David says, but he sounds tired. 'C'mon, Oisín.'

Oisín puts a hand on his arm. 'Please.'

After a moment of silent fighting between them, David relents and follows Mom down the passage.

David returns to the waiting room ten minutes later,

111

folded white sheet in hand. Mom follows behind him. Her face has gone tight and she can't meet his eyes. He pulls out a worn wallet and puts a few notes on the counter.

'See ya, Zara,' David says to me, lingering a moment.

Mom looks up sharply. She turns away when they thank her and she's still not talking on the walk home.

'What was wrong with him?' I ask as we near our road. I know she can't tell me, but I want her to say something about it.

She shakes her head.

'Mom?'

She stops. 'Keep away from those boys, Zara. I don't like them. Especially David.'

'You've only just met them.' It's not like Mom to be this hasty to judge. Mom's the kind who'd argue the devil himself is just misunderstood. Mom will pick up stray demons on the side of the road and invite them home so she can heal them.

She walks faster and I chase after her. 'Sometimes once is enough,' she says.

'I thought you said no one is beyond redemption.' I'm getting cross.

'People have to want to be redeemed.'

'And how do you know they don't?' I challenge her.

But she won't say anything more.

When she examined David she discovered something she really doesn't like. Like maybe he's addicted to whatever drugs he was looking for. Something that made her decide that David is beyond fixing.

We walk the rest of the way in silence. It's uncomfortable and heavy, like I've done something wrong. Even during dinner and after, the mood doesn't lift. Dad's out again and I have to escape.

I go out back and up the steps into the wild garden that Laila loved. I've avoided the garden because it reminds me too much of last September, when Adam and Laila and I would waste time out here. Laila would tell stories about the Horribles or we'd just be quiet, stare at the sky, the trees, the many rooks that fly overhead.

I lie back on the grass as the evening finally begins to darken around me. I turn over the things that weigh on my mind: Breanna and Sibéal. Cillian and Canty. David. His brother. Mom's certainty that David is bad news.

A large yellow moon is rising against the indigo sky. I think it's the new light that helps me see what I hadn't seen before. Looking at the hedge, I notice how the thin trunks of the trees are a little bent. How they make a small opening, like a gateway.

Getting to my feet, I move closer and peer inside. There's a deep hollow formed by the hedging trees.

It's the Horribles' ditch. My ditch. Here's where Horrible Laila cut her first Awthrack, the vicious biting creatures with blood on their teeth. Where Horrible Adam sang his Death Song, the dirge that lured a hundred rats to their death, and Horrible Zara trained her insect circus. I can't believe I haven't found this before. Leading through the hollow is a small trail. Overgrown, but distinct. And through the trees at the other end, I can see the green of Jarlath Creagh's fields.

I step inside the hollow, moving towards the Rookery.

Where Laila had a key.

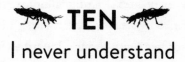

TEN

I never understand

David

Had I realised Aisling was the new receptionist at Ryan's dad's practice, I would have broken into their house, empty this weekend, and helped myself to Bryce Kelly's prescription pad. Anything would have been easier than this.

Dr Salie examines my eyes in her consultation room and I realise, with dread, that she's one of those doctors. Earnest, with a burning need to help. She'll want to understand everything. I can only imagine that she's responsible for hiring a fucking augur.

Headaches, I tell her, but she knows it's more. She knows I'm injured. I curse Bryce Kelly for not finding a less observant doctor to take over as he retires.

'Did someone hurt you, David?' She examines my bruised jaw, my cut lip. The compassion in her voice nearly breaks me. So I put on a stony face and tell her I've been in a fight.

'Fight?' She wrestles her disappointment, trying to

reconcile well-mannered son of landlord with violent thug. 'Were you attacked?'

I glance up at her. Does she think I am a victim? Has she seen me? I'm a soldier. We get hurt.

'Nothing like that.' I want to leave it there but, as with her daughter, I have this urge to explain myself. It's the way they look at me, that steady gaze that sees beyond the surface and finds me wanting. 'A disagreement. It got physical.'

Cassa would have me back on the cradle without hesitation if I drew unwanted attention to us. But the ritual of the seed is tonight and I will be expected to contribute as if I hadn't spent the previous night chained and bleeding.

'I never understand how that happens.' The doctor Velcroes a cuff to my arm, agitating the wounds there. 'Must have been something important. A girl?' Her eyes are on the blood-pressure monitor.

I shrug. I can't exactly tell her the truth: You see, Dr Salie, the wounds all over my body are evidence of ritualistic punishment, carefully designed to be excruciatingly painful without totally incapacitating me. Performed with cold precision by my mother's half-sister. Which I opted for, to spare my brother, who was seriously fucked up by augurs back in December. What are augurs, you say? They're a bunch of mean, hard-drinking bastards who think they can tell the future but it hasn't seemed to help them much.

Dr Salie's face is carved with distaste. I realise I've been smiling, because it's so absurd. I must look a sick bastard who amuses himself with violence and jealousy. Her words are clipped as she turns away to print out the script, warning me how to use it, like I haven't gotten it off Ryan's dad many times before.

The pharmacy is thirty minutes each way and by the time we get back to the Rookery, we've not long before the ritual of the seed.

The reparation last night was only the beginning. There'll be a cloud of suspicion over us, over Oisín especially, until the Eye is returned.

I have to find a way forward, and there is only one thing for it.

I have to use my words.

I wolf down the dinner Lucia's kept in the oven, anxious to go down the back fields. To the old oak, thick and moss covered, with a hidden hollow near the base.

At the oak, I reach my hand into the cavity, feeling under the leaves. At the touch of small legs, I pull out my hand and examine the beetle there. It stays on my hand, the black legs ticklish.

'Hey, little fella.' I run a light finger down its wings and the plates covering its abdomen, the tail that's slightly raised even though I know it's not at all agitated.

And all my pain and tension disappears. I sit there, letting the devil's coach-horse crawl on the palm of my hand.

Lucia knows the secret magic of trees, how alder may be used for protection or whitethorn for heart's desire. Dad, Oisín and Mamó are bound to the rooks with a respectable blue magic. Cassa, who is touched by silver magic, has her flowers. Rumour has it they can steal secrets and then whisper them to each other, all the way back to Cassa. Some swear they've seen her make a rose bloom in thirty seconds. I know for sure her plant salves can bring a man to his knees. She is never stronger than when surrounded by flowers.

And me? Insects like me.

This is my magic trick, my dull, grey superhero power: insects come to me. I'm an invertebrate pied piper, luring beetles, termites, moths. But beyond this magnetism, nothing more. I do not command an army of ants, I can't wield the mysticism of bees. Insects find me. That's all.

It's never going to help me save the world.

The devil's coach-horse gone, I reach into the tree, feeling for the metal box I keep there.

With enough words, we can form a law. In my pocket, I have the strip of leather that I cut from the steering wheel. And in my box there's a stone, a blade of grass, some jagged plastic, a thumbtack, a metal pencil parer, a button, a girl's shoelace and a lock of bloodied hair. My words are encased in these objects, and I can use them to help me find the Eye.

This is not an immediate abracadabra kind of magic, or else I would have come here before reparation. Rather, when a law passes, a path to the desired outcome opens up. It's up to the judge to follow this path and it's not always easy. There will be events, opportunities that will help me find what I'm looking for. I have to be ready to take them.

I feel around beneath the leaves but my hand hits only dirt. The panic doesn't start at once. No one knows I keep my words here, and even if Dad or Oisín or Lucia did, they wouldn't move it. Not even Mamó, who has little respect for the rights of others, would touch another judge's words.

My box isn't there.

My words have been stolen.

I can't pass a law. I feel myself curling up tight and then reaching out as I roar. Everything has been fucking horrible and now it's worse.

I have no words.

I stand there, helpless. Furious and inert with this large sense of awfulness that is about to overtake us.

Think, David. Where could they be?

Who could have taken it? Sibéal? Possible, but the rooks would go mad if an augur came to the house and fields. There'd be blood and feathers to show.

119

When last did I see the box?

A while ago. It's been pretty dry with the old words lately. Aside from Keep, encased in the steering wheel leather, I haven't received one since Stephen's Day just after Wren stabbed my hand. Nearly six months ago. As luck would have it, that word wanted hair. I'd checked up on the box a couple of times, but probably not since March.

Laila.

She'd been in our fields. She'd very possibly stolen the Eye. My box has to be in the tenants' house. Or wherever the hell she'd hidden the Eye.

I want to go there right away. But running into Dr Salie's house breathless and demanding to search Laila's room will get me nowhere. I have to be smart about this.

Back at the house, Dad is in foul humour at the loss of another field and he can barely look at Oisín. He's locked himself in his study with a bottle of wine.

Oisín and I are alone in the kitchen. I open the glass cabinet for the Langstream crystal. But reaching up, I'm unable to help the grunt of pain that escapes.

'Why did you do it, Davey?' His face is blank. But he called me Davey. He hasn't done that in months. 'My reparation?'

Placing the whiskey and glasses on the table in front of him, I twist open the bottle top.

I push a glass in front of him. He looks at it.

'What happened that night you were attacked?' I ask.

The silence drags out. And just when I think that's it, that he'll shut himself off again, he surprises me.

'I don't remember much.' He's fiddling with the glass on the table. 'One minute, I was spying on three augurs who were humming binding songs at the megalith. Next, a bunch of them had surrounded me. We fought. I was holding them off. But I must have been hit on the head because I blacked out. Later, I was in a farm shed some-where. Chained to a post, and drifting in and out of consciousness.'

'Did they drug you?' I take a deep slug of the whiskey, remembering too late Dr Salie's warnings about the pills. Small sip won't hurt.

He thinks for a moment. 'It was like being drugged, but I don't think I was.'

'Did you see anything? Hear anything?'

'They said they'd take me to the woven room.'

'The woven room? What the hell is that?' Sounds like some kind of old people nightclub.

He shrugs. 'No idea. I remember a harsh white light. It would be on for a few minutes, then go out. And there was music. Like carousel music. It felt like I was in a theatre. On stage and part of an act.'

This is the most Oisín has ever talked about that night.

'I lost all sense of time. I was chained in a corner, the light flashing on and off. The rest of the place in darkness. But it felt like it went on for months, the music playing as I drifted in and out of consciousness. There were other things that I can't explain. The sense of something large swinging across the room, then back again, like I was inside a giant clock.' He glances up at me. 'I've always been strong, both physically and mentally. That's come easily to me. I used to despise weakness because I couldn't understand it. But in that place, in that woven room, I was broken.'

There's more. I wait.

He stares at the tumbler, struggling with what he's about to say.

'I told them one of the Badb's offerings.'

If Cassa hears this, she'll never forgive him. It doesn't matter if the augurs used thumbscrews or blades, he'll be guilty of collusion – no matter how unwilling.

'We have to keep this to ourselves,' I say quietly. These are words that could disqualify me from the War Scythe contest.

'They're here.' Lucia is at the door. From her troubled eyes, I know she's heard enough. 'Cassa's impatient.'

'Better go.' I stand. The bite from hundreds of cuts has been clawing into my flesh with rising intensity. I pull the

122

blister of pills from my back pocket. It's going to be a long night.

Outside, the garraíodóirí are waiting. We cross the fields until we reach Cassa's new acre. We're carrying an assortment of tools, as if heading to work the land. But the rising moon is yellow against the evening sky, and there's time before it's dark.

'You up for this?' Tarc is beside me.

'Sure,' I lie. I don't want Tarc to shield me or bear the brunt of the work. And he'll do that even though he has his own pain, and even though he is wary of me, because he is good. But if word gets back to Cassa, she won't be happy. Elliot and Ian walk behind us, their heads bent together. They're all right, but we're rivals. And they won't hesitate to push me down to keep themselves ahead.

Raising tools, we break the soil. The earth is hard and stony, resisting our efforts. Gritting my teeth, I force the shovel down and dig.

ELEVEN
Get out of here

*I wish Zara would come with me to the woods
sometimes. She's been so distant since we moved
here. I worry.*
LAS

Zara

I hesitate. I'm not worried about being caught, because
that's unlikely given the size of the grounds. But it feels I'm
crossing a threshold, going through the hedging trees.
I'm stepping into Laila's world.

It's after ten and the sky is an array of grey-blues and
oranges in the dying throes of daylight. To my left is the way
to the Rookery. On the right, the hedge thickens and turns,
a gate connecting to another field. I pause a moment, then
head right.

I climb over another cattle gate and walk on, wildflowers
and tall grass slapping at my sandals.

Then, on the other side of a thick line of trees, I hear it.

A regular *thu-thunk* breaks the silence of the evening. Orange light from a flaming torch.

Peering out, I see them. Four half-naked boys, and they're digging. I hear the sound of their tools hitting the ground in a discordant tattoo. I watch one pull back his spade, tossing the dirt into the heap beside him. Another lifts a pickaxe, swinging it down to break the hard ground. The first thing that occurs to me is that they're digging a mass grave. Because that's what's on my mind: graves and dead people. But the pit is wide and I don't see any bodies. I edge a little closer.

I watch as the boys dig.

Their skin shines with sweat and dirt in the torchlight. They're more than knee deep when they stop, and another boy wheels over a barrow of soil. It is disconcerting, watching these boys with their beautiful bare backs and shoulders working the empty field late at night. It feels dark and secret and I want to know more.

David's there. He's concentrating hard on this inexplicable task. His skin has some kind of marking on it, but I can't make it out. The smell of turned earth is sharp and fresh in the air. One boy stops to pick up a bottle of water and as he drinks, he pauses as if he hears something. He looks around and I duck behind the tree as his gaze turns my way.

'Gallagher,' David calls him. 'Chuck that water, will you?'

Gallagher tosses another bottle of water. David catches it, drinks it down. He wipes his mouth with the back of his hand, streaking dirt on his chin.

Gallagher scans the trees again. I press against the tree, wishing myself invisible. I don't know what this is, but these aren't farm boys working the fields. Something feels off. They toss earth, filling the pit with new soil. They work mostly in silence, apart from the occasional word. David throws his spade to the ground and stretches out.

'Back in a few,' he says as he ambles off. I watch him jump over a gate and disappear.

My phone vibrates: Where are you?

Mom. Now she wants to know where I am.

The phone buzzes with another, angrier message from Mom, when I feel the large hand cover my mouth, taste the grit. My back is pressed against muscle and bone, there's sweat sticking to my long-sleeved T-shirt.

'Looking to start another fire?' a voice says in my ear.

He turns me around to face him and I can see the surprise on his face. Whoever David thought he was grabbing, it wasn't me.

'Zara?' he says.

He takes my arm and leads me from the trees, back through the field. When there's some distance between us and the boys he stops.

'Why are you here?' He is cold and distant, unsmiling. Not the charmer I met the previous day, nor the well-mannered boy at Kelly's practice. Tonight he is something else entirely. Then I see him, properly see him. I'm staring and he doesn't like it. There's ink on his body: his inner forearm, and the hint of something emerging from his waistband. But that's not what caught my attention.

'What happened to you?' I want to reach out a hand to the cuts on his skin. It wasn't markings I'd seen, but a myriad of incisions on his chest and arms. New wounds. Is this why Mom was so tight-lipped?

'Fell through a window.' He's curt and I know he's lying. 'You have to get out of here.' Taking my wrist, he strides across the field and into the next.

'Stop.' I'm breathless at keeping up with his pace. 'Look, I'm sorry I was in your field. I shouldn't have.'

'Not my field,' he mutters.

We're at the hollow in the hedge when we finally stop. The dark is drawing in, closing around us.

'What were you doing back there?' I can't help asking.

'Had some tubers to plant. It's a good evening for it.' He shrugs uncomfortably and turns back to the direction we walked. 'I've got to go, help out.'

'David,' I call out.

'What is it?'

'You know what's the hardest thing?'

His eyes are hooded and I'm not sure I like this version of the boy I met yesterday. But then something gives. He shifts, relaxes slightly: 'What?'

'That I didn't ask questions. That there's so much about my sister that's a mystery to me. She had this whole other life, this whole other world that had enraptured her. I knew nothing about it, and I wish I could change that.'

I don't know why I'm telling him this. It's an apology. An explanation. I'm trying to tell him why I'm here where I shouldn't be. And perhaps I'm trying to understand it myself, this strange new appetite that's stirring.

He looks at me with an odd expression, and I turn away, making my way through the hedge.

At home, Adam's in the den. He's watching something violent and I sink on to the couch beside him. I watch the screen but none of it makes sense. All I can see is boys digging, the dusky indigo sky, the burning torch.

He glances at me. 'What have you been up to?'

'Hmmm?'

He gestures to the muck on my arm.

'Mom was looking for you. You might want to wash up.' His attention is back to the wild shooting on the TV screen.

Upstairs, I duck into the bathroom and drop my clothes. There's dirt on my shirt from when David grabbed me, long streaks of sweat and soil on the back. My hair is half undone and when I catch my reflection, I see my eyes are impossibly large. I look like a girl with a secret.

I look like Laila.

TWELVE
Beloved

David

When I get back to the digging, Cassa and Dad have arrived.

Dad's got swagger tonight as he lights the small pyre, feeding it with bonemeal, oakmoss and sage. He's glowering, pissed about losing this field. He doesn't understand why Cassa gets to tell him what to do, when he's so certain of his own greatness.

Even in the near dark I can see how much Cassa loathes him. And he her.

'Find anyone?' Tarc examines the peony tubers in a brass dish. Their odd little bodies were sprinkled with garraíodóirí blood at the equinox. They blindly stare at me with their pink eyes.

We'd both sensed it, someone hiding by the trees. With the field now belonging to Cassa, the rooks won't alert us to augurs. I wouldn't be surprised to find Sibéal here with leg-hold traps. Or landmines.

'No one there.' I really shouldn't lie during a ritual, even an informal one like this. The stink of the bone fire, sacred fire to lure silver magic, burns my nose and eyes.

Zara's confession, made in the darkness, bothers me. Whatever Laila was up to, doesn't look like Zara was in on it. But spying on us? Not cool.

'No one? Really?' Tarc's surprised. I get it, the uneasiness he feels. I feel it too. Something ugly is coming our way.

Tarc hands the tubers to Cassa, who kneels in the dirt to plant them. She'll do this herself, just as she's prepared the soil brought in from the walled garden at HH. She chants in Old Irish as she places the tubers in the new bed.

Beneath the burning torch, I see the lines of the Bláithín mark, the five-looped knot, near Tarc's hipbone. I was thirteen when I received mine. Made to stand unflinching when the inked needle branded my skin. Set me aside as a special little soldier.

I hate this tattoo, which says I am from a long line of soldiers, as much as I hate the snake on my forearm that marks me as garraíodóir. I hate their smothering permanence. Sometimes, when they catch my eye, I can't breathe and have to fight the urge to scrub them off my skin with some corrosive surface.

Cassa calls us to take our positions for closing, one in each of the five loops of the large Bláithín mark carved into the soil. Her eyes are troubled, and I know why: this ritual feels weak. Even with the sacred fire, it doesn't have the charge it needs.

Later, back at the house, I want only a shower and bed. Dad's in his study, nursing a drink. Hunched over the amber liquid, his eyes are troubled.

'I'm going to fix it.' He stands, throwing back the drink.

'Fix what?' Because there's so much that's wrong. 'How?'

'Everything.' He glances at me. 'For too long we've been sitting back just letting things happen. It's time to take control.'

Dad's always been a weird mirror of the future for me. In him, I see the man I'm meant to become. I've been taught to idolise his strength, his way with weapons. To be gruff, blunt, abrupt. Relentless. Without mercy or remorse.

But lately, what once seemed like vigour and fortitude now looks like bluster and stubbornness. His scrabbling for power seems desperate.

It's unfamiliar, this pity I feel for him as he pours another whiskey. He's in no way unsteady or slurring, but I can tell from the rigid way he moves that Dad is hammered. This is all he has: drunk, angry plotting that will come to nothing. Powerlessness sits poorly on him.

'Sure, Dad.' It's painful to watch.

'I've a job for you. In a few weeks.'

'OK.'

'I can count on you?'

'Of course.'

'Promise me, David.'

'Promise, Dad.'

I leave him to his whiskey-fuelled dreams of power.

I can barely drag my feet up the stairs. But I stop at Oisín's room. I want to test if that tenuous connection we forged at the kitchen table still holds. Knocking at his door, there's no response, so I push it open quietly.

Oisín is bent over his desk. From his profile, I can see the fierce concentration on his face. The room is lit only by the desk lamp. He doesn't realise I've come in, that I'm halfway across the floor, watching.

On his desk are several objects. The lid of a jar, a shard of glass. A leaf, a pressed flower and bit of twine. Oisín is positioning them carefully. I see his mouth moving as he whispers the words enclosed in the objects. I should leave, but I'm so relieved to see him doing something to help himself that I'm rooted to the floor.

Oisín is using his words. Finding a way out. Making sure we can track down the Eye and lift the cloud of suspicion that hangs over us. It feels like a weight has been lifted from my shoulders.

'Beloved.' He picks up the leaf. It's mottled and brittle. He places it at the top of the black velvet cloth he's laid out on the desk. The twine, a button and jar lid are already positioned.

'Molten.' A dull, thick shard of glass is at the opposite end of the leaf.

'Princess.' The pressed flower at the centre.

It's not the strongest law, with only seven words. Ten is best; after that words are wasted as adding more doesn't achieve much. The words themselves have to match the intention: you can't use the word Love to make yourself rich, or Brave to cower. But Oisín is good at investing, and that counts. It could shift a law from grey magic, low level and mildly effective, to blue. He's infusing the law with the strength of his feeling, which is why he doesn't sense me watching. He's silent for some minutes as he bends over the cloth in silent supplication.

I'm about to back out – I really shouldn't be watching this – when he speaks his intention. The sentencing.

'For David. That he may be free.'

I watch him sweep a hand over the objects to set the intention. He has passed a law. The air feels thick and charged, like he's channelled blue magic despite having only seven words.

'Oisín!' I yell, but he doesn't even look my way.

I'm horrified that he's wasted his words. Words that would have taken him the better part of a year to collect, on some insane notion that I need to be free when he is so utterly, utterly fucked right now.

I stare at the objects on the black velvet. They're now husks, useless. The words have been removed from them and something has been set in motion.

'Why did you waste them?'

'You need them more than I do.'

He picks up the husks and throws them in the bin. Ignoring me, he potters around his room, looking at his bookshelf and picking up a book. Then, pulling off his T-shirt and jeans, he drops them to the ground. He's pale, and though there're remnants of muscle definition, he's painfully thin. Oisín gets on to his bed, pulling up the covers as if to hide from my scrutiny.

'Get out, Davey.' There's a bite in his words. I stand there, still trying to figure out what's going on with him.

'Out,' he roars, and throws the book at me. It hits me on the head. I smile.

'Get the fuck out.' He picks up the Langstream crystal carriage clock beside his bed and hurls it at me. I dodge and it hits the wall, landing in pieces at my feet. He falls back on his bed like all his energy is spent.

I leave his room, laughing. I sound crazed. I am crazed. The incisions in my skin are burning, my muscles ache. My head smarts from where the book hit. And I'm pissed that

Oisín wasted his words when he could have used them to find a way out of this mess.

But it doesn't matter. Because I feel lighter. Because I caught a glimpse of him, the brother who tormented me all my eighteen years. A fleeting glimpse, but it means everything. It means that Oisín is still there.

THIRTEEN
The school road

On the green, this woman wearing a dress with giant flowers was waiting for me. She asked me how I like it here in the village.

LAS

Zara

Mom is cross. She's loading the car, dumping the crate of bottles with more vigour than is necessary.

'You need to tell me where you're going when you leave this house. Especially at night.'

Nearly three months of barely noticing us, and now she wants to know where I am. This must be a new stage of grief.

'I was in the garden. Then went for a walk.'

She drops a shopping bag of jars in the boot, they clink angrily. Wiping her hands, she stops in front of me.

'Did you wear a vizzie vest? Were you alone?'

'I don't exactly have any friends around here,' I say nastily.

'I saw how that boy looked at you.'

'That's nuts. Why are you being like this?' I'm almost shouting now, but I can't help it. One time, three words. She saw David say three words to me, and now she's constructed a disaster narrative around it.

'Look.' She takes a deep breath. 'Just let me know where you are, OK? I need to know that you're safe. And stay away from the Rookery.'

'It's too late.' I almost hiss the words. 'Laila's dead. And tracking my every move is not going to bring her back.'

It's a horrible thing to say. She freezes, her face a mask of pain, then turns away and gets into the car.

'Nice one, Zara,' Adam snaps at me as he gets in beside her. She reverses into the road and they're gone.

I stand in the drive, filled with this hollow, guilty pain. I am an empty girl, with gaping cavities inside.

Since moving here, I've felt like I've been slowly unravelling. Like someone pulled a thread, and as I move, I come undone. And since dead-on-the-grass, it's been faster, as if nearing the end. And I suspect that in my unravelling, I'm going to find something different at the core.

Something both unexpected and known. Something Horrible, honest and true.

I start walking down the road, so fast that I'm nearly

running. I've no destination in mind, I just don't want to be at home.

I reach the yield in the road to the village, when a man stops me. He's wearing overalls and wellies, and has a round smiley face.

'Take the top road,' he says.

'What?' I'm wondering if this is some kind of arcane life advice. But he gestures to the higher road that runs parallel to the one we're on.

'Go by the school road.' He gestures down to the blind corner. 'They're moving cattle down here. It'll be faster that way.'

'The school road?' Many of the roads around here aren't named. There aren't any signs, so the informal names of fields and roads is oral knowledge.

'There used to be an old school up there. Closed down about a hundred years ago. It's a nicer walk that way. Fine day for it.'

A magpie lifts off a tree, disappearing down the top road and I follow. The hedges are wild with growth, and it's quieter; there aren't many houses up here. I pass what must be the ruin of the schoolhouse, stopping to step inside. There's not much left of it, just the thick walls, the shape of rooms over-grown with ivy. I wonder if Laila came here. She probably did. And again, I'm so sorry I didn't explore this with her.

When I realise it, I'm so sure I'm right that my heart is beating excitedly.

The card I found tucked behind Laila's corkboard. *Find Meadowsweet on School.* It had to be referring to this narrow road. I continue down it, and after a little way, I find a place where meadowsweet grows in abundance.

I go a little further and see the old gateway. It's pretty overgrown, but it's clear this was once an entrance. And down at the bottom of a meadow stands a small ivy-covered house. A magpie hops in the garden, and I wonder if it's the one I saw earlier.

Going closer, it's obvious no one has lived here in a long while. The roof is sprouting leaves, and the ivy is thick and unchecked. Tattered curtains hang from grimy windows.

Beside the front door is an old nameplate. It's cracked and spotted with mildew, but says *Meadowsweet House*.

This is what Laila had been looking for.

The front door is locked, but that's kind of irrelevant since at least two of the windows are broken. I lift up and swing a leg over the ledge. Inside, the smell assaults me. It's wet plaster, damp, mould, old piss, and who knows what else.

The room is empty, stained a greenish grey. Large water marks pattern both the walls and cement floor. The ivy has crept in from outside. Built-in shelves line the walls, holding a random selection of objects: a dusty china shoe, a stained mug, a ladle. An old broken couch sits in the centre of the room.

Leaving the front room, I'm in a small, dark hallway. Faded, blackened wallpaper peels from the walls and some of the floorboards are missing. I peer inside the kitchen and see an old wooden table and a cabinet with missing doors. I continue down the passage.

I've watched enough horror movies to be uncomfortable. The bath is ringed with blackish brown, and I get a fright when I see myself in the distressed mirror.

At the end of the passage, beside a closed door, is a pile of stones. Crouching down, I touch the smooth texture. They're not as dusty or grimy as everything else.

Mom, years ago, told us about wishing stones. We would write a fear on a slip of paper and fold it up. Then write down a wish and fold it along with the fear. We'd heap stones on the papers, thinking of ways we could defeat the fear and make the wish come true.

I can see now that it was Mom's way of understanding what was going on inside our heads. That when we weren't looking, she'd read those slips of paper with our wishes and fears, so she'd know how to help us better.

This pile of stones, too new for the house that time forgot, looks exactly like our wishing stones.

I begin to remove them from the pile. At the bottom, on bare cement, are two slightly damp squares of paper. My fingers shaking, I unfold them. The ink has bled a little, but Laila's writing is large and clear:

I wish to be one of them. I wish they'll fulfil their promise to bring me into the grove. I wish for a talent, one with strong magic.

Laila *was* looking for magic.

I unfold Laila's fear:

I am afraid they are lying to me.

Who? I am so frustrated I want to scream.

I stand up, placing a hand on the doorknob. The floor is warped and the door struggles to give. I push my weight against the door several times until it gives way and I fly into another room.

Despite the thick growth right outside, the room is filled with bright sunlight. It doesn't smell as bad as the rest of the house. The wooden floors are still intact. At the centre of the room is an old cane rocking chair.

But it's the table that runs along the side wall that takes my attention. I recognise the red silk with silver swirls, I think Mom bought it in India. I've seen before the battery-operated fairy lights that still turn on when I push the switch. The table is covered with small statues, all women. Candles, large and small, are arranged around stones and feathers and spirals. Celtic knots are painted in gold. An eye inside an open hand, to ward off evil. A knife with a carved handle. Rune stones painted in Laila's hand. Is that the delicate white skull of a small dead animal? The entire wall is covered with marks I recognise as Ogham, the ancient Irish system of writing using strokes and lines.

This is Laila's sacred space. I found my sister's shrine.

FOURTEEN
A little different

David

I'm rapping at the door of the Scavenger Hunt. The sign is turned to '*closed*' but I can see the figure inside.

'Open up, Canty,' I holler, and the door buzzes open.

I don't trust John Canty, but he has his uses. He trades information with both augurs and judges, depending on what he gets out of it. He's been known to cause mischief. Sometimes I wonder if Canty wants to see us destroy each other. If it's true, if he is descended from the third group of the draoithe, the lost bards, as he claims, I can't say I'd blame him.

'What can I get you today?' Canty leans over the counter like it's an ice-cream parlour.

'I need help locating something.'

'Oh? Something you've lost? Or are you seeking something new?'

My blank stare shuts him up. He's nuts if he thinks I'm giving him any details.

'No need to get so pissy.' He holds up his hands, a smirk on his face. 'What are you looking for? A chant? Something stronger?'

'Something stronger.'

He nods thoughtfully.

'C'mon back.' I follow him into the back room. While Cassa turns a blind eye to Tarc getting information off Canty, she would be livid to find out about the chants and artefacts. Canty's able to do this only because it's clandestine.

'I have something that I've been holding for the right person.' He passes the cabinet and turns the dial on the heavy floor safe.

'Just show me.' I get weary of Canty's performances.

In his open palm is a small silver compact mirror. It looks like something Mamó would use.

'This mirror tracks magical objects. You have to tell it what you're looking for, and as long as that item is in use, the mirror will show you who wields it.'

'Rubbish.' I don't believe him. Scavengers don't find magic like this. Even Cassa or maybe Mamó, who have more silver magic than most, would be surprised to find it.

He holds the mirror in his hand, with his eyes shut. When he opens them, he holds out his palm: 'Where is my Healer's Amulet?'

After a few seconds, the reflective surface clouds over.

Then, in his open hand, is the image of Canty's mother, Dorothy, asleep in bed. She's deathly pale. The amulet must only be soothing her pain. It's uncomfortable to watch.

Canty swallows a little. And I appreciate this small vulnerability that he's shown me.

'I'm sorry,' I say to him.

'It is what it is.'

'Where did you find this?'

'Got lucky.'

'How much?' I ask him. I want the mirror. Badly.

'The pricing on this one is a little different.' He opens the cabinet and searches among the vials.

'Different how?'

'You will give me complete honesty. For one year. I won't pry unnecessarily, nor will I demand garraíodóir secrets, but whenever I have a question I need answered, you will tell me. You'll drink from this vial to ensure compliance.'

'No.' I can't give him that. Nothing is worth that.

'Then we have no deal.'

FIFTEEN
Death wish

*I overheard some women talking about an abandoned house
on the old school road. This might be what I've been
looking for: a place to build my shrine.*

LAS

Zara

The next few days pass with Mom and me in silent battle.
Determined to keep me busy, she hands me brochures for
coding camp, camogie camp, horse-riding camp, nun camp,
how-to-avoid-dying-on-the-village-green camp. OK, not
those last two, but her intentions are obvious. She wants me
away from any possible danger and temptation, and she's
decided, based on nothing, that the boy next door falls into
this category.

But I am looking for Laila. I want to find traces of my
sister in the village she loved.

I visit Laila's shrine. I leave her disgusting hair spell there.
It seems the right place for it.

Most of the figurines on her shrine are women. I recognise Medusa by the snake hair, Baba Yaga with her mortar and pestle. There's an old hag, forged in iron. A woman with a melted middle, like she's given birth to a monster. Some have deeply lined skin and breasts that touch their stomachs. One woman in her three forms: maiden, mother and crone. Another that's half tree, half woman.

Today, I've brought the ash chant from Canty. I figured I may as well use it. Not saying I believe in magic, but things are definitely odder than I'm used to, so who the hell knows?

I pour the ash on my hand and blow it over the shrine. I'm not sure what I'm expecting, but after a few minutes of nothing, I'm disappointed.

I've been staring so hard at the table that when I notice the wall, I'm not sure if it's my eyes playing tricks on me. A small section, immediately above the ring of black candles, seems somehow brighter. Perhaps it was like that before and I hadn't noticed.

Or perhaps the wall is glowing a little.

The glow highlights a small selection of Ogham marks. Like it's telling me, *Hey, Zara, check this out.* I pull out my phone and take a picture.

When I look up, the wall appears normal again.

This place. My imagination is working overtime.

Something bangs in another room. I freeze. Then I hear the tread down the passageway. Slow and heavy. And coming closer.

I fix my eyes on the door, wondering what's on the other side. A creepy clown. A shadow man with reed-thin arms and legs and glowing eyes. A little girl with a stitched-up mouth.

I've watched too many horror movies.

It would take weeks to find my body.

I'm at the window, one of the few in the house that's still fully intact. I'm about to open it when I see the massive wasp nest outside, right there at the corner of the window.

Wasps or killer clowns?

And then the door pushes open. It doesn't catch on the warped floor, opening smoothly and silently.

An old woman stands there. She leans on a stick, watching me with surprisingly clear eyes.

'I wouldn't. Those wasps have a terrible sting.'

I'm at a loss for words. She's no apparition, dressed in black trousers and a red-and-black jumper. Her hair is silvery and tied in a low bun.

'I've frightened you.' She smiles. 'I must be a sight for sore eyes.'

'I'm sorry,' I say. 'I was just … visiting.' An old derelict house. A shrine built by my dead sister.

'I've been watching you coming in here these last days. I wanted to see what you were up to.' She glances over at the altar while coming closer.

'Is this your house?' I say.

'It belongs to my family.' She looks around the room. 'Been many a year since it was lived in.'

'Looks it.'

'Houses need families. They ruin without humans to live and love and fight and weep inside them.' She taps her stick on the wooden floor. 'Rotten. Mind it doesn't give in on you.'

'These walls must know many stories.'

'That they do. So many stories. I know them all. This place has seen a lot of strife. People arguing with each other. Endless fighting and squabbling.'

'This house?'

'This village. This world.'

Can't argue with that.

'With all this greed and gloom, no one visits an old woman any more.' She sighs. 'I'll leave you to your sister.'

'Wait,' I say, and she turns. 'If you've time, I'd love to hear your stories. No one visits me either.' I mean to say the last bit lightly, but even I can hear how wistful I sound. How lonely.

She fixes me with her sharp blue eyes. Then, holding both handles, she sinks into the cane chair. I sit on the floor.

'A very long time ago, there were two families who couldn't abide each other,' she begins. 'Now, these weren't ordinary families. They were superstitious folk, and believed in the old ways. They were united in their love for nature, but this is what caused the conflict between them.'

'A love for nature?'

She nods. 'One family believed that nature was about design and order and that those who couldn't perceive that order were inferior. The other family was more severe, but they honoured the wildness of nature. So, they could never see eye to eye. And then they began to argue about land.'

Listening to the old woman's stories, I lose track of time. She tells me about people knocking down stone walls to settle disputes over property. Of people releasing each other's cattle into the road out of spite. She talks of murder and mayhem that grow from small disagreements.

'Would you give me a hand up, there's a good girl,' she says eventually, and I help her out of the cane chair. 'Will you visit with me again?'

'I'm Zara,' I tell her as she makes her way to the door. She looks at me over her shoulder.

'People call me Callie.'

'Where can I find you, Callie?'

'I'll be here, among the ghosts of the living, with the dust of the dead.' I must look startled because she lets out a bark of laughter. 'I like coming to this house, picking through the bones of the past.'

'Me too.'

'I like you, Zara.' And then she's gone.

I'm reaching the fork in the road when I see them. Cillian, Breanna, Ryan and Sibéal. It's obvious from their body language they're having a disagreement.

Another disagreement. Three against one.

They haven't seen me coming and I creep closer to listen. Cillian and Sibéal are having an intense staring match.

'We told you to get out of here,' Ryan says.

'You're blocking my way.' There's no emotion in Sibéal's voice. She's still staring at Cillian.

'That's the intention, Captain Obvious.' Breanna sounds impatient. 'Look, it would be awful if you found your home trashed or broken into. We wouldn't want anything bad to happen to you or your sister.'

'Is that a threat, Breanna?' She breaks her gaze from Cillian's with a small smile. He's breathing loudly, sharp and shallow.

'Just expressing our concern.'

'Noted. Now get out of my way.'

Breanna looks up and sees me watching: 'We have a little spy.'

Their attention now on me, Sibéal pushes through the gang, not looking back. I don't want to pass them, but I can't turn tail and hide. I step forward.

'What's your problem?' I say, heart pounding, as I walk up to them. Cillian and Ryan stare, arms folded. Breanna is smiling, a mean little grin.

'Oh, for God's sake.' Sibéal stops. She turns around and yanks me away. 'Do you have a death wish? Just ignore them.'

'You don't.'

'I'm me. You're not.' Her hand grips my wrist and she pulls me down the road.

'Sibéal,' Cillian roars after her. I look back and see the rage coursing through his body. He's rigid with it, like it's bound him so tight he can barely move.

'Leave her alone,' I say to him.

I can practically hear Sibéal rolling her eyes.

'Don't talk to them. Don't look at them. Pretend they don't exist, OK?'

'Why do they hate you so much?'

'Family stuff.'

I'm thinking about Callie's stories of discord in the village. I guess I've walked right into one of the feuds.

Breanna comes running up behind us. I'm expecting her to launch herself at Sibéal, but it's me she's headed for.

I feel my small backpack snatched from my shoulders as she laughs.

'Give that back,' I shout.

'Make me.' Breanna throws it to Cillian, who runs forward and out of reach. Ryan calls from the side, 'Here, here.'

He's enjoying this. My attempt to get my bag back is laughable to them.

My anger at them, at the universe for taking Laila, is building and it wants out.

Cillian has my bag. He dangles it in front of me. I grab for it, but he snatches it back. I throw myself at him, and I don't know how I do it, but now we're both falling on to the patchy grass. The bag lands about a foot away.

I'm leaning over Cillian, so furious that I want to pound him. I want to claw my nails down his face. I stare down at his small eyes, the sharp cheekbones. I've never before hated anyone. It's strong and alive, I feel it like it's in my bloodstream. I feel powerful with it.

'You going to let me up?' I hate Cillian's lazy voice. 'I mean, this could be fun and all, but I don't think here's the place.'

I hate Cillian's small piggy eyes.

I hate his smiling mouth.

I hate Cillian.

I register Sibéal's biker boots beside me. She picks up the bag.

'C'mon, let's get out of here.' Sibéal speaks like none of this has happened.

I stand up, still wanting to hurt him. It doesn't help that he's wearing that smug smile.

He's lying on the ground as we walk away, his elbows angled out from his head as he whistles up at the sky.

'Best ignore Cillian.' Sibéal must see how shaken I am as we walk away. 'He'd like to be more dangerous than he is.'

'Why are they like that?' I say.

'Some folk are just rotten.' She shrugs. 'I don't know.'

'They really hate you.'

'The feeling is mutual.' She laughs. 'And now I think they hate you too.'

SIXTEEN
A variation

David

Towards the end of the week, Lucia takes me down to the ring of stones at the lake. We're lucky to have this nemeton on our land. Most gairdíní, groves too, share these sacred places, and the battle for ownership of them is as old as our feud with the augurs.

'On your knees.' Lucia arranges branches around me, placing an alder staff in my hands. This is a ritual for warriors between battles. It's a gentle song to offset the harsh rigours of warfare.

It's easy to underestimate my mother. She appears vague, uncommitted. But this is a weapon, a tool in service of the steel beneath. Dad, who values decisiveness, doesn't realise how much she, whimsical and distracted, manipulates him.

She murmurs softly as she seals me inside a circle.

'Your name means "beloved", you remember that?' she says.

'I remember.' Lucia doesn't let me forget it.

Drawing a knife, Lucia pricks the tip of my finger, an apology in her eyes. She doesn't usually use blood for this ritual, and I'm not sure what she's doing as she smears my finger across the staff.

I lose track of time, and when I glance up, Lucia is ethereal, her golden hair glowing as she draws ash and alder branches in sweeping circles around me.

Like Tarc and Cassa, Lucia's affinity is plant. And like Tarc, her totem is tree, but her guide is oak. It's how she survives the din of the Rookery: the trees keep her grounded while Dad, Mamó, and Oisín thrive on the chaos of noise.

I am drawn to neither birds nor trees. Dad hasn't forgiven me this. He sees it as a slight on his virility that I don't share his guide, the rook, nor his totem, the bird. I am the broken link in a proud chain. In thirteen generations of warriors, every son has been guided by the rook. Until me.

The bug boy.

Our totems are blood drawn, we get them from our parents. Less frequently, a child shares a totem with a grandparent.

Insect comes from my flighty maternal grandmother, commonly referred to as my grandfather's midlife crisis. It's a nothing totem, only found in unimportant families; it's a

157

totem weak enough to make a girl step back from a boy she might like.

When younger, Dad couldn't understand why I was so traumatised by the loud, relentless noise at the Rookery. He was perplexed when I put my hands over my ears and cried, instead of finding the music in the guttural cries of the birds. It didn't occur to him that I would be anything else.

And then they started coming to me, the bees, the wasps and earwigs. I'd find them in my bed, my shoes, my toothbrush as they tried to tell me the one thing I wouldn't hear.

I was eight when I finally realised my totem was insect. In the old ballroom, my aunts were squabbling. Suddenly everyone's attention was drawn to the persistent buzzing of a large fly.

The fly landed near Odile, the unreliable sister, then up again, dipping in towards Cassa, who swatted at it, a near kill.

It buzzed off, landing beside my nose like a big green tear, where it stayed for a happy moment. My happy moment. Bewildered, and more than a little terrified of my aunts, the fly on my face was both itchy and right. Better than sweets. Then Cassa swatted, slapping her hand across my face.

The fly landed on a large portrait. It walked up the gauzy dress of Granny Jenny, Lucia's mum, once a nursery maid, always an insect lady.

The fly lifted and flew back to me, losing itself in my hair.

It was clear: I was an insect child. Lucia, who'd been hoping I'd follow trees, like her, stifled a sob.

Insect is not so bad, Lucia later comforted me when Dad could barely look at me. Look at that dragonfly, it's a noble creature. Choose your guide wisely. Which meant: Don't embarrass us with fleas or cockroaches.

I found as my guide the devil's coach-horse beetle. Or rather, it chose me. It didn't crawl to me the way the earwigs and ladybirds did. Instead, it waited at doorways, watching. Such a fierce, ugly creature. I knew, when one first settled on my palm, I could have no other guide. Lucia was dismayed, Mamó was furious, even though they knew that choosing a guide was more than act of will, that it was a connection that defied easy explanation.

The devil's coach-horse has always been an ill omen, a sign of corruption. This beetle is a little predator who eats carrion and lives in rot.

We are well suited.

In the grove this afternoon, Lucia's hands are on my shoulders, telling me to rise. I feel a deep peace and resolve. Like an armour has settled around my heart, my mind. It's unlike anything I've felt before. I don't know what Lucia's done, or how she knew I needed it, but I'm grateful.

'What was that?' I say as we walk back to the house.

'A variation on the soldier's fortification ritual.' Lucia is

159

deliberately vague, which means that she's done something big. That this ritual is important.

'Why?'

'I worry about you.' She puts a hand to my cheek.

I wonder if it's the War Scythe contest that's troubling her. It's been ten days since the four contenders were announced. The first fight has to happen soon.

'Did Dad ask you?' Pricks of worry push through the armour. Is this a way to manipulate me into doing what Dad wants?

'Oh, Davey,' she says. 'Not at all. This is so you can find the bravery within. True bravery. Not bluster, not posturing.' Her hand moves from my cheek to my heart. 'It's there. You just have to allow it out.'

SEVENTEEN
Welcome

When I walk through the woods, I feel a pull. Zara says it's only stories, but I know it's more.

LAS

Zara

I'm on my way home from a camogie match at the club two villages over when the car pulls up beside me. The same car I last saw careering down the road beside the village green.

'Hop in.' David leans over, opening the window.

'I'm nearly home.' I gesture up the road with my hurley. I haven't seen him since that strange night.

'I know.' David glances curiously at my sports skirt, which is more like shorts if you lift it up.

'You drive like crap.' I nod to the car.

'I'm sorry about that night.' He looks sheepish as he cruises beside me. 'I ...'

He gives up on the explanation.

'I'm going to yours.' He leans over and pops the handle, the door falling open. 'So you may as well get in.'

I'm sure Mom would have something to say about my getting into a car with him, this boy who needs repeat prescription drugs, who digs pits in the middle of the night. This boy with eyes that know pain.

But I get in.

The silence is uncomfortable. I don't know what to say. And he doesn't seem to either.

'Finally fixing your window,' he says eventually.

I can't think of a reply. I hate how tongue-tied I am. I'm awkward, he's awkward.

'What happened there?' I leap upon the only words I can find and point to the steering wheel. A patch of leather has been cut out of it.

'Seriously?' His shoulders shake with laughter and it makes me smile. 'There's any number of things wrong with this car, like that smear there that looks like a vomit stain. Or the damp smell and water marks.' He knocks on the roof. 'And you ask about that?'

He's genuinely amused. It softens his face and seems to lift some of the tension from his shoulders.

The three cookie-cutter mini-mansions are beside us. But instead of stopping at the end house, my house, he drives on to the iron gates.

'Grabbing my tools.' The gate swings open.

The house appears at the end of the winding road, the imposing grey stone surrounded by ancient trees.

And there it is: the place from the photograph.

'Laila took a picture of herself there.' I gesture.

'I know,' he says. 'I saw it.'

'When?'

'At your house. It was on your bed that day I fixed the shelves.'

'How well did you know my sister?'

'I met her a few times walking our fields.' He's silent, looking out ahead. Something's on his mind. Then he turns to me. 'We spoke about the weather, the village.'

I don't know if I'm disappointed or relieved.

'Don't move,' he says, and reaches out a hand. 'You've made a new friend.'

There's a long black beetle on my thigh. My skin tingles where it moves.

'That's one ugly creature,' I say. 'Does it herald plagues? Foretell my doom?'

'It's a devil's coach-horse, so my guess is that your doom is pretty much guaranteed.' David reaches over and quickly lifts the beetle from my leg. 'That's what you get hanging out with me.'

Cupping the beetle in his hand, he looks at me strangely.

163

We get out of the car, our shoes crunching on the loose stones. Outside the door, David sets the beetle down gently.

Wearing Laila's charm bracelet, I look for a crow-shaped lock but it's just an ordinary old-fashioned doorknob. David opens up without unlocking it at all.

So much for John Canty's crow key. But I shouldn't be surprised.

'I'll just, uh, grab the tools.' He rubs the back of his head, flustered. I don't know why he's suddenly so distracted. Even more awkward.

He walks me down the passage with its black-and-white floors. I peer into rooms, struck by the clutter, the worn antique furniture and threadbare Persian rugs. The height of the ceilings and thickness of the walls. The whole house conveys a sense of faded grandeur, something that was once the height of fashion, now fallen into disrepair. We pass the curving stone and iron staircase.

'Wow.' I can't help myself. 'This house.'

And I see how perfectly David fits in here, this dark, sad prince in this house that was once luxurious.

'It's been in my dad's family a few hundred years.'

There's a massive chandelier with missing crystals. A huge family crest on the wall. It's hard to make out the spiky letters between the swooping crows, the menacing eye at the centre.

'*Red the blade*,' I read aloud.

'It's a call for blood.' He disappears down the hall. 'Our family war cry.'

Family war cry.

Maybe we need one of those.

The kitchen is big and bright. The windows are large, the worktops black granite. But the vanilla paint is chipped and breakfast dishes spill from the sink. The milk is out of the fridge, the cereal boxes not packed away. Mom would evaporate if we left our kitchen like this.

David's gone through into the utility and I follow. The room smells of laundry detergent. A mess of clean, loosely folded laundry spills out of baskets and I think he's embarrassed about the half-in, half-out underwear.

I lean against a cabinet and he searches the shelves. Then suddenly he stops. David turns to me and looks at me. Really looks at me. Boy-fixes-on-girl looking at me. He seems bewildered.

'I've never brought a girl to the house before,' he says, as if he's just realised that I'm one. And that I'm in his home.

'Never?' I swallow the word. The gear change is abrupt.

'The tools are just behind,' he says, inching closer.

I might know that look, but I can't be sure. It's searching and slightly dazed. Mesmerised. Not one I know well, having kissed Nathan only twice before we moved away and one time after.

It's a question, waiting for me to answer.

But then something catches my eye. Hanging out of the laundry basket is a large scarf. Grey with red stripes at the bottom. I've seen it somewhere before but can't think where.

'Zara?' David follows my eye.

'Yeah?' I move from the cabinet, chasing the connection. But I can't put it together.

'What's wrong?'

'Nothing.'

He's looking at me intently. And I realise I've killed the moment. That he'd been declaring an interest and I was too distracted to notice.

But maybe that's for the best. I can't figure him out, this boy who is awkward and defensive. He has a family war cry, for heaven's sake, and one that uses 'red' as a verb.

I suspect that kissing David will yank me out of my carefully created numb zone and I'm not sure I'm ready for that.

'We should probably head.'

David smiles. It's a smile that says, *Hey, no big deal*, which miffs me a little. Couldn't he be a little disappointed?

David reaches on the shelf behind me for the tools, his T-shirt inching up and exposing creamy skin. It rides up further and I'm thinking about changing my mind, about touching my finger to skin, when I see them. The scars. I notice what I didn't two weeks ago: the precision with which they're laid out. The regularity. His shirt falls down as he turns, unaware of what he's inadvertently shown me.

I look away too quickly. Not understanding what I've seen, he frowns.

'Can I get you anything?' he says as we walk into the kitchen.

'I'm grand.' But I can't look at him. Outside, the birds are loud, they're cawing and screaming and I can't hear myself think. How do they live with this noise?

'You get used to it,' David reads my mind.

Around us, the raucous cries fill the air.

Oisín is standing near the fridge, watching us.

'Hello, Zara,' this haughty, withered boy says. 'Welcome to the Rookery.'

David and I cross the fields, go through the hollow and into my back garden. I'm carrying my camogie stick hooked into the helmet, while he holds the heavy-looking box of tools.

'You're from the city, right?' He seems almost shy. 'This place must be a change.'

'You can say that.'

'Do you like it here?'

'It's taken a while, but yeah. I do.' I pause. 'It's hard, fitting in to a place like this.'

'It's a strange little village, all right.'

'Laila really loved it here. She was excited by the stories and decided that she'd be part of things and no one would stop her.'

'She sounds a real character.'

'That she was. She made this shrine that I found in this old …' I shut up abruptly. Laila's shrine is a secret. I'm not ready to talk to anyone about it. And when I am, I want to tell Adam first.

'A shrine?' David glances at me.

'It's nothing.'

I open the sliding door and we step inside. He looks like he's about to ask a question, but then we hear them.

Unexpectedly, my parents are home.

Down the passage, low, urgent voices are going at it. Fighting voices, doing their best to destroy the other person in an even-pitched, slightly hissing tone.

'You don't get to walk away from me,' Mom says.

'Watch me.'

'We're having a conversation here.' Mom sounds thin and desperate.

'A conversation?' Dad hisses. 'You call this a conversation? I don't hear any sense out of you, Naz. You just say the same thing over and over again.'

'Do you hear me now?' There's a loud crash, like Mom's thrown something against a wall. 'Do you hear that?'

In these moments, I don't know how my parents ever loved each other. I don't know how they got married, defying their parents, who tugged them in different religious directions which only confirmed their position as diehard atheists. I don't know how they decided to leave their home countries, both of them, and start again where they knew no one. I have no idea how they thought they'd have enough love to fuel that.

I'm rooted to the floor as their voices continue the endless circle of accusations. David is behind me, and I am so very embarrassed. I can't face him.

'I can't take this any more.' Mom's voice is rasping. She's close to tears.

'And you think running away will solve things?' Dad.

'We need a clean start.' Mom.

'They need stability right now.' Dad. He punctuates 'stability' in a particularly arsehole-ish way. Not clever. He's goading Mom.

I don't expect her to storm out of the kitchen and into the dining room, where I stand with David. She's startled when she sees me.

'Zara.' She can barely look at us. 'I didn't realise you were here.'

'Apparently not.' My cheeks are hot.

'And you brought a friend.' She's livid David's here. That he's caught a glimpse of how dysfunctional we are, that her perfect doctor facade has snagged.

'You've met David.' I still can't turn to look at him, but I can feel him behind me. 'He's here to fix the window.'

'I'll come back.' David sounds so stiff, it's almost endearing.

Fast, angry footsteps sound down the passage to the front hall. The door opens, and bangs shut. Dad's gone out.

'Please excuse me.' Mom sounds watery. 'I have a headache.' She disappears up the stairs, and I'm left alone with David.

'Zara.' David sounds tentative. I've turned to stone as I watch the door where Mom has just left. I want him to shut up. There's nothing he could say that won't have me in tears.

I wish Adam would appear so I could pretend this never happened and I wouldn't have to see pity or judgement or disdain on David's face. I couldn't bear it if he were kind.

I wait a few seconds but no one comes to save me. I turn reluctantly to him.

'Dads suck.' His words are wooden, like he knows, and there's a sandpaper-rough scrape to my heart. He forces a grim little smile and I let out a choked laugh-sob.

'Sure do.'

What is it about this boy, his awkwardness and discomfort, that draws him to me? I think it's because we're both jagged, we're the people who fit in wrong. We need to be a little uneasy, it's how we are.

'Thank you.' The words are so quiet I'm not sure he hears them.

After a moment, he opens the door and leaves.

Someone else witnessing a family fight is unpleasantly definitive. It takes the horrible out of the realm of nightmares and into the real. It brings our ugly that bit closer to the surface.

Upstairs, Mom is on Laila's bed. She's lying on her side, watching out of the window. She knows I'm there, but she doesn't move.

I'm worried. They haven't had one of these rows in weeks. I'd thought Mom and Dad were finding their way back to each other.

Later, when Mom's shut herself up for the night, I go down to the small room Dad uses as a study. I type in the password to his desktop – he uses the same three for everything – and check up on him.

There's nothing dodgy with his email, just boring work things. Nothing in the private account he thinks we don't know about; it hasn't been used since last year. It doesn't look like there's a new Lindy, but I'll probably need to go through his phone to be sure. Before I put the computer to sleep, I check his recent tabs.

The last three are job adverts. Two chairs in English Literature and the director of some institute. Two in Australia, one in the States. Dad is looking for a way out.

I walk out of the study and lean against a wall, breathless.

How little I can trust my parents. How they lie and sneak around with their secrets. Secrets that affect us, that threaten to uproot me and Adam. That take us away from Laila.

The door to the hall closet is slightly ajar. My denim jacket hangs there. In the top pocket is John Canty's love chant. If they can't sort themselves out, I'm going to do it for them.

Even sticking my fingers into the tight pocket, I don't believe it. I don't buy that a love charm will magic them back together.

But I want to bend them to my will. I want to hiss at them, *Just behave like my goddamned parents. Just do what you're supposed to do.* I want so badly to make them do what I need them to do, to be as I want them to be.

I want to take away their agency the way they're taking away mine.

I want to be horrible.

I dig into the brown paper bag and pull out John Canty's ring with its black stone. It's pretty, so I slip it on. I take the grassy oil from the hand-holding ceremony and, before I can second-guess myself, decant it into Dad's empty shaving oil bottle. It's rubbish and desperate. But if there is even the smallest chance I can get Dad to stay with Mom, I'm going to try.

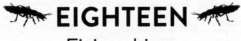 EIGHTEEN
Fixing things

David

I really wish Zara hadn't taken my key because climbing into their house through the back window is further down the wrong side of shady.

I leave the tools in the back kitchen so if they come home, I have an excuse. A weak one, but it's better than nothing.

Coming out of the back kitchen, I see a figure in the doorway, watching.

'Oisín,' I say, playing it cool. Like I'm not surprised he followed me. 'What are you doing here?'

He raises an eyebrow. 'What are you doing here?'

'Fixing things.'

Oisín watches while I search the kitchen drawers. At Birchwood, we spent a few weeks learning to search houses, supposedly to be able to find magical artefacts hidden in augur homes. I'm systematic, leaving no trace. After a few minutes Oisín joins in.

'It would help if I knew what I'm searching for,' he says.

'Information about a secret shrine. And maybe a metal box.' My voice is gruff. 'Should be locked.'

The only indication that Oisín is aware of the significance of what I lost is the way he doesn't react.

'I've been called in,' he says, searching through a pile of recipe books. 'Cassa wants to question me. Seems like there's new information.'

I frown. I've heard nothing about this.

'Did she say who'll be questioning you?'

'Three commanders.' He throws away the words like it's nothing, but it's not.

This is a tribunal, and Cassa wouldn't call Oisín before a tribunal without good reason. Like having cause to believe that Oisín was somehow complicit, that the Eye is lost because he allowed someone to have it.

I hide my worry.

I leave for the den, and beelining to the shelves, I hear a light scratching from the side console.

'Jaysus.' A pair of eyes are locked on mine.

A rat, in a cage.

It watches as I search the shelves. I have a cousin in the city whose guide is squirrel. With silver magic, she could quiz the rodent. Like a scientist in a lab, using objects and movements, she could ask the damn thing questions and give us some idea of whether the Eye had been in this room. But my cousin really fucking hates us, she'd sooner stab herself in her eye than help me, and silver magic remains elusive.

As I'm checking the skirting in Laila's room, Oisín appears. 'We'd better make tracks.'

I am, unusually, enjoying the idea of Oisín and me as 'we'. Even though we're breaking and entering, so wrong, I know, there's some satisfaction in our shared purpose here. That Oisín is helping me. I don't think he's ever done that before.

'Just a minute.' I go to Zara's room. I've remembered the knee-wall door part hidden behind a chest of drawers. I pull it open and crawl into the attic space. Nothing.

'In sight,' Oisín calls from the hall window as I move the chest back in place.

Leaving Zara's room, the card in a shallow box on the desk stops me in my tracks. THE SCAVENGER HUNT. I look inside the box. There are several objects in it: the picture of Laila outside the Rookery, the red purse we found in the hot press.

'Leave. Now,' Oisín calls.

And it's almost like old times.

I turn over the card and see 'nemeta' scribbled and circled in red. How the hell did Laila know about nemeta? And then I see the damning words: *Badb Eye is a Knot*.

Oisín, who's sidled up behind my shoulder, sees them too.

His face falls as he sees the confirmation: Laila knew about the Eye, that it isn't just an antique family heirloom. There's no way she didn't steal it.

'I'm sorry.'

I put the card down, but not before making a note of the last line. *Find Meadowsweet on School.* I know this, but I can't get it. It's there in my mind, just out of reach.

Oisín has visibly wilted. I hear the sound of something dropping on the front path. Grabbing Oisín by the arm, we scramble down the stairs, two at a time. The key turns in the door when I grab the tools, and she's inside the front passage as we climb out of the window.

I yank Oisín up the garden stairs and through the hollow. Once he's in our field, I go back, slip around the house and to the front door.

I knock at the door and wait. Zara opens, she's wearing that skirt again, and there's an old scar on her knee, and a mole on her thigh, a bruise on her shin.

I forget about judges and totems, Cassa and Dad. I forget that I've just broken into her house, and I stand there, looking at those eyes. Her ponytail falls over her shoulder, half undone. I look at her cheekbones, full mouth, her waist. The way she holds herself together so carefully. Her forehead creases at my scrutiny but I don't, can't let her go.

I am so very, very distracted.

'David?' Zara sounds worried. 'You all right?'

'Come to fix the window.' I hold up the toolbox.

Wickerlight. Threshold time. Like nemeta are threshold places. Wickerlight is when time cracks, when magic gets in. It's a rare star alignment, or maybe a blue or blood moon. Equinoxes, solstices, dawn, twilight and midnight, all of these are favourable for wickerlight. But sometimes, without rhyme or reason, wickerlight just happens. Sometimes, for a few intense seconds, you know time feels different. Like you've stepped into pure magic.

I feel that right now as I step towards Zara.

Brushing up to her, closer than I should, the word pushes up, surprisingly delicate. It's a leap from a high place on to the squashiest feather cushion.

Save.

I cast around to see what it wants to be encased in. It wants something soft, but a little scratchy. Not the awful stiffened silk flower on the window sill, this word wants to be swaddled. A thick, stretchy fabric.

Zara is puzzled as I hover just inside the doorway, trying to place this word before I lose it.

Then I know what it wants.

'Please don't take this the wrong way,' I say, though I probably do mean it the wrong way, just not right now.

And I reach for her skirt.

 NINETEEN
The ugliest thing I'd ever seen

*The woman with the flower dress, Maeve, asked me if
I want to earn a little extra money.*

LAS

Zara

David is more than a little odd today. He's bent over, physically uncomfortable. I'm beginning to think that I draw it out, this uneasiness with the world around him.

'Please don't take this the wrong way,' he says, and reaches for my sport skirt. He lifts the bottom of the clinging fabric and squeezes, rough knuckles brushing my skin. It feels nice.

Maybe I want to take it the wrong way.

'Would you mind very much if I borrow this?' he says. And it is so utterly strange, his perfect manners, the bizarre interest in my camogie gear, and those fingers against my leg.

'You want to borrow my skort?' Stupid word, skort. My cheeks are hot.

'Just a small part.' He's holding the edge of it tightly between his fingers. 'Have. Not borrow.'

'Why?' I say.

'Please?'

But that's no answer.

'And if I say no?'

'Then you say no.'

He releases the fabric.

'You can have it,' I say and he picks up the edge again. 'Anything else you'd like? A button? Some thread from a jacket? Maybe a shoelace?'

And when he looks up, he is so pained, so tormented.

'David?' I say, worried. But he shakes his head. And takes out a knife from his waistband. I should be alarmed, but I'm not. I'm not alarmed by any of this. I think of boys turning the fresh earth beneath the moon. I think of the Horribles waking up in their ditch.

'I'm sorry, Zara.' And he looks so sad. I don't know what he's apologising for, but he's sincere.

'I dreamed about you last night,' I tell him even though I don't mean to. I hadn't even remembered the dream until just this moment. It seems like the right thing to say because it feels like he's showing me something vulnerable too.

'You were standing outside. A field, I think. There were flower bushes behind you. Peonies. You wore a black jacket, the collar turned up at your neck. You were wearing your crown that day, just a thin iron band of … leaves? No, feathers. And your black jeans. Your jacket had a symbol on the sleeve, nothing I've seen before. Your cheeks were pink from the wind. You were waiting for the storm, the sky a deep purple, the dark clouds hanging low. There was something on your shoulder, I thought it was a rook, but it was an unnaturally large black bug. The ugliest thing I'd ever seen.'

And I talk to him while he gently slips the knife into the stretchy navy fabric and then again until a small square has been cut out.

'Thank you.' He doesn't look at me as he puts away his knife. He folds the square of skirt into his hand.

I look down at my ruined skirt, the shorts beneath. Nothing special about it at all. Nothing to warrant that desperate need to have a piece of it. And I remember the cut-out patch on the steering wheel. The precise line of cuts up his side, beneath his ribs. The strange dream. And they feel like pieces of the puzzle that is David.

But this isn't the puzzle I'm meant to be solving. David is a distraction that I don't need right now.

'I'll be upstairs,' I tell him, and turn away.

In my room, I take Laila's spell from my grey bag.

I've lied to Mom. I'm fed up of her trying to manage my

time. So when she told me she'd paid for this week's camogie camp after I'd asked her not to, I just smiled and dressed in my gear. Left the house, as if going for the bus.

Instead, I went to Laila's shrine. To sit there a while, looking at the eclectic collection of symbols; she'd plundered every known magic system and ancient civilisation to create her sacred space. So very Laila.

Her spell has been bothering me. I thought leaving it at the shrine would make me forget it, but the reverse is true. I wake up at night thinking about it. I have this weird feeling like it's been calling me back. Like it wants me to *discover* it. When I left the shrine today, I just had to bring it back with me.

I turn the hairball, wondering what Laila was doing when she made this hideous thing. It reminds me, sort of, of the time she gave me a beautifully made origami horse. There was a faint trail of writing on it, disappearing under the neat folds of the paper.

'What does it say?' I'd asked Laila. She just shrugged, smiling a secret smile.

I could make out the C followed by a U, then an R.

'It's a message for you.'

'I have to know what it says.' I glanced up from the delicate horse.

'Then do what you must.'

I followed the letters, slowly unfolding the origami

horse. When it was just flat paper again, the exquisitely made animal destroyed, I saw the message: *curiosity killed the horse.*

Laila laughed.

There's something beneath the hair, I can feel the weight and shape of it, but I can't see how to get to it without cutting Laila's hair. Which feels like a violation. Like killing the horse.

Before I can think too much, I pick up my scissors and do it. As I cut, there's the edge of something hard pushing through the hair.

In my hand is a disc, either gold, or maybe gilded silver, with a blackish inlay. About three inches wide, a quarter-inch thick. Intricate loops and knots are carved into the surface. Worn and uneven, it seems very, very old.

I study it from every direction. Where did Laila get this from? Why would she hide it inside her hair? And what is it?

TWENTY
Full of surprises

David

The window fixed, I call up to Zara. A minute later, she comes down, still wearing the skirt I vandalised. She looks troubled and I feel bad.

'Zara.' I say it again. 'I'm sorry.'

For breaking into her house. For going into her room without being invited. Because I can't be honest with her.

But she thinks I mean the skirt and she shakes her head.

'Don't.' A smile breaks through her worried face. 'I have plenty.'

I take her hand and she furrows her brow, like she's wondering what odd thing I'm going to do now. I should come with a warning sign: proceed at your own peril.

I ease her phone from her hand, as she watches me, I save my number under Handyman. More like handsy man.

'Can I have yours?'

'You want me to call you?' She looks at the phone and

laughs. 'Handyman sounds like a hammer-wielding maniac from B-grade horror.'

'That's probably about right.' I'm grinning like a fool as she gives me her number. I'm feeling lighter than I have in the longest time. Maybe my entire life.

'Call if you need anything fixed.' And I hesitate. 'Or if you just want to chat. Hang out.'

My heart is beating like I'm running with an armed grover yapping at my heels. Never has a girl made me feel this, I don't know, nervous. Stupid.

I've not done this, made friends with a girl like this. All my friends are judge kids, and I haven't found myself trying to kiss any of them against the back-kitchen cabinets.

'David.' She hesitates. 'Can I ask you something?'

My phone rings. It's Ryan.

'You need to get to the hotel right now.' He doesn't waste words. 'Sibéal just sat down at Mamó's table.'

'The Huntsman?' I mouth an apology to Zara. As I turn away, she shuts the door.

'Get that girl away from my grandmother,' I say, already running down the road. It takes me five minutes to reach the hotel, and I'm a sweaty mess by the time I walk up the front steps.

Breanna meets me at the entrance.

'On the patio. Ryan's watching. They're just chatting, but Mamó got really mad when we tried to break it up.'

Outside, my grandmother is at her usual table. The crisp white tablecloth, the pot of tea and scone, all of this is ordinary for a summery afternoon. Except for the girl across the table from her. They're talking, and it's so utterly bizarre.

Seeing me, Sibéal stands up and leans over Mamó, dropping a kiss on her cheek. Sibéal waves to me, then goes down the steps to the garden where a bunch of tourists are milling.

I go to Mamó, who is still at the table. Cold tea in front of her. Her scone untouched.

'Mamó?' I try to hide my anxiety. 'You OK? What did that girl want from you?'

Mamó is deep in thought and it takes her a moment to shift her attention to me.

'Mamó?'

'Sit down for heaven's sake. Don't make a scene.'

I'm incredulous. Why has Mamó gone schoolmarmish on me? She's not that kind of grandmother. My mamó loves a good scene. But I do as she says.

I cast an eye over Mamó as she examines her scone with disapproval.

'These are yesterday's scones,' she grumbles.

It doesn't look like any damage was done. I don't know if Sibéal is a grover, if she's an armed augur trained in guerrilla tactics. But if she hurt my grandmother here in this hotel, owned by a judge family, she wouldn't have made it out alive.

Mamó is looking out across the lawn, watching Sibéal push through the hedging trees that border the back garden.

'She's a fine girl.' Mamó slices through her scone, and my blood runs cold. 'Reminds me a little of myself.' That any girl should be like Mamó is her highest compliment.

'Mamó.' I'm suddenly very frightened. 'Don't drink that tea.'

Has Sibéal poisoned my grandmother? Slipped some potion in her tea? I examine her face. She looks the same, her eyes haven't gone weird or anything.

'What did she want?'

'We just talked.' Mamó examines the jam, then goes for the cream. 'She asked me about Badb.'

'Badb?' Why is Sibéal poking about my family lore? 'What about Badb?'

'She wanted to know about my family.' Mamó is lathering cream on to the scone, unperturbed. She looks up, and I'm horrified by the single tear that runs down her cheek. Mamó doesn't cry. The tear splashes on to the white tablecloth. Another follows, but when I look up, her face is clear, her eyes dry.

'About Badb's Eye.'

'What did she want to know about Badb's Eye?'

'You know, David, you underestimate Sibéal. She's a fine girl. A fine girl. David? What's wrong?'

David. Mamó never calls me David.

I'm up like a shot, leaping over the banister and into the garden as I sprint after Sibéal. Through the trees and into the lane. I jump the cattle gate down the other end and see the solitary figure walking. I'm running so fast, not even winded, yelling her name.

She turns, like she's not surprised to see me there. I get right into her space. I know that somehow she's messed with Mamó.

Mamó would never disclose anything she shouldn't. That woman could be buried beneath the weight of her untold secrets. She'd never reveal the offerings.

'Worried?' Sibéal gives me a sympathetic frown.

'What did you do to my grandmother?' I snarl the words at her. I'm so terrified that whatever Sibéal did may never be put right again. That I'll have a well-behaved grandmother who calls me David and cries delicately, rather than a chain-smoking badass with the sharpest tongue I know.

'Did she tell you that you underestimated me? That I'm a fine girl?' She's smiling, and I can't bear it. 'I thought that was a nice touch.'

'What did you do to her?' I'm shouting right in her face but she's laughing and it's making me madder. Then she takes me by surprise. I feel the knife right above my heart.

'I should put you out of your misery,' she whispers. 'But where's the satisfaction in that?'

Grabbing her hand, I twist it away from me, oblivious to whether I'm hurting her or not. I'd just rather she didn't have a blade to my skin.

'Don't ever –' I spit the words – 'go near my grandmother again.'

She holds my gaze. I turn away. I have to get out of here.

'The first offering is Entrap.'

It's only a whisper, but it makes me stop.

'What?' I turn around slowly.

Sibéal gives me an infuriating Mona Lisa smile.

'And the second –' she steps closer '– is Sever.'

I think she's about to pull the knife on me again, but instead, I feel this weird whoosh inside me. The force of it reminds me of when the rooks fly really close to my face.

Suddenly thoughts flood my head. Feelings push to the surface. Zara wearing the tiniest skirt in the world. Zara slipping away from me in the back kitchen. The brutal, crushing disappointment of her rejection. I'm thinking of Dad. How he'd ignore me in favour of Oisín before he broke, and how stupid and useless it made me feel. Mamó poking her stick at my ribs. Cassa lifting her small blade to my skin. Lucia's love as her hair sweeps over my cheek while I kneel in ritual.

The weight of my emotion is unbearable.

My head is throbbing. A bird caught inside a small bright room, flapping furiously to find a way out. Bashing against this glass window and then that one. I want to put my hands over my head to stop the weirdness inside.

Sibéal is looking at me intently with bloodshot eyes, and I know that whatever is happening to me is her fault. I want it to stop. I would rather a hundred days on Cassa's cradle than this. It's too much. It feels like my head is going to explode. I will it to stop.

Desperate, I shove her. Hard.

She lands on her arse and everything is right again. I don't know what that was, and it's left me breathing heavily. But I can't help thinking that even though she's on the ground and I'm standing, she's won this battle.

'You're full of surprises, David,' Sibéal says. '*That* girl?'

I'm totally confused as I look down at Sibéal. What girl?

Then I see the figure standing on the side of the road. She's hanging back, keeping out of sight. Zara.

She looks at me with complete disgust.

'Zara,' I say, moving towards her. But she glances at Sibéal, and suddenly I see what she sees. What this looks like. Me, having shoved a girl so hard that she fell to the ground.

I did that. I was feeling bad, and I lashed out. It doesn't matter that my head felt weird in the moments before. In my anger, I hurt someone smaller, weaker than myself.

And it wouldn't be the first time.

Zara goes over to Sibéal, who fends her off with a hand. 'Don't.'

'I'm sorry,' I say to Sibéal, who arches an eyebrow at me.

She picks herself up and saunters down the road. I don't know how long we stand there, Zara staring at me. Me seeing myself through her eyes.

And finding a monster.

'You pushed her,' Zara says. 'You hurt her.'

'I know.' No excuses. 'I shouldn't have done that.'

I feel the heat of Zara's revulsion. Of my own self-loathing. I don't want to be this. I don't want to be what I am.

'I'm sorry.' I don't know what else to say to her. I'm without words.

'You seem to say that a lot, David,' she snaps, then walks away.

On my way back to the Huntsman, everything is in turmoil. I am confused, uncertain. I feel that armour from the fortification ritual, when Lucia did something to me down at the lake, but now it's tight and hurting.

My head is a mess. Ten minutes ago, I knew with utter certainty what I most wanted, what was right, what was wrong, and now I'm fuzzy. I'm not sure what anything is any more.

But there's no time to examine these unfamiliar, conflicting feelings. I have to see if Mamó is OK. And find out if Sibéal was simply repeating what Oisín revealed to the augurs when he was chained and unconscious, or if she somehow tricked another offering out of Mamó.

Back at the Huntsman, Mamó insists I sit down as she orders another pot.

She's quiet, distant. And slowly she returns to herself. A discomfited, slightly more fearful version of herself. I don't know if she seems like an old woman, frailer than I like, who is churlish with the waiter because that's what she is and always has been. Or if it's something else. But I've never looked at her like this. Since that awful moment with Sibéal, with Zara, everything seems different. It's like a picture taken out of its frame and suddenly the whole image reassembles in an entirely different way.

After not drinking her tea, Mamó and I walk back from the village to the Rookery. We're quiet. Moody. I'm trying to deal with this new identity that Zara gifted to me, cursed me with, in that awful moment.

Monster.

'What happened, Mamó?' I say eventually. 'With Sibéal?'

'The augur girl?' She's stalling.

'Yes, the augur girl.'

Her lips are pursed like there's something unpleasant in her mouth. I wait for her to respond.

'Nothing,' she says eventually.

'Mamó, please.'

'I said nothing, Davey.' This evening, the bird in Mamó is not a wondrous, strong thing, but fragile and delicate, and it scares me.

It scares her too.

TWENTY-ONE
Wishmaker

*Is David really this obtuse and oblivious to my hints? A
pretty boy, but perhaps a little dumb?*

LAS

Zara

I'm walking from the Huntsman trying to take in what
just happened. One thing is certain: I saw David shoving
Sibéal. Hard enough to push her to the ground. I'm haunted
by her red-rimmed eyes.

I'm less sure, but it's possible, that I saw a glint of steel in
Sibéal's hand. Had she pulled a knife on him and that's why
he shoved her? Does it matter? A big fella like that, surely he
could have just taken it from her without hurting her?

An hour ago, he stood on my doorstep. I thought he
seemed the gentlest boy, both awkward and graceful, that
I've ever crushed on. And now this. This is not something I
can just brush aside.

And still, I can't help but feel that there's a large chunk of things that I'm missing. That I'm not seeing. Like trying to read a secret document where half of the words have been redacted.

A few minutes after David left my house, I decided I'd go to the Huntsman. That I'd catch him on his way out. I wanted to tell him everything: explain how I'd found the disc in the hairball, and how I was sure it was linked to Laila's death. I'm so tired of doing this alone, of having no one to talk to.

Now, feeling shaky, I stand outside the Scavenger Hunt. This wasn't the plan, but I'm glad I'm here.

The sign on the closed door says '*Gone Hunting*'. I cup my hands against the window and peer inside. Someone is sitting at the counter, and I bang a hand against the glass.

The door buzzes open. Canty's wearing glasses and doesn't seem to have his poet persona on. He's looking even more dishevelled than before, if that's possible.

Inside, the smell of musty coats and polish is comforting.

'I found something,' I say, and pull the strange disc out of my pocket.

Canty looks at it, mildly irritated, but this quickly changes to shock.

'Where did you get that?'

'Laila.'

Canty looks like he wants to touch it, but I hold it back.

'Is it valuable?'

'You have no idea.'

'Why would Laila have this?'

'I'm wondering the same thing.' He comes a little closer. 'Do you want me to hold it for you? Buy it from you? It's not safe to go around carrying things like this.'

I shake my head. This is my key to finding what happened to Laila.

'I think this is connected to why Laila died.'

Canty tries to keep his face clear but he's too much of a drama llama and I see it at once: he thinks so too.

'What is it?'

Canty turns away, straightening teacups on a shelf.

'I shouldn't be telling you this.'

'Please.'

'It's a trinket called Wishmaker.' He goes to the counter and pulls a bit of silk from a drawer. 'Worn by young girls such as yourself at Lughnasa in order to wish for their true love.'

Oh. It looks a lot more impressive than that. I feel inexplicably disappointed. Something this majestic should be more than a love charm.

'It's very strong magic.' He hands me the silk and I see it's a small, neatly stitched rectangular bag. 'So it's best not handled too much.'

'Why not?'

'For your own safety.' He nods for me to put the disc inside the bag. 'You need to keep this hidden. Very well hidden. You also have to hide it from your mind. Forget about it.'

'How do I do that?'

'Disguise it inside your head.'

Right, OK. Laila's world is making my head ache with its strange logic.

'Every time you hide the disc, imagine it looks different. Maybe it's copper, maybe more delicate. Then put it in an iron box in your mind. Put your iron box inside a silver box, and then inside a gold. Use the strongest, most beautiful key you can imagine, lock it and throw your box in the lake. Then imagine a cottage, keep it small because the detail is important. Imagine it very carefully and put the key on a hook. As you do it, take a sip from the chant I'll give you. If you need to retrieve it, go to the house, get the key and take the Wishmaker out of the boxes.'

'Why would I do this?' It's too much. Too weird. And way too much bother.

'Why would you not?' he says. 'It's the best way to protect valuable things. And if anyone, anyone at all, asks you about it, don't tell them you have it. This can be dangerous, Zara.'

He's enjoying the theatrics again.

'Promise me, Zara Swart.'

'What?'

'That you'll hide the Wishmaker. Or else, let me keep it for you.'

I don't miss the look of longing on his face.

'I'll hide it. I promise.'

He fetches something from the back while I think about what he's just told me. It's without a doubt the strangest thing I've been told to do. But when he brings me the small vial with a darkish liquid, his face is sombre.

'This will help you cover any traces of it. There are people who want this very badly.' His worry is genuine. 'Even if you don't believe me.'

Busted.

I'm about to leave the shop when his voice stops me.

'I'm a selfish man, guided by my own interest. But Laila's death haunts me. I will always wonder if there was something I could have done to prevent it. So please be careful, Zara. Things aren't as they seem. Trust no one, not even me. But know this: Laila was a good person and she didn't deserve what happened to her. I will do what I can to help you stay safe.'

I leave the shop chilled by Canty's warning. Mostly because of the words he used. *She didn't deserve what happened to her.* For the first time, someone else has acknowledged what I've always felt. That Laila didn't just die. That it was caused by something, a chain of events that I can't understand. That it could have been prevented. And for that, even though I do not trust or believe him, I will do as Canty says.

At home, I pull the silver disc from the silk bag and examine it again, tracing my fingers over the elaborate knotting. Then I stuff it back into the silk bag, open the knee-wall door behind the chest of drawers and hide it in the attic.

Taking a sip of Canty's chant, I imagine placing the disc in an iron box, the iron box inside a silver, and the silver in a gold. I lock the box with an old rusted key. Standing on a rock, I drop the box with the Wishmaker into the lake. Behind me is a small cabin. I can see the faded red of the front door. I go inside, seeing the scuffed wood floor, the worn leather couch. On the wall, beneath a painting of a beach, is a row of hooks. I put the rusted key on the hook.

Leaving my room, I follow the sound of music until I find Adam on the patio strumming his guitar.

I must be very suggestible, because for the first time since I found it, the disc isn't an urgent nudge that demands my attention. I haven't forgotten about it, but it feels well hidden. It feels safe.

I sit with my brother, listening as he sings the songs Laila loved, thinking over the strange afternoon.

It's there that I remember: the scarf, the grey scarf with red stripes from David's utility room. I *had* seen it before, when I was last in Canty's shop and he showed me that photograph.

I'd seen Laila wearing it.

TWENTY-TWO
Sorry

David

The Eye isn't here.

I want to rip the red silk cloth from the table and send it all crashing to the ground. I am so frustrated.

I search around Laila's witchy altar, around the figurines and objects arranged there. I lift the girl/flower Bláithín, shift the stones, examine a detailed iron cailleach, an old hag. But no Eye.

I test the floorboards and feel the undersurface of the table. Nothing.

This broken-down, half-rotten house belongs to my family. As a young woman, Mamó lived here briefly. It's the spillover home, where Creaghs go when we squabble too much. When it suddenly came to me what 'Find Meadowsweet on School' meant, I legged it here.

At the centre of the shrine, half-burned black candles circle the small antique glass and gold casing. The last time I saw this casing, it held the Eye and now it's empty.

The entire wall is painted over with Ogham script. I recognise the song of the Crow-Mother, which takes up most of the surface. But immediately above the empty casing are three words that aren't part of the song. Three words, in Ogham, that stand out. Words that are sacred to my family: *Red the blade.*

This was no accidental stumbling, despite the mishmash of different kinds of magic that's displayed on the shrine. Laila knew.

It's never felt right that Laila died in the same place on the same night that Cassa, through her ritual, changed Wren into the Bláithín. Under the wickerlight. Was Laila somehow injured by the changing ritual? Could she have been trying to salvage the remnants of Cassa's magic and it backfired and killed her?

I ring Canty to ask him about salvaged magic. He can't talk, and says he'll call me later. Hanging up, I hesitate, my finger hovering over Zara's number.

I put my phone away. My world is volatile and uncertain. And she wouldn't want to talk to me now. It's better this way.

Leaving Meadowsweet House, I set off home. There's only a short while before Oisín faces the tribunal at HH.

Empty-handed and out of ideas, I'm fighting a rising dread that the augurs have found the Eye.

Just inside the gates to the Rookery, a lanky shape peels from a tree.

Sometimes Cill gives even me the creeps.

His affinity is animal and his guide is mink. Cute, right? Until I remember how one of them got into Lucia's chicken house. Crawled right through two-inch mesh wire and killed all ten chickens. Bite marks in the neck. Several heads ripped off. I'd found the bodies arranged against the wall in two neat piles.

'Davey.' Cill stops me. Never forget: minks kill for pleasure.

'Cill.' I shove my hands into my pocket, hunching my shoulders against the sudden chill.

'Long time.' He pulls a half-cigarette from his shirt pocket, tapping it against his hand. 'Want one?'

I shake my head. It's been months since I took one of his smokes.

'Grab a beer?' He cups his hands around the cigarette and clicks his Zippo. The smell of lighter fluid is strong.

I feel guilty. I've neglected him, when I know he's down about being out of work.

'Going in to HH this evening.' I walk, inclining my head so he'll walk with me.

'A quick one?' He's pleading. 'At the Huntsman?'

'Can't. I have to bring Oisín in for his tribunal.' And I've had enough of the Huntsman.

'I'll come along for the ride, so.' Cill takes a deep drag.

'It isn't a party, you psycho.'

We turn the bend and the house is in sight. Laughing, he claps a hand on my shoulder. 'Can't stop me.'

He's right. And since I have a night shift followed by a day, Cill can use my car to bring Oisín home after the tribunal. Saves me some driving.

'I've heard the augurs are still searching for the Eye.' Cill glances at me. 'They haven't found it.'

'Good.'

'What's the deal with your tenants?' Cill exhales hard. 'The foreigners?'

'Don't be a dick, Cill.' The stones crunch beneath our trainers.

'Sure, that's what they are. They're not from here.' He tosses his cigarette end.

'Here's their home.'

'What do you know about the girl?'

My attention is taken by the figure at the tree. Mamó.

'Leave her be, Cill.'

Mamó's staring at an oak tree close to the house. She's eerily still and I'm suddenly terrified. Picking up speed, I race to the tree, Cill close behind.

I stop when I see something shiny on the ground. It's round and gilded, with knotwork detail. The Eye.

But when I bend for it, I see it's only Mamó's replica brooch. It must have fallen from her dress.

'Holy shit,' Cill breathes, looking at the tree. I move closer, trying to make sense of what I'm seeing.

Hanging from the oak are black shadows.

Not shadows, rooks. From the low branches, rooks are suspended, twisting in the breeze. They're arranged, like maudlin decorations. Easily thirty of them, and all lifeless.

The horror of it. The dedication. How long did it take to trap and kill the birds? Weeks? Months?

It breaks my heart. Even though I don't follow the rook, I'm attached to them. I can't bear to see them hurt.

Mamó's face is both furious and devastated. She can't take her eyes off the birds.

How could an augur get in here long enough to do this? Even if they were dressed in some kind of protective gear, they would not have made it away unscathed.

It's only then that I realise how silent it is. It's unnatural that there isn't a single rook, hooded crow, jackdaw or magpie calling in the early evening. Even when the birds are resting, there's the odd cry or shriek. Silence this complete is unusual. Wrong.

And I realise it's because the rooks are sad and angry. Rooks are smart. They know.

Dad and Lucia are out and I find Oisín in his room,

staring at the ceiling. Since the attack, this is his favourite hobby.

'Did the rooks go wild earlier?'

He looks at me, bored, then back to the ceiling.

'What was the offering? The one you told the augurs?' I nag him. 'Oisín!'

'I was asleep.' He's communing with the cobwebs up there. 'I had these awful nightmares of rooks in cages while sharp spikes pushed up from the ground to impale them. They were screaming so much. It hurt.'

'That wasn't all dream,' I sigh.

But Oisín is lost in the aftershocks of his nightmare. It's like I'm not even there.

'We have to go. Your tribunal.'

I pick up a shoe and throw it at him. He doesn't blink.

After a minute, Oisín gets up like he's getting out of his grave. He's in one of his funks again.

'Get in the shower.'

He can't face Cassa like this. I herd him to the bathroom we share and run the taps. There's barely any hot water from this morning but he'll survive. I start pushing him in, clothes and all, when he shouts, 'Hey.'

He pulls off his clothes and gets into the shower, leaning his hands against the tiles. The bones show through his skin.

From beneath my annoyance, I allow another feeling to

rise to the surface. I let myself name it: fear. Seeing Oisín come to this makes me very afraid.

And I acknowledge what perhaps only Lucia has. That Oisín is not pathetic. That he's suffering a kind of post-traumatic stress disorder. And he's not able to work through it, because he doesn't even know what the trauma is.

The water must be freezing and still he stands there, bracing the wall like he's holding up the house. And I want to say something. Help him somehow. Let him know that I care. So, I flatten my hand and bang on the glass, shouting, 'Hurry up, dickwad.'

The water off, he shivers as I reach out a towel.

'Sever,' he whispers with chattering lips. Which means Sibéal wasn't lying. The augurs know two of the four offerings.

We've underestimated them. Again.

At HH, Cassa insists Oisín must face the tribunal alone.

While we wait, Cill wanders off, probably to annoy Ian and Elliot. I stay outside Cassa's court. I'm jiggling my leg as I sit on the hard chair, then I'm standing, then pacing outside the door.

What is taking them so long? Is Oisín able to speak for himself or is he self-destructing in there? I really don't want another of Niall's rows.

But what I'm most afraid of is that he's confessed to telling the augurs Badb's offering. I don't want to think of the trouble that would cause.

I go downstairs to the Harkness Foundation office to see if Laney is around. She might have some idea of how bad things are. Laney may be Cassa's assistant, but she's our childhood friend. Oisín's first kiss.

She's not there, but at the tall windows near her desk is Wren. Cill's there with her. He's leaning over her, not too close, but his stance is aggressive. His smile is a sneer.

And again, I'm hit by the shame from yesterday. It's like being slapped in the face with a wet fish.

'Go on then, use your magic to make me go away.' Cill looks down on her with outright hostility. 'Oh right, you don't have any.'

'Cill,' I warn as I approach them.

'I don't have to explain myself to you.' Wren is annoyed. I wonder how many of these conversations she's had. How many times she's been sabotaged by pissed-off judges who want answers.

'You may have Cassa fooled. But we don't believe you are some magic flower girl. Right, David?'

'Cill.' I'm closer. 'You really need to stop.'

'What do you tell your grover boyfriend, Wren?' Cill ignores me. 'When you sneak out to meet him?'

208

'Would you ever just shut up?' Wren tries to sound bored but I'm not buying it. He's rattling her.

Cill moves closer to Wren. She's uncomfortable but stares him down. She won't show how much he's intimidating her.

I place both my hands on his shoulders and steer him away.

'Give her some space, OK?' I pat him on the back. 'If you have concerns, take them to Cassa.'

Cill is looking at me with astonishment. I've gone so far off script that he's gaping at me like he doesn't know me.

'Fuck you, David.' He marches to the door, slamming his hand against the wooden surface.

Wren's looking at me with those eyes that dissect. Lucia's armour pulls again, but this time I feel stronger for it.

'I'm sorry.'

They are difficult words to say. Words that choke a throat. Funny how my stupid pride, all the things that once seemed important, just aren't any more.

'I'm sorry,' I say again, and this time it's easier. 'For terrorising you. For making you afraid.' For being one of those boys.

She takes a sharp intake of breath and looks away. I'm glad for it. But I sense my strangled apology means something to her. And saying it has made me feel lighter.

I leave the Foundation office and head to the marble staircase. Canty rings, just as I see Oisín coming down. He looks wrecked.

'Canty, I'll call you back, OK?' I say, not taking my eyes off Oisín. 'Give me five.'

Oisín leans against the wall.

'What happened?'

'They don't accept that the Eye is lost. They think I was compromised during my capture and gave our family heirloom to the enemy. I have two weeks to prepare my defence.'

'Did you tell them about the offering? That they got one off you?'

'Not yet, but Cassa knows I'm hedging. It's going to come out.'

This is bad. The only thing that will save Oisín is finding the Eye. He sinks to the ground, head in hands. I help him up before Cassa finds him on her floor and fines him for untidying the place.

We go out the garden door, down to the garage. Cill is in the car and gives me the stink-eye. I deposit Oisín.

'What did Canty want?' Oisín says to me. Cill looks up sharply.

'Nothing.'

'You doing business with Canty?' Cill says.

'It's nothing.'

He snorts, and starts the ignition. He shakes his head with a small laugh. Like I'm a lost cause. 'You need to get your head right.'

I turn away. He's not wrong.

Once Cill and Oisín pull out of the drive, I ring Canty.

'I'll give you one year. Not a minute more.'

'The terms have changed,' Canty says.

'You can't do that.'

He sighs. 'I thought you'd want to change them.'

'I don't trust you.'

'And you shouldn't usually. But this time is a little different.'

'What is the change?'

'It's just a small adjustment.'

'What do you want, Canty?'

'There's a girl I think might be in danger. She's stumbled into a mess and I'm worried for her. You will pay your debt to her instead of me.'

'This is unexpected. What's going on?'

'Let's just say I didn't speak up when someone else was in danger. This is the only way I can think to make it right.'

I'm clutching the phone tightly. I could be getting myself into a whole lot of trouble here.

'So I have to promise to answer questions honestly to this girl? Who?'

'Do we have a deal?'

This is insanity. But, Oisín.

'Not to an augur,' I say.

'She's not an augur.'

'Fine.' Agreeing to this stupid deal is making me almost light-headed. 'Who then?'

'The girl who lives in your rental. Zara.'

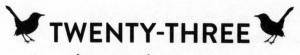

TWENTY-THREE
Love to have you

*Maeve Lawless paid me two hundred to spray paint a
black, large smiley face on a stone in a field in Gortashee.*

LAS

Zara

This week, I continue my quiet rebellion by mitching
camogie camp. I have a sense of purpose, a mission even. It's
like I'm tracking Laila, searching the quarry, the woods for
echoes of my sister. I can almost sense her, just beyond that
tree, or reading behind that fallen bough. Tramping in and
out of fields, I imagine her boot-covered feet on winter
grass. But when I look down, it's my Havaianas part hidden
in long grass, buttercups and wild flowers.

'There you are,' Sibéal says.

It's late afternoon and I'm walking from the Spar. Her
face is covered in red, angry scratches. There's bruising near
her eye, puncture wounds on her hands and arms.

'What happened?'

'I did something I probably shouldn't have.'

'What do you mean?'

'I mean, do you ever do something you know is wrong? But you do it anyway because the bastards deserve it?' And the way she looks at me, with that mild disdain, she knows the answer. No.

I suppress my Horrible. I put a lid on my baser, instinctual self. I let things fester inside. And I do as I'm told. I hold my darkness close while being the good daughter and behaving as is expected of me.

Except the love juice in the shaving oil thing.

Sibéal starts walking, gesturing for me to walk with her. 'Look, I wanted to say thank you. For the other day.'

'I'm sorry that happened.' I sound dull.

'Do you want to come over?' Sibéal says.

'Come over?' The invitation is abrupt, unexpected.

'To ours. You can eat with us. Mam would love to have you.'

I hesitate. But then I think how lonely it is at home. Laila's not there, and Adam is always visiting Patrick these days.

We walk to the old quarry road mostly in silence, until we reach a cottage and a seventies bungalow. There are no other houses around, just fields and the woods.

'Mam,' Sibéal calls, 'I've brought Zara for dinner.'

In the kitchen, a short woman with curly hair comes towards me and pulls me into her arms. I'm a little startled by the sudden intimacy.

'Oh, my sweet girl, your sister.' Her words are sugary. 'Such an awful, awful thing, dead on the grass. Now. You'll eat with us this evening.'

She steers me to the table on the opposite side of the room. Through an open door, I see Aisling in the living room. She's wearing a jacket and pencil skirt like she's just home from Kelly's practice.

'You've met my sister, Ash, right?' Sibéal says. 'She works with your mom.'

Sibéal drops into a rocking chair and starts humming. With each rock, the chair squeaks. Maeve looks at her sharply, then calls Aisling in.

Maeve talks to me, about the weather, the village, their summer holiday plans. She's chopping vegetables with the ease of an efficient and systematic cook. Aisling sits beside me, tapping a pen.

The window is open, and wind chimes chant intermittently through Maeve's mindless chatter. On the patio are dream-catchers and colourful objects that spin around in the breeze.

It's all strangely soothing: the even taps of Aisling's pen. The knife slicing through onions, through celery, through carrots. Sibéal's wordless song that weaves in and out of Maeve's talking. The rocking of her chair.

'Tell me about Laila,' Maeve says.

How jagged and agitated my home is. Not like this place, where everything flows. Even the people are in tune with each other. I bet they don't fight. I bet they don't throw things at each other.

Suddenly, I'm achingly jealous. I'm jealous of Sibéal, that she has a sister who is alive. A mother who isn't floundering. I'm jealous of this house, of the togetherness I sense. It's so beautiful, so out of my reach. These are people who love each other fiercely, who'll do anything to protect each other.

'It must be so hard. Do you know what happened?'

'I don't.' The words are difficult to form. 'Yet. But I will find out. I must.'

The chair, the song, every small movement, is like a dance. Movement art, set to music. The colours twirling outside. I shut my eyes and see a brief image. A memory of a David Attenborough video of a spider spinning its web. The ring with its black stone feels tight around my finger.

'Have you found anything unusual?' Maeve's voice is far away. Soothing, and I feel such peace.

When I look around me, the light has changed.

It doesn't feel like I've fallen asleep. More like I blinked, and the scene changed. I'm still at the table but Maeve and Sibéal are no longer there. I am disoriented, like I've been spinning too fast and come to an abrupt, giddy halt.

I hear voices in the next room. See Sibéal and Maeve through the open doorway, their heads bent together. I hear the words, but struggle to make any sense of them.

'... doesn't know anything,' Maeve says. 'We're wasting our time.'

'So let's rule it out then. Besides, he likes her. I can use that.'

'You don't have enough control.'

'I can do it.' Sibéal sounds frustrated. 'Just give me a chance.'

'Too risky.'

'You're awake.' Aisling's voice is startlingly loud. She's standing over the stove, stirring something there.

'Did I fall asleep?' I push my hair out of my face. I'm mortified.

'Yeah, Mam can talk all right.' Aisling laughs.

'I hope I didn't offend her.' I stand up too quickly and hold on to the table until the dizzy spell passes.

'You're grand,' Maeve laughs as she comes into the room. 'I'm delighted you're comfortable here with us.'

'I didn't think I was tired,' I say. 'It doesn't even feel like I've been asleep.'

But the light outside has shifted. The chopped vegetables are soup.

Maeve drops the bowls on the table and the sisters are bickering over spoons. We eat together and too soon, another hour has passed.

'I should get home.' I'm reluctant to leave. 'Mom will be wondering where I am.'

'Come again.' Aisling smiles. 'We'd love to have you back. Here, my number, go on, put it in your phone.'

I oblige and she gives me Sibéal's too.

'We're friends, Zara.' Maeve hugs me as I leave. 'You look like you could do with a few of those.'

Her eyes run over me, maternal and concerned. And leaving, I feel a deep sense of calm. Of love. I leave the house, feeling certain that I've found good people.

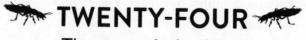

TWENTY-FOUR
The wounded soldier

David

The dungeon at HH is tiny, with only a six-by-six-inch square of light. This is the cage in Cassa's beautiful garden.

It's state of the art, with retractable spikes that push up from the floor, blades that slice out of walls. For some crimes the disgraced judge, or accused augur, is made to sleep, sit, walk on the bed of spikes. For others, the nails creep up from the floor on an unknown schedule, the anticipation part of the punishment.

And upstairs the house is filled with flowers and music and art. People drink champagne and flirt and laugh. Further up, on the next floor, is Cassa's court. In her chambers is her selection of tools, some antique, plenty more modern. She takes pride in them, their strength, what they symbolise.

She is not a bad woman. Rather, she's a woman always on the back foot. There are a few, like Dad, who would like her power for themselves.

This time, I've been lucky. Three days of solitude to

reflect on my actions, no nails, no blades, no blood. Cassa was being kind.

She called me in after Cill expressed a concern about me and Canty, hinting that I was using scavenged magic.

Cassa was even more disappointed than usual, possibly perplexed. But if she knew the details of the bargain I struck with Canty, aiding a girl who doesn't like me, I'd be getting a lot worse than the cage.

I pull the small compact mirror from my pocket and open it for the hundredth time. Again, I see my own reflection. When I picked it up three days ago, Canty made me drink a disgusting tonic and swear an oath. This had better not be some elaborate con with a dud mirror.

The cage is not the worst punishment, though the boredom and isolation could drive a boy too deep inside his head. I'm OK, solitary confinement was a Birchwood module where I excelled.

But the dim, lazy light. The way it never quite gets into the room with its lacklustre reach. And I hate the stale air. Being deprived of light, of outside air, affects me far more than being alone. I struggle for not hearing the crawl of insect feet, the soft sound of wings, butterfly, moths, bees through the air. I touch a finger to the beetle I've etched into the skirting.

So much for Oisín wishing me free.

On the third morning, Cassa comes for me.

'In our brokenness we find our strength.'

I don't know who she's quoting this time, if she's even quoting anyone at all. But there's a look on her face, and it's almost a plea. Or maybe I'm imagining it; that's what three days, three nights locked in a near dark room will do for you.

'The wounded soldier makes the truest save.'

I'm stiff and sore. I tried keeping an exercise routine, but the room's too small and really, how many push-ups can you do while in a cupboard? Dad is going to be furious that my training is yet again compromised.

'The sword passes through fire before it becomes a weapon.' Cassa is still muttering while I pull on my T-shirt. I just want to get out. I want to move. I want to run and soak up the sun, feel rain on my face.

'You're well able for it, David,' she says to me as I pass through the door.

'Able for what?' I hope she doesn't hear the anger in my voice.

'For more than you think. Don't let fear dictate your choices. Sometimes the thing that breaks you is what makes you.'

Yeah, put that on a greeting card. Or make a fucking meme with cute kittens.

I'm up the stairs two at a time. I want to be outside.

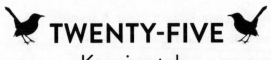

TWENTY-FIVE
Keeping tabs

I prepare my shrine.
LAS

Zara

By Thursday, I give up all pretence of going to camogie camp and Mom's lost inside her head again because she doesn't even notice.

Most mornings I visit the shrine and Callie calls in for a chat. She tells me unhappy stories, with terrible endings and I find them strangely consoling. Leaving Meadowsweet, I might go to the woods, the main street, the green, the abandoned quarry, the lake.

It's become an obsession, this need to keep close to Laila. To find the places where she's been. I match my own wandering with the photographs on her corkboard. I find the small hidden boathouse, the round stone bench by the lake, the broken TV in the quarry. I mark off each one, like I'm playing a kind of game. A scavenger hunt, where I'm searching for Laila's destinations.

'Zara,' Sibéal calls from her front gate as I walk back from the old quarry.

I stop. She blows hot and cold, this one. I never quite know where I stand.

'You look thirsty, will I get you a drink?' she calls. 'Come on, I won't bite.'

She turns down the path and as I enter the gate, I hear the soft words: 'This time.'

Over her shoulder, she gives me a broad smile, and I follow her into the house.

'Elderflower OK?' she asks as we go to the kitchen. There's a sketch pad on the table which she flicks shut. 'Mam makes it herself.'

'Sure.'

'Whenever I see you –' she hands me the glass '– you're just wandering around. Aimlessly. Alone.'

She looks at me intently while I think what to say. Tracking my dead sister doesn't seem like the socially acceptable response.

Sibéal breaks her gaze suddenly, like she's forcing herself to turn away.

'I could say the same about you.' I drink from my glass.

'Except I'm not aimless.'

'Who says I am?'

'What is it, Zara?' Her eyes are dark and intense. 'What are you looking for?'

A loud noise, like a gunshot, sounds. So close, it reverberates through my body, propelling me forward.

Sibéal's face pales, her mouth opens. She spins around, black hair whipping my face. She's at the door first, pushing it open. Me on her heels. When I go in, she's shielding herself from an explosion of light and colour. There's a loud whistling as another firecracker goes off, lighting up the room. Sparks fly, and I raise my arms over my face.

'You bastards,' Sibéal bawls, a deep guttural sound. Outside, an engine starts. Tyres squeal as a car pulls away.

I run out the front door and see a blue Micra down the road. Too far to get a registration, but I take a picture anyway. Inside the house, Sibéal hurls a torrent of foul words.

I turn, and see black words sprayed on the wall: THE CROW WILL AVENGE.

Inside, Sibéal is furious as she stamps out embers on the scorched rug. The wall is smudged black and the flame licking the curtain is growing. I scramble to the kitchen, Sibéal following after. She grabs a bucket and I take a pot from the drying rack. Water spills on to the floor as we run to the curtains. Half my first attempt ends up on the wall.

We rush between the kitchen and curtain, trying to

stop the growing flame. Sibéal slips on the wet floor and goes down with a bucket of water. Her hair is wet, her clothes patched with damp, but her face is set with grim determination.

It takes a few trips before we put out the last of the flames.

'This is a mess,' she says, looking at the smudged walls, burned curtains, and wet floor.

'We should call Garda Creagh,' I say. Calling the police is the only option here. But Sibéal makes a strange sound, half a laugh, half a snort.

'That's not going to help.' She's bitter.

'He could find who did this.'

'I know who did this.' Her mouth is tight. She looks like a girl plotting her revenge.

'Who?'

'Who do you think?'

It takes a moment before I realise who she means.

'Breanna and the boys? No.' I don't believe it. 'They wouldn't go that far.'

Sibéal's face is grim. 'They would go that far, and a whole lot more.'

Later, I'm unlocking the door at home when I hear his voice behind me.

'Zara.'

I turn around, and there's David.

'What do you want?'

'Was just passing. Thought I'd see how you're doing.' He can't quite look at me. He seems ashamed.

I shrug. 'The same.'

He's uncomfortable, but I don't care. I don't want to chat or hang out with boys who shove girls.

'I have to go.' I jerk my thumb back to the door.

'I know. I get it, I do. And I'll stay out of your way. But ...' He scratches his head, like he's feeling stupid. 'Just, I spoke to Canty, and if you have any trouble, call me. No matter how late.'

He shoves his hands in pockets and walks towards the Rookery gates. Slowly, the gates gape a little before they swallow him up.

I sit on the top step, watching him walk away. Into the green.

A car approaches, heading towards the Rookery. It slows down, and the driver cruises by me with a deep scowl on his face.

I know this car. I'd seen it just an hour ago. Driving away from Sibéal's house.

'You need to make better friends, little girl,' he calls to me through the open window. Cillian.

Oh, for God's sake. Here? Really? He gets out of the car, taking the time to smirk at me, and punches in the code.

I scramble for my phone camera and snap a picture of the car to get the registration.

'Can't get enough of me, can you?' Cillian calls.

'Why are you here?' My lack of enthusiasm is evident.

'Visiting friends. You keeping tabs?'

They're friends. The boy who threw a firecracker through Sibéal's window is friends with the boy who shoved her. I shouldn't be this surprised.

I shake my head and blank him before he drives off. Opening my photos, I see one that I'd completely forgotten about: the photograph I'd taken at Laila's shrine. I'd disregarded it, certain that the glow in the wall had been a false impression.

I look at the photograph again and, in the picture, it's obvious. One small section of the wall is definitely brighter. Like a light is shining right down on it, drawing attention to a strip of Ogham.

Sitting on the front step, I find an Ogham translation site and forget about David, about Cillian the psychopath. After a little while, I've replaced the strokes and slants with letters.

I examine the letters: D-E-R-G-A-N-L-A-N

I mutter it out loud, trying to break the words up in a way that makes sense.

Derganlan. Looks like Irish, maybe?

But David. The solitary figure walking into the light, into the green.

Give him and his friends a wide berth, Canty had warned me weeks ago. *They're dangerous.*

I have to stop thinking about David.

Derg an lan? Maybe the Ogham is in an older form of Irish? And if that's the case, what would happen if I changed the letters a little? I play with a few versions until it hits me.

Derg an lann

Dearg an lann.

Red the blade.

Oh shit.

David's family war cry.

TWENTY-SIX
You will be held

David

Today the Rose will descend upon the Rookery for the midsummer rites. We will serve a feast we can't afford. We will welcome our gairdín into our home, hoping the broken floorboards and peeling paint aren't too visible. And in return, they'll whisper about our problems just loud enough for us to hear. And we will smile and serve them, because we are good subjects. We do as our Cleave commands.

It's busy downstairs. The courtyard, surrounded by semi-derelict outbuildings, is set up with tables and chairs for the dinner tonight.

I find Lucia arranging sprigs of rowan and blackthorn in the courtyard.

'Take this down.' She hands me branches to carry to the lake field, to place inside the stone ring. Dad prepares the bonfire.

When everything is set, I change into my day uniform,

the black wax jacket with the Bláithín insignia over a black T-shirt. I'm almost happy.

As the afternoon draws, members of the Rose trickle down to the lake for the summer rites. Some weave garlands. Cassa arrives with Tarc and for the first time in months, Wren isn't with them; she's travelled to Boston to meet her father.

Children run, screaming in delight. Everyone looks nicer with flowers strung in their hair, looped around shoulders and trailing down dresses. The scent of roses and wild-flowers, sunshine and laughter. This is the Rose at its best.

Cill arrives and it's still tense between us. He hasn't forgiven me. Can't say I'm happy about the cage.

When there're more than eighty of us gathered in the field, Cassa begins chanting. She moves searching hands over the stones. Children gather around her, each bringing a different sprig. When she finds the right stone, she touches two wooden staffs to it, signalling the beginning of the duel of light and dark.

This year, Dad takes on the role of dark. He clashes his staff against hers. The movements are choreographed, but Dad is rougher than is necessary. He hits her staff with too much force and Cassa stumbles. A murmur goes around the Rose. These movements are ritual, which means every small gesture matters. Stumbling does not bode well.

Cassa rights herself and they finish the duel. Dark vanquishes light, as it must at the summer solstice.

Wreaths are laid at the stones, new alder and blackthorn staffs are hallowed, and the rites completed. Dad lights the bonfire and as the flames catch, the crowd cheers. The band starts from the side of the field and it's just perfect. Lucia grabs my hand, laughing as she pulls me up to dance. Even Cassa is barefoot and dancing in the field.

When the band takes a break, Cassa stands in front of the crowd, who are fuelled with sunshine and wine.

'Liscarron has asked me to announce the first round of the War Scythe finals,' Cassa says, and the Rose goes wild.

I'm not too surprised. An already assembled audience, of course there'd be fighting. Nothing like spilt blood to complete a Rose party.

I glance at Elliot, who doesn't look happy. He ranks fourth and he's probably had a beer or three.

'Today's elimination round is a knife fight. The fourth rank will fight the other contenders. If he loses two, he's out. Our soldiers will fight until blood stains the earth.'

More cheering. The Rose just loves eliminating losers.

We draw tokens for the order of fights, and the first is between Elliot and Ian, then Elliot and Tarc. If he loses both fights, he's out and I'm off the hook for today.

Ian and Elliot face each other. Judges circle them, with bets taken. While Elliot's cheeks are a little red, Ian is ready. It doesn't take long before Ian holds Elliot down on the ground, taking his knife and running it down his arm. Blood falls, turning a patch of grass red. The Rose gives a frenzied cry and hands pound the grass, feet stamping their delight.

Cassa allows Elliot a minute. He's sobered up, and he's entering the zone. I've spent years training with these boys and Elliot performs better when he's properly warmed up. He focuses best after he's taken a few hits.

He launches into Tarc with new energy. Elliot is nowhere near as good as Tarc, despite the leg that still gives him trouble. He gets a few jabs in before falling to the ground.

But still no blood has stained the earth.

Tarc allows Elliot to clamber to his feet. Tarc leans forward, knife out. But Elliot is fast, feinting left, then going for the back of Tarc's leg, right where he took a bullet three months ago.

Gasping, Tarc slices Elliot's hand but it's awkward, not the neat cut he was aiming for earlier. As Elliot's blood falls to the ground, Cassa raises her hand to call it. Tarc has won.

But Elliot ignores the signal and jabs his knife in the back of Tarc's thigh. Tarc stumbles. I'm running out to him, yelling at Elliot.

'What the hell was that?' I curse him. Anger's always made him mean.

'He'll be all right.' Bryce Kelly is beside me. 'Get him to the house, I'll treat him there.'

Tarc's face is strained. With Ryan's help, they go back to the house.

I'm ready to tear into Elliot. This is not how brothers-in-the-garden behave. But Tarc won the fight and with two fights lost, Elliot's out.

Then I look up and at first I don't understand. They're backlit by the sun, the line of them on the slight incline staring down at us. The haze from the bonfire warps the line of men and women. My scalp tingles, and I think maybe it's head lice, even though I've asked them to show their affection otherwise. But my body is alert, and I'm drawing a knife. I don't see any augurs as I scan the field.

Something is wrong.

As they draw closer, I see garraíodóirí and wardens, the very best men judging by their badges and decoration. Dad's there, right in the centre.

The bonfire is at full blaze. The Rose is uncharacteristically quiet.

Cassa watches them approach. Her face reveals nothing, but she's small and strong as they move towards her. They draw to a standstill.

Dad steps forward.

'Calista Harkness, First Cleave of all Cleaves, Grand Magistrate, Hand of Justice and Second Commander of Garraíodóirí. You are charged with consorting with augurs. That through your complicity, you have put the brithemain in danger. You will be held until the time you stand trial.'

TWENTY-SEVEN
Not going to make it

*I don't think Adam knows the boy he loves is keeping such
a big secret from him.*

LAS

Zara

It's the best kind of summer's morning, sunny and sleepy.
Flowers are in full bloom, birdsong fills the air. A magpie
hops on to my window sill.

I'm in bed, still thinking about David's family war cry.
Why was it above Laila's shrine? And why was scarf she
wore in their laundry? When Canty warned me of dangers,
did he mean them? Cillian is violent and has an agenda.
And David, who is no angel, is his friend.

But what is the link to Laila?

Adam comes into my room and stretches beside me. He's
been so absent these last weeks, it seems like he's grown
since I last looked at him properly. His legs nearly reach
over the end of the bed, and yet he is so unfinished. He's an

artwork in the making, eyebrows that are too heavy for his still-narrow face. His fingers are stained with ink and I couldn't tell you if he loves sport or music more.

'They're not going to make it, are they?' Adam is looking to me for reassurance.

'You've been busy.' I avoid the question. 'I've hardly seen you.'

'Anywhere else is better than being with them.' He turns away, staring ahead. 'It's easier at Patrick's house.'

A pang of guilt pricks me. My family might be dysfunctional, but they're mine.

We're both quiet. The sound of a door opening and Mom's footfall down the passage, then on the stairs.

'Dad wants to leave.' I have to tell him. 'He's looking for jobs overseas.'

Adam chews on his lip. 'I can't move again. I've made friends. There're people …' He pauses. '… I don't want to leave. I'm not letting my team down. I can't do it all again.'

'And Laila's here,' I add.

He closes his eyes. 'And Laila's here.'

'Then we have to make sure we stay.'

Mom knocks on the door and comes in. She is surprised to find Adam on my bed. His hairy toes on my white covers.

'Dad and I thought we'd drive into the city. Do some shopping, get lunch.' She's trying to sound bright and breezy but her voice is a little strangled. They've not said a word to each other for two weeks. And now they're suggesting a family outing. I want to shout at Mom, but that's not going to help anything. I look at Adam, our pact fresh in our minds.

'Sure.' He plays it cool. 'If I pick the music.'

'God help us,' I mutter, trying to push him off the bed.

'Go feed the rat,' Mom says. She can't hide her distaste for Laila's pet rat, Silas. Adam has taken on its care, but none of us has the same enthusiasm as Laila did. 'We're leaving in twenty.'

In the city, I remember why I don't go shopping with Mom. If she picks up another mid-calf-length dress, I'm going to smack her over the head with it. She's frowned at everything I've shown her, complaining they're too short or too flimsy like she's never looked inside my wardrobe.

Dad lasted ten minutes before he disappeared for a newspaper and coffee. Adam abandoned me right from the get-go. The traitor texted old friends and met up with them, leaving me shopping with my mother.

I settle on a playsuit which bothers Mom marginally less, even though it's as short as any of the skirts. I've worn her down and I celebrate my victory by annoying her and putting it on right away. She's emitting random long-suffering sighs when we see Dad at the coffee shop.

I'm thinking how well we're doing. How effectively we're managing to ignore everything broken. I realise that even though our conversations are stilted and our smiles are strained, it was a good idea to come out together. To get away from the village for a little while.

'You're earlier than I expected.' Dad looks up from his book while Mom goes to order. 'I think this must be a record. How have you managed to finish shopping so quickly?'

'We came to an agreement.' I strike a little pose to show my new outfit, and his eyebrows go up.

Laughing, I sit across from him. This is almost like before. This is as normal as we've been in so long. We're a forced grimace that eventually becomes a smile.

'Professor Swart?' a voice says. Slinking down my seat, I see the woman in front of us. She looks around thirty. Long pale hair.

'Margaret.' Dad smiles at her. She stands there, hovering at the table, and something rings odd. I don't know why she doesn't move on, or why she's looking at me so intently.

'This is my daughter Zara,' he says, still holding his book. 'Margaret is doing her PhD in the department and she was a teaching assistant on my first-year course.'

He's over-explaining, and looking across the large, crowded room to the counter where Mom's getting lunch.

238

The worry is a prickle down my spine. Suddenly, I'm cold. My legs are covered in goosebumps.

Margaret is wearing a demure sundress with a cardigan. To put it bluntly, Margaret is hot. But Dad has always stuck to middle managers in pencil skirts, avoiding the murky waters of dalliances with students. Surely he's not that dumb?

'Meg,' she says stiffly. 'I prefer Meg.'

'Is there anything you wanted, Meg?' Dad is beginning to sound strained.

She pauses, then says, 'No. Nothing.'

'So how was that talk?' I look up from beneath my lashes. 'The one on Byronic heroes in twenty-first-century stories?'

'Oh, it was really good.' Her enthusiasm falters and she flushes. 'I mean … I should go, I have a family thing on. See you on Monday, Professor Swart.' I'm sure the other graduate students call Dad by his first name.

I'm confused. Terrified. I don't know if I've become as neurotic as Mom. Maybe checking Dad's computer isn't a good idea. I don't know if we've just been burned so much that any innocent encounter begins to take on significance that isn't there.

I don't know if Dad had a particular reason for wearing his Rage Against the Machine T-shirt that brings out the green in his hazel eyes and makes his brown arms glow. It shows off his shoulders, the biceps that are surprisingly defined for an English literature professor pushing fifty.

What if Dad, thinking he had an extra hour before Mom and I finished shopping, decided to take a chance to meet up with Meg? I don't know if this was arranged, and Meg was pissed off, or she's just one of those awkward people who are better with ideas than social niceties. I don't know.

But it's left a bad taste. And I hate that I've become so paranoid.

In the car, I catch Mom's face through the mirror as she rummages in her bag for her lipstick. For a moment, the mask slips. The strain, the weariness around her eyes and lips are pronounced. She exhales slowly and I see the deadness in her eyes. She pulls out the lipstick and holds it up to the mirror. She watches herself, and by the time the Velvet Teddy is pasted on, so is her smile.

And it occurs to me, maybe she *should* go back to her real home. Maybe she should find happiness again. Who am I to keep her from that? But Mom will never leave Adam and me, she'd rather stay in a bad marriage than leave us with Dad. Than have a Lindy replace her in our lives.

We're just outside of Kilshamble, and everything is heavy again. I don't know how to untangle this awful knot.

I allow myself an Insta peek, to scroll through the many pictures of the life I no longer live.

Then I see it: the late evening sun behind them, Hannah and Nathan are kissing. Really kissing. Devouring each other actually. It was posted by Ciara two days ago. The filter is dramatic, blurring details and rendering them ethereal. Magical.

While I feel so dull and ordinary.

This is why Laila longed for magic. I'm beginning to hope she found it.

Maybe I'm beginning to hope I find it too.

I don't mind that Nathan's kissing Hannah. My old friends are so far off my radar that it doesn't hurt. But the picture unsettles me. It highlights that feeling of missing out. Life is happening around me, but I skulk in the shadows. I hide in abandoned houses, talking to an old woman and her ghosts. It doesn't feel like enough. Looking at the picture, I realise the problem: I don't feel alive enough. Laila's dead. She's literally dead. Can't do anything at all. But I can.

I stare at the picture a long while. My legs are hot and sticky against the car leather. Then I delete the app and say to Dad, 'Can you leave me here?'

We're near the school bus stop.

'Where're you going?'

'It's a nice day.' I'm clawing at the handle. 'You know, fresh air and exercise.'

I have a sudden longing for Maeve's house. I want to talk and laugh with Sibéal and Aisling. I want to belong, to matter.

I want to live.

Dad pulls over and I'm out of the car, half running, half walking towards the quarry.

I've lost so much in such a short time. Laila, my friends, my very sense of who I am. But as I walk, I know I will keep on going on. There will be new friends, new places. And I will shift, like a snake with its skin, into new versions of myself.

I knock at the door of Cairn House. No one answers, and yet I can hear voices and scuffling inside. I shouldn't have pitched up uninvited. I'm about to leave when the door opens.

'Zara, this is a surprise.' Aisling doesn't sound as friendly as before.

'Sorry, I should have called. I can come another time.'

She steps out of the front door and pulls it nearly shut behind her. Inside, I can hear Maeve talking to a man.

'I think that's a better idea.' Aisling glances back inside. Her voice is quiet. Maybe I'm paranoid, but it's like she doesn't want anyone to know I'm here.

'Hey, look who's here.' Sibéal pulls the door wide open. 'I've been hoping you'd come.'

'You have?'

'Yeah, come on in. Mam's baking.'

In the hall, a guy, maybe twenty, stands with his arms folded.

'That's Simon,' Sibéal says, and leads me to the kitchen. 'Aisling's boyfriend.' Her tone is teasing. 'It's new, so I'm still ragging them.'

She leads me to the kitchen, where Maeve is at the counter sifting flour in a bowl on a stand mixer. There's a look between Maeve and Aisling, and I wonder what it means.

'Hope you like cake.' Maeve smiles at me as I cross the room to the table.

'Want to play?' Sibéal holds up a pack of cards. The others are hovering, watching. When I turn, they scatter. Aisling goes to the tractor stool, Simon leaves for the living room, leaving the door open. The wall's been painted and the curtains replaced.

'Sure.' I pull out a chair at the table and watch as she shuffles the pack.

An unpleasant sensation shoots through me. Like that stomach dip on a roller coaster, but in my head.

It's been a day, I tell myself. That odd encounter between Dad and Meg has left me rattled.

Behind Sibéal, Maeve's got the stand mixer going on a low speed. The rotary blades are turning, the bowl moving in circles. Simon's on the couch, and through the open door, I watch him bounce a small rubber ball on the coffee table.

That odd dissociation becomes worse as I watch Sibéal shuffle the pack.

'I think they're shuffled now,' I say to her.

'Will I read your cards?'

I don't quite understand until she hands the pack and says, 'I can't tell the future but I think the present is always more interesting.'

She nods for me to cut the deck and I do. Sibéal takes the pack and starts laying cards out on the table. She shuts her eyes for a few seconds, then she looks at me with a penetrating gaze.

'You're sad, and I know that's obvious but it's so thick around you, you can barely see your way. You're going to be sad for a while longer, this kind of sorrow takes a long time to clear.'

In the background, the stand mixer is going. Aisling sways on the tractor stool and it emits a long thin whistle each time she swings it. I feel a pressure around my face, like something invisible around me has been disturbed.

'You want something very much.' Sibéal's eyes are on mine, like she's reading me and not the cards. 'But it will bring dangers that you've never dreamed possible.'

That odd nudging pressure moves down from my face, travelling down my arms, pushing at my legs, then back up to my head.

I'm transfixed. What has started as a game seems to be something more. I feel like Sibéal is somehow able to look into me and see things that I can't begin to understand.

'You've been following Laila.' The pressure increases, except now, I'm feeling it inside me. Like it's somehow crossed my skin, these light tingles in my head. 'You found something. Hair? Something else?' Sibéal frowns, like she doesn't agree with herself. 'No, just the hair.'

Her gaze is becoming too intent and I'm beginning to feel dizzy.

'Laila made a shrine,' Sibéal breathes out. 'But I can't see where it is.'

Nausea rises and I curl my fingers around the seat of the chair.

'There's a wall up, it's blocked somehow.' The tingles are stronger. It feels like invisible hands rummaging inside my head. I'm so light-headed.

'I don't understand,' Sibéal is muttering to herself.

'There's something very strong here, but it's dark and damaged.'

'Focus, Sibéal.' Maeve's voice drifts over. 'Does she know about the Eye? The offerings?'

'You were both close to Laila and not close.' It's like boxes being upended, drawers opened and contents tossed aside. 'You don't know …'

'David.' She smiles like a hacker who got into a government database. 'Ah, you really liked him. You were so disappointed in him when he pushed me. But Zara, I'm no fragile flower. David can't hurt me.'

The nudging is harder, more urgent. I hold my hand up to my head and bend over.

'You dream of him.' She's still smiling.

'Please stop,' I breathe out.

'Here's what you have to do, Zara,' Sibéal whispers to me, concentrating hard. She's as white as a sheet, with her sleek black hair falling into her bloodshot eyes.

'Sibéal, you've got to stop.' Aisling's spinning ends abruptly.

'You've got to get David to tell you the last two offerings. Go to him. Forgive him, really he didn't hurt me.'

'He didn't?'

'No, Zara, silly girl. I'm fine. Now, you go to him. Kiss him. Let it happen. He wants it as much as you do. And then ask for his deepest secret. Ask him if he's ever been told an ancient truth in a vision. Ask him to tell you the offerings.'

It feels like the invisible hands have taken something and pushed it into a fold inside my head.

'What must you do?' Sibéal's voice is so gentle.

'Go to David. Kiss him. Two offerings.'

'It won't work, Sibéal,' Aisling argues. 'You're crazy if you think he'll tell her.'

'He likes her. A lot. Enough to be stupid. Stupider, rather,' Sibéal snaps at her sister. 'I don't see you coming up with anything.'

'Because I'm not rash.'

Sibéal touches her hands to my head.

'You're going to forget that I asked you to retrieve the offerings. I can't make you forget all of this afternoon, but you won't remember me talking about David. Right?'

'Right.' I feel so very far away from myself. I feel myself falling off the chair and pulling up my knees.

But there's something I need to remember, something about David.

'Mam, make her stop the Delve,' Aisling pleads. 'Zara's in a bad way.'

'But I can see what she knows about—'

'That's enough for now, Sibéal.'

Everything is quiet for a moment, and I can feel them all looking at me. I sense Aisling's fear and worry.

But David. I must remember David.

With everything I have, I get to my feet. I am so light-headed and nauseous I can barely stand. Moving away is like breaking an invisible hold. I stumble forward, bumping the table and knocking over the chair.

I have to remember that thing I have to remember.

Sibéal is still staring at me, her eyes are huge and blood-shot. She wipes a tear and it streaks red across her cheek. I don't know if it's because she rubbed a scratch too hard, or if she's crying blood.

'Mam.' Aisling is staring at me, panicked. 'Zara's all over the place. We've got to do something.'

It takes all my energy to get out. Out through the door and into the bright sunny day.

I push open the garden gate and run out into the road. There's nothing but woods and farmland around. Keeping close to the road, I run along the trees.

Ahead is a thick oak and I'm moving towards it. I hear Aisling calling from behind and I go faster. I'm nearly at the tree, nearly touching the trunk, where I can just take a moment to breathe—

And then I'm sitting further down the road. I don't know how I'm there. There's something I must remember. But inside my head is all basic shapes and primary colours. I can barely think, never mind chase elusive thoughts.

The tree is gone. No one else is around. I'm on the ground with my knees pulled up to my chest. I'm shivering, despite the warm day.

I get up, unsteadily, and begin to walk home.

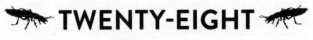

TWENTY-EIGHT
Answer her

David

Cassa's dress lifts in the breeze as Dad lays out the charges against her.

'What evidence do you have?' When Cassa speaks, she is still every bit our queen, wearied by incompetent underlings. She's small but majestic as Dad puffs himself up in front of her.

Don't let him bully you, I want to cheer her on.

'You will be held until your trial can be arranged.' Dad ignores Cassa, nodding for soldiers to cuff her.

'Why won't you answer her? What evidence, Dad?' I call across the field. The silence is jarring.

Dad turns to me, a cold fury defines his stance.

'In the interim, I am the highest authority.' Because Lucia signed over her claims to him years ago. 'And you will address me with respect, soldier.'

'Where is the evidence, Commander Creagh?' I load Dad's title with just enough sarcasm to spare myself a backhand later.

'We have proof that Cassa Harkness knew an augur infiltrated Harkness House before the nemeta locations were leaked.'

Bluster and bullshit. Dad's grasping. None of that matters any more.

All eyes are on me. Cill's beside me, gripping my arm. I try to jerk out of his hold without drawing too much attention to us. But Cill clenches tight and hisses in my ear, 'Don't be daft.'

Then, far along the shoreline, I see her.

Where the water meets land stands an old, old woman wearing a black cloak. She's watching us and I want to point to her because she is so magnetic and I don't know why everyone else isn't staring at her in awe.

A murder of crows flies over and Dad puffs up even more. He's feeling validated by the crows. They settle on the old woman and still Dad doesn't acknowledge her. She smiles at me and it's the smile of a thousand years. Of damp moss, of secrets. Of true power, not the bluster that Dad thinks is strength. Of service, not the pride that had fuelled me before.

Truth.

I hear the whispered word inside my head and I feel like a child held by loving arms. Everything else has disappeared and it's just me and the old woman.

I look back at the gathering, and my stomach drops. Everyone has fallen. They're strewn across the field, their bloodied bodies twisted and broken. The bonfire burns high and there's a stink of charred flesh. The sound of keening fills the air as a few solitary figures hunch over the dead. Following a pounding sound, I turn to see a heavy grover hacking a body with an axe.

Everywhere is death and desolation.

I turn back to the woman, who watches without expression.

'No,' I whisper.

Then don't let it happen.

'Jesus, Davey, you're making a right fool of yourself.' Cill pushes me forward. Everyone is exactly as they were. Not dead.

And I realise where I am, gaping in the middle of the field. I look back to the old crow lady but she's gone. Like she was never there.

Truth.

An offering. I received my first offering. And, with it, a warning.

I *am* deserving. And what does it mean that I receive my first offering, like some kind of late adolescence, just as I stand up to Dad?

Lucia takes my hand and squeezes it. I recognise the

conflict she has, her loyalty and love for her sister against her duty to Dad. I feel it too. She squeezes a second time before letting go, and I find solace in standing with her, a mirror image to Cassa with her quiet strength.

The Rose loves blood, but not like this. Not when we turn upon ourselves in a way that threatens to destroy us.

'Take her away.' Dad is enjoying this.

Cassa allows herself to be escorted to the house. Dad announces dinner and I can't face it. I see some people have slipped into the shadows. They will leave, they will refuse to participate in this. But most of the crowd follow on to the courtyard. Their allegiance is easily swayed.

My world has become infinitely more perilous in the last few hours. What did Mamó say? Dad is hungry. For power, but also for revenge. He will make the augurs pay for what they did to Oisín. And when they strike back, he will be ready.

I stay out there at the bonfire. Oisín appears at some point, telling me to get food. But I shake my head. Around me ants gather, bees hover. I open the mirror, see nothing, snap it shut again.

Then I hear her approach. I turn around and there she is.

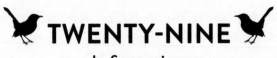 TWENTY-NINE
Infestation

*I approached Jarlath Creagh today but he brushed me off
rudely. Arrogant tosser. If he knew what he's just turned down.*

LAS

Zara

I'm walking home from Aisling's house and it's slow going.
Everything looks different. Luminous and too much, like
the filter from the picture of Hannah and Nathan has been
transposed on to everything I see. The road and trees are
covered in an Insta glow.

I'm feeling a deep, sharp terror at the strangeness of
things.

The woods are behind me and I can't look. Because I'm
sensing something hidden. Something with a beating heart.
I think of Laila and her certainty that there was truth to the
stories of the tree people. I think of the Horribles, and how
afraid they were to venture out of their ditch. I feel the
touch of the Inky Black there in the forest.

I should get away, but my legs are shaking. I sink down, just for a moment, beside the road.

There is something wrong with that family.

They did something to me.

My head feels odd, like it's been put back together wrong after Sibéal rummaged through it. Something really strange happened when she was reading the cards. But I'm too woolly. I can't put this together. Exhausted, I put my head in my hands.

I hear the car pass and pull up a little way ahead. First I think it's Aisling, but then when I look up, I see it's Dad's car, which is odd because he doesn't come down the old quarry road.

But I don't think it through. I run up to the passenger door and just before I open it, I see them through the window.

Dad's not alone. There's someone else in the car and it's disconcerting to see a woman who's not Mom in the front. I can't see her face, but I recognise the hair and the sundress.

Dad's with Meg. And it's utterly horrific. He's leaned back in the driver's seat while she straddles him. Both of my hands fly to my mouth. She's kissing him, and it's more than I can bear. I turn away, heaving.

Unsteady on my feet, I lurch towards the car. I have to make him stop.

But when I look up again, the clouds have shifted. The car is gone. I'm further along the road. I've never lost chunks of time like this. Once again I'm terrified. What if Laila and I have some rare genetic condition that makes us lose control over ourselves, like wind-up dolls running out of juice? What if it's my turn to switch off?

I need to get home.

And then, I'm barefoot in our drive. One of my Havaianas is broken and I'm just standing there. Dad's car is parked in the drive, and it makes no sense. I guess it is possible that he went out down the quarry road and came back but it seems unlikely. I've no idea how much time I've lost, so I can't even begin to piece it together.

I push open the front door and find them in the living room. They're all there, Dad, Mom and Adam. Their laughter sounds unfamiliar in this house. It looks like some other person's family. On the coffee table, a game of Risk is under way. Mom's stretched out on the duck-egg-blue couch, with Dad's head brushing her legs. I'm floored by the ordinariness of this. A family playing a board game on a Saturday afternoon.

Except, we never do. This is not my family.

Dad calls out when he sees me. 'Zara. Come and save me.'

'How long have you been playing?' I say to them, noting the time. It's been two and a half hours since I went walking.

'Hmmm?' Dad's intent on the game. He moves, playfully threatening Adam. Mom is reading Laila's autopsy report again, which is more normal.

'Little more than an hour? We took a break because your mum had some calls, so we're not too far ahead if you want to join?'

I'm agitated and hot. I can feel my hair sticking to my face, the taste of vomit in my mouth.

'You all right, Zara?' Mom looks concerned. 'You don't look so good. Did you get too much sun?'

'Yeah, a little hot.' I go into the downstairs bathroom to wash up. I must have dreamed it. I must have dreamed Dad and Meg in the Lexus. I don't see how he could have dashed out for a ten-minute shag in the middle of a family game of Risk unless he is a psychopath. Or maybe he is. Maybe he is that kind of liar, one who enjoys the game. Maybe the thrill of sneaking around is what Dad chases. I close my eyes and picture Meg on Dad's lap, his hand snaking up her dress. I open them, and the world looks different.

Through the mirror, the room has become wider, the angles of the doors and walls curve in. I can see everything down the passage, the details on the brass vase are in clear focus. I see myself: my eyes have changed. They dominate my face. Large and bulbous, there are thousands of small lenses shimmering like a mesh screen.

I have insect eyes.

Horrible, Zara.

I close them, clutching the sink. This time it's not Dad and Meg in the Lexus I'm mis-seeing. It's me. Dark hair, dark insect eyes. Thin antennae reaching above my head. I can't look.

When it's been long enough, I cautiously open my eyes. Back to normal.

I get it. Whatever happened with Sibéal has messed with my head. I'm seeing things. Dad wasn't in his car with Meg. I didn't have weird bug eyes.

Or did I?

'Where've you been?' Mom is standing in the doorway.

'Just walking.'

'You hungry?' She's watching me too closely, her doctor's eye dissecting my posture, my shallow breathing.

'I'll be out in a minute.' I want her to go, but she knows this and that's why she hovers in the doorway.

'Have you been drinking?' she says sharply, and I hear what she wants to know: have you taken drugs?

'Really, Mom, I'm fine. It's hot. I've a headache. I walked too far too fast, and got a little dehydrated.'

She nods, not entirely convinced, and leaves.

I open the tap and bugs burst out. A spray of beetles and hopping things and flies spurt out with the first rush. I squeak and Mom is right behind me, holding a box of ibuprofen.

Without taking her eyes from the sink, from me, she takes her phone from her pocket and it rings a long while before it's answered. We're both mute and unmoving as we look at the insects scrambling to get out of the sink. Not a drop of water has come out. Mom moves to the bath and turns on the taps, another spray of bugs is released. The flies have lifted off and are buzzing around the room and Mom's mouth is downturned with revulsion.

'Jarlath, yes, this is Dr Salie. We've a problem with our pipes … No. No it can't wait … It looks like an insect infestation … Yes, I said insects … Tonight. And please not your son, no offence, but this isn't a job for an eighteen-year-old.'

She pauses impatiently.

'I don't care how talented he is. I want a plumber right now.' She bats away a fly.

In the kitchen, I grab a bottle of water and go to my room to wash my teeth. I don't know what's happened, but I'm furious. The rage runs through my body, needing a release. I need to walk or run or punch something. I can't stay in the house, pretending that everything is normal when it's not.

One thing is becoming clearer: I am caught in something bigger than I understand.

Only this morning, I'd been sure that Sibéal was on the side of right. That David and Cillian were persecuting her. But what Sibéal did today has turned everything upside down.

I pull out a hoodie and sneak out the patio doors. From the back garden, I slip through the hollow and into the Creaghs' field.

I only see the cars when I've crossed over to the Rookery. There're lots of them lining the drive and parked on a field. I can hear the voices and music coming from behind the house. I take out my phone and call David, but it goes straight to voicemail.

Skirting the house from a safe distance, I walk along the lake. In the distance, I see a dying bonfire and head that way.

And then I see him, the solitary figure at the bonfire. I know it's him right away. David is so lost in thought that he doesn't hear me approach.

'I'm not much company tonight,' he says, but pats the grass for me to sit.

Maybe this is all part of becoming Horrible, but the rules here are different. Girls die for no reason at all, I see the truth of people in my dreams. Boys dig holes and walls glow. People hurt each other, and it's strangely normal. And ladies trick you with their smiles and homemade soup while they break into your brain and want things from you.

I sink down beside him, watching the fire flicker over his face. He looks so forlorn, so weary. On his jacket, I see the five-looped symbol from my dream and I understand.

Somehow in the last few weeks, I've passed a threshold. Not an obvious door or portal, but something like an invisible dolmen. I've entered into the world of impossible things.

THIRTY
Made you Horrible

David

When Zara appears in front of me, she's angry or upset. Her mood is dark. We're well matched.

'I'm not much company tonight.' I touch the grass, gesturing for her to sit.

She drops down beside me. The world is falling apart, my whole sense of who I am is in turmoil. And here I am, my heart speeding up like some giddy schoolboy because this girl is here.

Last midwinter, I was in bits after Oisín was captured, presumed dead. This midsummer, the other side of the winter solstice, I feel an immeasurable peace because Zara has come to me.

She sits close, our shoulders touching, her knee brushing mine. She looks at my face, reading the worry and fear that I'm too exhausted to hide.

'That bad?' she says.

'Worse.'

The silence is comfortable, but the words want out: 'I am so ashamed.' I have to say it. 'Of what I did that day.'

'Why did you push her?' Zara asks.

'No excuses.' I shake my head. 'I should have walked away.'

'Did Sibéal do it to you?' Zara is looking out to the lake. 'Nose around inside your head?'

I turn sharply to look at her. 'You too?' Is that what it was? And how does an augur have that kind of skill?

'It was a violation.' She looks down. 'Invasive. I would have shoved her too, given the chance.'

'You're not …' A trained soldier with a whole lot more pounds on him. 'Me.' I finish lamely.

She bumps my shoulder. 'You should have told me.'

But Sibéal isn't the problem here. She's just the fly on top of the rubbish heap.

'There's more.' I can't look at her. 'I terrorised Sibéal's friend. I understand why she hates me, because I deserve …'

Zara's hand is on my mouth.

'Stop. I know. I know you're Horrible.' She breathes the last word and I hear the emphasis on it. Horrible, with a capital H.

And the way she's looking at me, I think she really does know.

'But Horrible isn't cruel. If you've done wrong, and

understand how it's wrong and are truly sorry, then you need to fix what you damaged. You know your heart.'

She pulls her hand away.

'What has made you so broken?' She watches me another long moment. 'What has made you Horrible?'

It's not a question looking for an answer. We're quiet, watching the lake. We stay out there for a while, until near dark on the longest day of the year.

'David –' she sounds hesitant '– have you been honest with me?'

'I won't lie to you, Zara.'

'Whose grey scarf was that in your utility room? Was it yours?'

'Do I look like I'd a wear a scarf? In summer?'

She chucks a blade of grass at me.

'It's Oisín's.'

'Then why was Laila wearing it in a photograph?' Her phone buzzes with an incoming call. She ignores it.

'Laila visited him sometimes. They'd talk.'

'Does he know anything about how she died? Did she tell him anything?'

'She stopped coming around at the beginning of March.'

'What … oh, bloody hell.' Her phone starts again. When it stops, I see the flood of texts lighting up the screen.

'I should go,' she sighs.

I don't want her to go. I don't want to get back to the mess Dad made. But I must.

'C'mon,' I sigh. 'I'll walk back with you.'

We stand up and I lead her down to the shoreline, avoiding the house.

'You're friends with Cillian, right?' Her words are stilted. I hadn't realised they'd met.

'Yeah, our families are tight. I've known him all my life.'

'He's a prick.' She says it with venom.

'I know.' I let out a breath. 'He's difficult, and it's been worse lately. Has he given you hassle?'

'He and Sibéal are always at each other. What's that about?'

'They are?' He's said nothing to me.

'He threw a firecracker into their house the other day.'

Not good. Sibéal will be plotting her revenge. And when their little war of attrition intersects with Dad's need for retribution, no one is safe.

Zara's waiting for an answer.

'There's a lot of hostility between Maeve's family and ours.' Damn you, John Canty.

'A feud? One of those village disagreements that run through generations and people knock each other's stone walls down?'

I frown at her; where does this come from?

'Definitely runs through generations,' I concede.

The music travels to us as we follow the shoreline, the raucous cheers and calls. The Rose sounds drunk.

We've crossed into the field below Cassa's when Zara suddenly stops, the tips of her fingers hooked into mine. I turn to her.

'What were you doing that night, out here?' she says. It feels like a test.

'Digging.' I step towards her. I shouldn't.

'Why?' Her hair falls over her cheek and I lift a hand to brush it away. I tell myself that's all. One small touch.

But with her fingertips, she tugs me nearer. 'Why were you digging?'

'Because my aunt instructed me to.' I inch forward.

'Instructed? Why?'

I put my hands on her waist.

'My aunt –' I'd rather not be talking about Cassa right now – 'really loves flowers.'

'But that's not all, is it?' Zara slips her hands up to my shoulders. Tentative, shy hands. Her touch feels good.

'No.' I tug her into me, her body against mine. Her face is turned up and I'm over the moon that she's letting me in.

There has been so much ugliness. But this moment, the moment I press my lips to Zara's, is reprieve. To feel her respond is absolution. Then I forget thinking and I'm just there with her.

Drawing back, she's smiling. So perfect.

Which is why the frown that crosses her face is unexpected. One minute she's looking at me in a way that I'd so hoped she would. And then she's not.

'What's wrong?' I lean back, trying to read her better.

'I don't know,' she says. 'There's something that I need to remember.'

We walk on in silence, Zara deep in thought.

We jump the gate into Cassa's field and my luck runs dry.

Someone's there. In the distance, near the peony patch. By the shape of him, tall, broad and moody, it's Dad. He's just staring, hands in his pockets.

'Can we not right now?' Zara sees him too.

We move stealthily along the hedge towards the copse of trees where Zara hid that night. Then I realise what has Dad so transfixed.

I knew they would grow a little faster than is natural, but the abundance of flowering plants makes me stop. The whole patch is covered with newly budding peonies, despite being planted at the wrong time of year. Tuber to bud, in just over three weeks.

This is magic. Real, strong magic. Not the subtle magic of my connection with my totem. Not the slow magic of our laws.

This is silver magic. It feels, smells different. What if Cassa is right? What if we're on the cusp of the third ré órga?

Just in time for Dad to reap the rewards. He couldn't have planned this better.

I tug on Zara's hand, but she doesn't move.

'The briars,' she says. The hedge is holding on to her.

There are thorns deep in her hoodie and on the cotton of her shorts and scratching her legs. This is not an accidental brushing up of the hedge, these are plants protecting their own. They're trapping her, for Cassa. They mustn't have realised that the Rooks have ascended.

A word attacks me, a fist to my face. I pull a briar from her skin.

Sting.

And it wants to be encased in the blooded thorn. I pause a moment, squeezing the thorn as I put the word inside, then slip it into my back pocket.

Zara slips out of the hoodie and we're both frantically trying to detach her from the twisting briar. Then I hear Dad's voice behind me.

'David.'

I shut my eyes a long moment. When I open them, Zara is looking at me with such kindness.

'Dad.'

'Who's your friend?' Even though he appears calm, it's obvious Dad is raging. The cold, clipped tone and the way he leans over Zara is meant to make her nervous. Afraid. He wants her to go away and never return.

'This is Zara.' Dad knows who she is. 'We were down at the lake.'

Dad keeps his eyes on her as he says to me, 'Make sure Zara gets home.'

'Yes, Dad.' He's not said a word to her. I'm embarrassed at his rudeness, but mostly I'm afraid for her. I don't want Zara on Dad's radar. I don't want him deciding that he doesn't need tenants any more and finding a way to end the lease or making trouble for them.

I take her hand and walk with Zara through the trees. Neither of us speaks, until we reach the hollow.

'Your dad was really mad,' she says. 'Will you be OK?'

'I'm always OK.' I shrug. 'It's really late. You smell of fire and you've lost some of your clothes. Right now, I'm more worried about your dad than mine.'

It's a lame joke but she smiles.

'But will you be OK?' I say. I don't want her in trouble because of me.

She nods and turns to leave, moving through the narrow cluster of trees and hedge. She looks over her shoulder.

'Mind yourself, David.' And then she's gone.

THIRTY-ONE
Nothing to do with curses
and magic

I wish I could describe to Zara how it feels in the woods.
How I feel like my real self there. I am Horrible Laila who
loves the feel of bark on her skin.

LAS

Zara

Mom's furious with me. Last night she was waiting up when I came home. My hoodie missing, and my hair and clothes smelling of grass and fire. She scorched me with one long look.

'Just tell me you weren't with that boy.'

'His name is David,' I told her. But I could see her fear, her grief at losing Laila, as she struggled to find her words.

'I'm too angry to talk right now.' She turned away as I went up the stairs.

One of my favourite Horrible stories is the one where the horrible children lock their parents out of their ditch. The horrible mother and horrible father watch between the tangle of branches. Let us in, they wail with their horrible little mouths. But no, say the horrible children, and they sit down to dirt and leaf soup. Let us in, wail the horrible parents again. But no, say the horrible children, and they lie down on their twig and mulch beds. The horrible mother and horrible father shiver and shake in their bare thread clothes but still the horrible children won't let them in.

In the morning, I'm thinking of the horrible parents peering through the brambles and briars when I hear her coming up behind me.

'Mom,' I say before she sits down on the velvet couch. 'Do you believe in magic?'

She pauses. It's not what she expected.

'No.' She is so certain, and yet …

'Does Ma?' I ask about her mother, who is like a woman from a fairytale. I vaguely remember stories from our child-hood, stories of curses and boys dancing with swords.

She gives a small laugh. 'She does.'

'Do you think Laila died because she was cursed, like in Ma's stories?'

'A doekoem?' Mom says, but she's not surprised. I'd guess she's thought about this herself. 'No. Of course not.'

She sighs and sits beside me. 'Sometimes horrible things just happen. Whether we deserve it or not. Nothing to do with curses and magic.'

Mom is calm as she hands me a cup of hot lemon water from the table beside her.

'Where were you last night?'

'Next door,' I say. 'They had a midsummer bonfire. I got caught in some briars. I'm sorry about the playsuit, I'll fix it.'

'It's not the clothes, Zara,' Mom sighs.

'It's him. David,' I say.

Some years ago, Laila and I were hanging out in the city. A bunch of young men were sitting in the sunshine, drinking beer. They laughed too loud, catcalling to the women who passed, each one trying to be more obnoxious than the other. And with them was a younger boy, maybe fourteen. He laughed at the jokes a beat too late, and when they left, he trailed behind, trying to keep up.

'I don't trust him,' Mom says. 'And I know you didn't go to camogie camp. What's going on with you, Zara?'

When I think of him, that boy from long ago, he breaks away from the older men. He wanders down a river path, the sun on his face.

'You don't have to trust him. David is not your child.' I sip the lemon water but it's too hot. 'Do you trust me?'

She nods, unhappily.

'Then that's all you need. Look, I know David's a little …
wounded.'

272

'That's not the word I'd use,' Mom says darkly. 'You can't change someone, you know.'

'I know, Mom,' I say, 'I know.' But people can change themselves. Not for anyone else, but because they want to be better.

David has his darkness. But there's also a vulnerable side. I saw more than David realised last night. I saw impossible things, the flowers growing and budding at an unnatural pace, the briars grabbing and trapping me.

I saw David, in all his brokenness. I saw David and his fear. I saw his dad, and the firm hold he keeps on David. I saw the boy trying to resist that hold.

'I like him.' A lot. 'I think he needs someone …' Outside of his normal.

'But why should it be you?' Mom sounds so broken. 'I've lost one daughter, I have to protect the only one I have.'

'Mom.' I take her hand and she's surprised. We never talk like this. 'You can't use Laila's death to keep me from living.'

There are so many things Mom wants to ask. I feel it in her restlessness, her dissatisfied sigh. She wants to know if I've kissed him. She wants to know if it was more. She wants to know what I meant when I said he was wounded, if I know what happened before he came into her surgery, whether he's addicted to whatever drugs she prescribed for him.

But she feels the brambles and briars. She knows that she's been locked out.

I take the same route, and it's like I'm trying to undo yesterday's broken journey home. I pass the spot where I saw Dad's car, the tree where I sat. Before I reach Maeve's house, I slip between the trees at the edge of woods and go around the back of the house. Hiding behind an oak with a split trunk, I watch.

I think through my visits there: something similar happened both times, but with very different results. The repetition of regular sounds and movements, different instruments in some weird orchestra, somehow affected my head. The first time, it made me feel unusually peaceful. Safe. The second, combined with Sibéal's fixed staring at me, was invasive and violent.

Whatever it was, it's not normal.

And then I see Sibéal. She's out in the backyard eating an apple. I crouch lower. I definitely don't want her to find me here.

'Come on, Sibéal, Ash will miss her train,' Maeve yells into the back garden.

'Coming,' Sibéal says, throwing her core to the trees. She goes around the side of the house. After a minute, I hear the faint sound of a car door, the engine.

They're gone.

A week ago, I wouldn't have dreamed of doing this. Of climbing over the back hedge and dropping into the cement backyard. The very idea of walking up to someone else's house, trying the back door and stepping inside would have been anathema. But here I am in Maeve's kitchen.

Things are different now.

Sibéal's cards are still at the kitchen table, a reminder of the previous afternoon. I don't know exactly what I'm looking for as I move through the house, opening drawers and cabinets. Between the girls' bedrooms, there's a small box room. The desk there takes up the entire width of the room. In the drawers, I pull out a folder titled 'Whitethorn Grove – Finance' and another 'Whitethorn Grove – Members'. There are several other documents related to Whitethorn Grove.

I remember Laila's wish and fear, written on the papers I found. She wanted 'them' to bring her into the grove. She meant Maeve and her family.

In Sibéal's room, the walls are cluttered with artwork. Beside her bed is her sketch pad. Just as I open it, I hear the voice from down the passage.

I scramble under the bed. There's a man in the house, and from the one-sided conversation, he's on the phone. He's walking down the passage to Maeve's room.

'No. Not at all,' he says. 'Tell Sibéal she's caused enough damage … Sibéal needs to hold herself back, it was a daft and dangerous thing to do … Yes, I know it was unplanned and she just showed up, but really, Maeve, you should have known better. Do you really think that boy is just going to tell her? It was reckless and won't achieve anything.'

He listens impatiently, then bites out, 'Stick to the plan, target the grandmother … Yes, I know, but she can't lock herself in her house forever. She'll have to come out some-time and we'll be ready.'

He ends the call and walks back down the passage. A few seconds later I hear the back door shut.

What grandmother? Could he mean Callie?

I crawl out from under the bed, still holding on to the sketchbook. The pages are divided into squares, and in each square is a drawing. It's perhaps a comic, or a storyboard.

I flick through, and towards the end of the book, I find a picture of a girl sprawled awkwardly on the grass, eyes to the sky.

It's Laila. That's Laila's faux fur. Laila's roughly chopped hair. I go back a page to the beginning of this two-page story. It begins with Laila walking by herself. She approaches something that looks like Stonehenge and goes inside. A cloaked figure stands over a sacrificial altar, holding a knife. He looks like he's trying to grab something from her.

Then there's a picture very like the Wishmaker disc I found hidden in the hairball. It fills the entire square with a twisting knot design. But on Sibéal's drawing, words are written on two of the four quadrants. Entrap, Sever. The remaining quadrants have question marks. Two pop-out squares with smaller drawings illustrate entrapment and severing: a hunched figure locked in a cage. Two lovers at the edge of frame, their hands reaching for each other but unable to cross a jagged tear.

In the next square, Laila's mouth is open in a silent scream. Her terror is obvious.

The back door opens again. Someone whistles a tune, banging in the kitchen. The fridge opens. The sound of the kettle heating travels down the passage.

Quietly, I put the sketchbook back in place. Footsteps sound down the passage. I hear a door, perhaps the bathroom, shut. I push the window open and lift up to the sill then drop down outside.

I run. I get the hell out of there.

I helter-skelter towards Meadowsweet House to check on Callie. I might be completely paranoid – sure, there are a good few old ladies in the village. But if there is any chance that man was referring to Callie when he said to target the grandmother, I have to do something.

There's no one at Meadowsweet House, and I haven't

seen Callie these last few days, so I leave a message. I don't want alarm the woman but I want her to be careful.

> *Callie,*
> *I'm a little worried. Please can you come to me? It's probably*
> *nothing, but please find me. My number and address are*
> *below. I'm looking forward to our next visit.*
>
> *Zara*

I ask at the Spar and the restaurant in the village, but no one seems to know her. I wish I'd thought to take her last name.

There's nothing more I can do, so I go home. I'm thinking about Sibéal's story. It's obviously fictional, Laila had no knife wounds, and there's no Stonehenge around here. But I know there's truth in what she drew.

I just have to figure out what it is.

THIRTY-TWO
Tell me their names

David

In the days after midsummer, the Rookery is busy. Garraíodóirí, both full-time soldiers from Liscarron, the military base disguised as a private research institute, and the older wardens are in and out of the house.

Cassa is kept in a locked room, and Dad has already found a way to delay her trial. I want to check on her, but I'm not allowed.

Her personal guard is disbanded, and Dad seems to take special delight in assigning the most unpleasant jobs to Tarc. He gets the 3 a.m. call-outs from grumpy farmers miles away to check on possible nemeta attacks. Dad wants Tarc worn out, so that when Liscarron calls the next War Scythe round, he'll be at a disadvantage.

'There you are.' Dad finds me in the hallway. 'I need your help.'

'Sure, Dad.'

I follow him but stop dead in my tracks as we enter the

old ballroom. It has been completely repurposed. Maps have replaced the paintings on the wall. There are charts detailing different augur groves with approximate geographical location. The arch druids are named, and the groves with the highest number of fighting-age men and women identified.

Dad is beginning a war.

He unlocks a cabinet and is reaching for something there. But I can't stop looking at Dad's war plan.

'David.'

I turn and Dad's right there, holding my metal box.

Dad has my words.

'There they are.' I am so relieved. 'Why didn't you tell me you had them? I've been frantic.'

'You're going to tell me their names.'

'Their names?'

'I need your words, David. Oisín needs them.'

'No.' I'm confused and can't help the small laugh that escapes. 'I'm not giving you my words.'

'I thought you wanted to help Oisín.'

'I do. I'll do anything to help him.'

'Then tell me their names.'

'But you're in charge now. Can't you just let it go? Oisín is obviously not colluding with augurs. You know that.'

'I can't just break the rules for my son. He's been charged. He has to defend himself or produce the Eye. You've made no progress on retrieving it. If you want to help him, then this is what you have to do.'

He's serious.

Dad doesn't stay anything, just watches me, his heavy brows at odds with his surprisingly gentle eyes.

'I'll make the law,' I tell him.

'Don't be daft, David.' He says it like this is what he expects, me being daft. I've done everything he's asked of me. I'm the second strongest soldier in my class. I've no love for augurs. But it's never good enough. I may not be guided by the rook, but I sure am controlled by it.

'I'm stronger,' he continues. 'I'll make a better law. There's a lot riding on this. Now's not the time for tantrums.'

'I'm stronger than you think.' But we're slipping into the usual pattern. Old behaviours. Even though Dad doesn't tower over me physically any more, it still feels like he does.

'Do you want to help your brother or not?' Dad's impatient. 'Do you realise he could be executed and there's nothing I can do to stop it?'

Defeated, I go to the table. When he takes my words from the box, I can't look.

'Are there any more?'

'No,' I lie.

I touch each word as I name them, just loud enough for Dad to hear. Then I stand at the window, watching the fields. I'm shaking with suppressed anger. With disappointment in myself.

But I am no victim. If I am trapped, it's me who's dug out the hole, who helped set the snare.

The room is quiet as Dad arranges them. Puts my words into his law. I watch the rooks flying above the trees, setting off and coming home.

'I will triumph over Cassa.' He completes the sentencing. I feel the words become husks and it's too much.

'But you said you would use them for Oisín.'

'I said my using them would help Oisín. This way, I am better placed to help him.'

He lied. Fury runs through me as Dad throws the husks into the fireplace and stacks the wood. He won't risk anyone undoing this law.

Dad watches the fire take hold. For him, nothing is changed, nothing different. Just another ordinary day for Jarlath Creagh. But it feels like an ending. This is a breach too far.

I stand in the doorway, waiting for my father to see my stricken face, my blotched skin and rigid stance. I want Dad to see me.

But, intent on the burning husks, Dad doesn't look my way.

THIRTY-THREE
So much I'm not telling you

With the crow key, the Rookery is mine to explore.
LAS

Zara

It's early evening, and I sneak through the hollow into the field behind to meet David. I haven't seen him since midsummer night. A weird mix of excitement and apprehension churns in my gut. I don't know what to expect.

Mom's been making me cover for Aisling, who's off work for the week. Out of trouble, she thinks. Under her watchful eye.

I still haven't heard from Callie. I've been back to Meadowsweet, and my note is no longer there. I've looked around, hoping to see her in one of the bright summer gardens in the village, or perhaps at the church. But I can't find her anywhere. Rationally, I know she's probably fine, maybe visiting grandchildren or down at the coast for the week. Irrationally, I worry that the tiny old lady, one I've become quite attached to, will sit down at Maeve's table expecting cake and get her head wrecked instead. That she'll end up on the village green.

He's there at the shoreline, looking out over the water. When David sees me, his face breaks into a huge smile.

We sit on the grass and he tells me stupid light bulb jokes, boarding school stories, but also talks about his dad. He tells me things have become even more difficult between them. When he mentions Jarlath Creagh, I see the simmering rage in his eyes, his jaw. But when he speaks of Oisín, I know he's worried and afraid.

David tells me he's begun to feel constrained in his job, working the security for his aunt's arts and heritage foundation. There's some big promotion that his dad is pushing him towards, that he wanted for a long time, but now finds himself without enthusiasm.

I tell him about the Horribles. About our safe, dirty ditch and the Inky Black.

We sit close, his hand on my leg, or mine in his hair as he lies on the grass with his head on my lap.

In our talking, there are gaps. Things we're not saying. That we know the other is holding back. Like how neither of our parents would approve of this, the secrets I know he's keeping. But being here this evening is my reprieve. Home is taut, stretched to that point where something has to snap.

We're there for hours. The day is still bright, with a light smell of rain in the air. But as the time ticks on, the things we don't say seem to push closer to the surface.

We're lying on the grass, eyes to the moody sky. I feel a light tickle on my arm and look down to see a green-bodied beetle.

'That's a tiger beetle.' David lifts it from my arm and looks at it. 'I've not seen one around here before.'

And I have never seen more insects than in the field down here by the lake. It's like Horrible Zara's insect farm, but for real. They seem to surround us, the bugs and butterflies and other little creatures burrowing in and out of the soil.

David looks at the beetle before setting it down. The bulbous eye and feelers remind me of that day in the mirror.

'Have you ever –' I'm feeling adventurous – 'seen something that isn't there?'

'What do you mean?' The first drops of rain fall, one lands on my cheek.

'On Saturday, when I came from Sibéal's house.' I flip on to my side, leaning on my elbow. 'I looked into the mirror and saw myself as a bug. My eyes were bulging, I had antennae. And I could see differently, like I had insect eyes. It went away, but it was disturbing.'

David is quiet. He's looking up, and I can see from his face that he's working through his thoughts.

'Zara,' he says eventually, 'there's so much I'm not telling you.'

'Do you want to?' I touch a raindrop that's landed on his forehead.

'I will if you ask me.' Strange answer.

'Then tell me just one thing.' But there's a shadow to my words. There's something else that's attached itself to them. 'Tell me a secret. Something you should never tell anyone else.' And it feels like the shadow is shaping my words, twisting them like vine growing over stone.

I lean over him, my lips inches away from his. 'Tell me something you treasure. An ancient truth.' I kiss him, just once, a quick brush of the lips. A promise of more. 'Tell me the offerings.'

David is looking at me like I've broken his heart. He doesn't answer for a few moments. Then he averts his eyes.

'I saw a very old woman, standing on the shoreline. And then she disappeared.'

'A ghost?'

'More than a ghost.' He hesitates. 'A vision. It was horrible.'

'I like Horrible.'

'She told me the offerings. But I'm not supposed to tell anyone.'

I drop down from my elbow to my back, feeling both

relieved and cross. The need to know this message is over-powering. The rain is beginning to come more steadily.

'That's fine.' But I can't hide the bite in my words.

Now he's on his elbow, looking down at me. 'Why are you asking me, Zara? Why does it matter?'

'All these secrets, David.' I stand up. 'I need to head back.' I don't want to push him to reveal the details he's nervous to share. But there's this strange twisting thing inside that's making me resentful that he's not talking.

'Don't go.'

'It's raining.'

'Then let it rain.'

'Mom will be looking for me. It's OK. About your secrets.' I mean it, but I don't.

And then he's standing in front of me, his hands on my shoulders. It's properly raining now, for the first time after two dry, hot weeks. In the distance, there's a growl of thunder. It's still warm despite the rain, and I can feel the heat of his body through his thin T-shirt.

'I will tell you.' He touches a light hand to my cheek. 'If you tell anyone else, it could destroy everything I love.'

Don't tell me, I want to say.

But I reach up and kiss him. I draw his face down to mine, holding my hand on the back of his head. It tastes like rain and grass and deceit.

'Tell me.' I don't sound like myself.

'Entrap. Sever. Truth.' The words are whispered. I think I feel him shudder. Horrible Zara stirs. There's something leaden and awful inside.

'Those are all I know.'

'I shouldn't have made you tell me that.' I step back, appalled at myself. 'I'm sorry.'

I'm staring at him, struggling to understand what I just did.

'I should go,' I say.

'That's probably best right now.' His eyes are glittering, and I don't know if he's sad or angry.

'Can we talk tomorrow?' I hold up a hand. 'I need to think.'

'Zara,' he calls after me. 'Wait.'

But I don't stop. I head back through the field in the rain and as I run, I'm beginning to remember. Sibéal telling me that I had to do something for her. Something about David. But it's all broken in pieces.

When I get to the house, I'm so angry with myself. For being used. For doing something I didn't want to. For manipulating David to tell me his secret. But mostly, I'm furious with Sibéal. Because, somehow, she made me do this. Part of me wants to run over there and have it out with her, but that would be foolish.

To get my mind off my anger, I take the Wishmaker from its hiding place. I mentally unlock it, retrieving the key from the imaginary cabin and taking it out of the imaginary boxes.

In Sibéal's storyboard, each quadrant had a name. The first was Entrap, the second Sever. Canty warned me that some people want this disc very badly. He also warned me not to handle it.

For the first time since finding it, I can feel a draw, a latent thrum. As if by learning its secret words, the disc is allowing me to feel its true power.

And David told me a new word: Truth.

I'm beginning to remember: Sibéal at the kitchen table. Aisling arguing with her that it wouldn't work. Embedding an instruction in my head: kiss David and get the last two offerings.

I'd been furious with Sibéal before but now I am incandescent with rage. She used me.

I squeeze my fingers around the Wishmaker. *Red the blade*, I whisper to it, testing the words. They feel right, so I whisper them again. *Red the blade. Red the blade.*

I'm thinking of Sibéal's drawings of the figure in the cage, the lovers' hands torn apart. And it's crystal clear, as if someone has explained it to me: this disc wants those actions. Offerings. And if I make the offerings, I could discover its hidden power.

I only know three of the four. That's not enough.

It's a start. I could try.

This hunger, having grown steadily, is intense. I am almost compelled to make the offerings. Like the thing in my hands wants me to act.

I want to handle it. I want to own it, wield it, master it. I want to know all its secrets. This is no love trinket. I don't know if Canty lied to protect me or for other reasons. But I know for certain that this thing in my hand is something of rare power. And I want in.

Red the blade, I whisper again. And again, like I'm repeating a mantra.

The disc grows warm in my hand. I drop it in surprise.

A car pulls up in the drive. Must be Dad. It's still bright out, but heading towards ten, it's later than I thought.

The doorbell rings. Not Dad then. Perhaps it's David. I feel a sudden giddy burst of glee. I hope so. I want to apologise.

I hastily pack everything away, locking the Wishmaker in my mind.

Mom calls to me. Hurrying downstairs, I'm fully expecting David.

And stop when I see Sibéal and Maeve outside.

Mom's stepped out, laughing at something Maeve's said.

I don't like them here at our house. I don't like them near Mom, who is too trusting.

No one is what they seem. That nice Maeve Lawless with her flowery dresses and pretty daughters can't be trusted. The big scowly man next door with his huge falling-down estate and family war cry definitely can't be trusted. Who knows, maybe the ladies who sit out on their lawns are actually secret assassins. Who bloody knows. Canty was right, I have to be careful, not trust anyone. Because I suspect Laila did, and she's dead.

The blue Micra passes our house. The window is open, and Cillian glowers at me from the driver's seat.

'Thanks for the offer,' Mom says. 'You've no idea how much I appreciate it.'

'What offer?' I say to Mom as I join them. Sibéal beams at me, saying 'Hey, Zara' like she didn't mess with my head and do some weird bullshit hypnosis.

'Well, I was on the phone to Aisling just now and she mentioned that your mom was a little worried. So I said to Sibéal here, we can help out.'

'Help out with what?'

'You know I'm leaving for Cape Town tomorrow,' Mom says. 'But there's an overlap of one night when Dad's flying back from his conference. Maeve's offered to keep an eye on you.'

'We're fine, Mom.' I'm annoyed. 'Adam and I will be fine.'

'I know,' she says. 'But after Laila, I'd rather someone was watching out. She's just going to check in. See that you haven't burned down the house.'

'I won't burn down the house.'

'Zara,' she warns.

'Fine.' I shrug like I don't care.

Mom continues to chat with Maeve and I walk down our drive. Sibéal follows. I knew she would.

I'm right where the brick paving meets the road when I finally turn to her.

'Look, I know what you tried to do. That you got inside my head somehow.'

'Never tried to hide it.'

'How? Was it some kind of hypnosis?'

She puts a hand on my shoulder. Leans in. Breathes into my ear: 'Maybe.'

She smiles. Then turns away, getting inside the car.

When she's sitting in the passenger seat, I lean in through the open window. 'You told me to get the last two offerings from David.'

I've surprised her.

'You remember that?'

'I didn't at first.'

'And did you? Have you learned anything?'

'I'm not your puppet, Sibéal.' The words tumble out in my fury. 'I won't tell you a single word of it.'

'I don't need permission, c'mon, you know that.'

'But you need to look at me. You can't get into my head if you're not looking me in the eye.' I lean into her. 'You can't make me open my eyes.'

I've touched a nerve, it's clear on her face.

I leave the car, going back towards the house.

'You've nothing to worry about,' Maeve is saying to Mom, and pulls me into a hug. 'I'll watch Zara.'

Why does she make it sound like a warning?

As Maeve reverses from the drive, Sibéal leans out the window, her hair whipping in the wind. She beams at me like we're best friends, and wriggles her fingers.

'See you Sunday, Zara.' She laughs at me as they drive off.

It's only once the car is gone that I see him.

Across the road, David watches. He's standing near the entrance to the Rookery, partially obscured by the trees. His face gives nothing away. But there is a strain to his body that makes me certain he doesn't like what he's seen.

I raise a tentative hand. But still he stares, not returning the greeting.

The gate swings open on a slow arc. We lock gazes with each other. Sure, he doesn't like Sibéal, but he looks angry with me. And then I'm cross too, because how am I supposed to know what's going on when there is so much hidden from me?

An old boxy Range Rover barrels through the gate. David steps into the road, gets in and they drive away.

THIRTY-FOUR
Use them wisely

David

Zara's gone and I'm not sure what just happened.

One minute we were together here at the lake, and everything was just right. Next thing, she's asking me for the offerings, and locked in by my agreement with Canty, I had to tell her.

She has to be working with someone, I think as I return to the house. There's no way she'd know to ask for that otherwise. It has to be Canty. This has all been a ruse to get close to me, so she could find out the offerings. He tricked me into telling her. How could I have been so stupid to agree to his deal?

I'm furious. Sore. Oisín is in trouble. Cassa locked up. Dad has pushed me too far. And now Zara.

Outside the house, I take out Canty's mirror from my pocket. Whenever I've checked it, I've seen nothing. But now, for the first time, the silver begins to cloud over. I'm seeing the vague outline of someone beginning to take shape. It's slow to form, but the person looks female. The background is a vivid green.

But why would Canty use Zara when I'd agreed to be honest with him? I don't get it.

A car skids to a halt on the chip and tar.

It's barely stopped when Cill's out of it. I look at the mirror again, the green has formed into leaves. The girl is still fuzzy, but I can see that she's wearing white and looking down.

'You need to get to the tenants' house right now. Guess who I just saw pulling up there? Maeve and Sibéal.'

Cill doesn't need to say any more. I'm sprinting down the drive, mirror in hand, so fast I'm nearly flying. Even if Zara and Canty have tricked me, I won't let Sibéal hurt her again.

Running down the drive, the mirror falls, hitting the stones hard. I stop to pick it up. A long crack runs the through the mirror but the image is clear: in the woods, wearing a white T-shirt, is Zara.

I falter.

Zara has the Eye? But she's not wearing that T-shirt. She's not in the woods. I don't understand what this means.

Just inside the iron gates, I follow the wall to the place where it's crumbled. I leap over, and run between the trees towards Zara's house.

And come to an abrupt halt.

Maeve and Dr Salie are chatting like old friends. At the bottom of the drive is Zara. And Sibéal. Zara is animated as she talks, it doesn't look like Sibéal is doing anything unpleasant to her at all. Her hand is on Zara's shoulder as she leans in, like she's kissing her cheek. Sibéal pulls back, smiling.

She turns to get into the car and it's then that I see that Sibéal has been kissed by our rooks. Her face is marked with tiny, fading scars. She would have worn protective gear when she strung the rooks outside our house, but in their rage the birds would have pecked through until they broke skin.

She killed our birds and strung them up to taunt us.

My phone vibrates and I step back briefly as Dad barks at me: the next War Scythe round is on. We need to leave, now.

As I hang up, Maeve pulls Zara into her arms and hugs her tightly before getting into the car. Sibéal leans out of the window, smiling and waving to Zara as they drive away.

'See you Sunday, Zara.'

I've been tortured and caged. My father has stolen my words, knowing how important they are to me. But none of that makes me feel as wretched as seeing Zara in the arms of my enemy.

I was wrong. Zara didn't get the offering for Canty. She got it for Maeve. It's all been a lie.

I glance at the broken mirror in my hand. Zara in her white T-shirt is frozen in the reflective surface.

When Zara realises I'm there, she smiles, steps towards me, but I can't move. I've nothing to say. Her smile falters. The Rover is idling on the other side of the gate as Dad waits for it to open.

I take a last look at her. Then the Rover pulls up beside me and I can't get into it fast enough.

Later, we're at the large farm shed, where I've just won the penultimate War Scythe round. Dad claps a hand on my shoulder. He's delighted that I left Ian a bloodied heap on the floor inside. He's thrilled we're a step closer to me becoming War Scythe.

I'm a mess. There is a darkness inside me that scrapes and pulls. My heart is a grover's mace, spiked with nails and studs. It *hurts*, and I need to lash out. All my rage, all my anger towards Dad, at being lied to by Zara, fuelled my fight with Ian.

I feel no victory. I wish I hadn't fought.

And it's suddenly crystal clear. I don't want this any more. I don't want to be War Scythe. I'll finish my Birchwood placement at HH, and when that's done, I'll do my duty to defend and protect when my gairdín needs it. But as a warden. I don't want to go to war, I don't want to lead an army. I don't want to become First Commander one day. I'm no longer Dad's good little soldier.

But now isn't the time to wallow.

'Well done.' A warden claps me on the back and I'm such a fraud, standing there receiving congratulations. In the corner, Tarc watches. He's also through and we'll face each other in the last round.

'For someone who's just won, you don't look very happy.' Tarc hands me a bottle of beer.

'I could say the same about you.'

'How's Cassa?'

I shake my head. Not allowed anywhere near her room.

'You know, you're different these days.' Tarc examines me. 'What's happening?'

I shrug. I don't know where to begin.

'How did it feel?' I sound raspy. 'When you found out Wren lied to you?' I take a glug of beer.

I'd been so disdainful of Tarc being blind to Wren's lies, and here I am. Suckered by the augurs.

'I was furious. Hurt. Went over every encounter to see what I'd missed. How she'd played me.'

Zara down at the lake asking about secrets. The night at the bonfire, kissing her. My hand on her skirt. Zara reading our family war cry.

Then it occurs to me: that day at the Rookery I'd been so focused on her. Stupid hormones. I'd been pleased and surprised when the devil's coach-horse seemed to favour her. And as I go over the encounter at the house, I'm certain: I did not whistle to rooks. I didn't even ask her in.

And yet she'd entered without making them angry.

Zara bypassed the rook protection. Which means that she could have gone into the Rookery at any time. She could have been spying on us, gathering information for months.

And the mirror says she has the Eye.

I take another deep drink. I need to figure out how to get it back.

'Before she left, Wren asked me to give these to you.' Tarc interrupts my thoughts. He holds out his hand. 'Says she has no instinct for words and she wants you to have them.'

In the palm of his hand are a coin and an acorn.

'Promise. Lucky. Use them wisely.'

THIRTY-FIVE
Patrick's cousin

I saw Jarlath Creagh doing magic. He was in his study and
I watched him through the French doors.

LAS

Zara

I'm messing with my phone while Adam and his friend
Patrick play music in the sitting room. Mom left earlier this
afternoon, and Dad will be back from his conference in the
morning. I've hardly heard from David, just one abrupt
message asking if we could talk tomorrow. I don't know
what's going on with him.

Adam ends the tune, saying, 'I'm going to Patrick's in an
hour. You OK with that?'

'Sure,' I say. 'Stay the night.' Patrick lives two villages over.

'Maybe.' He looks uncertain. 'I don't like leaving you
alone.'

'It's one night. Nothing happened last night or the
one before or before. I'll watch a movie, sleep. And if a

burglar decides that this is the night to break into our house, I'll lock my door and ring Garda Creagh. Between him and his scary brother Jarlath, I'm sure I won't be kidnapped.'

'You sure? I don't like asking Patrick's cousin to drive me home.'

'Adam, ask me one more time and I'll wallop you.'

Close to six, Maeve pulls up in the drive.

'Hello, Maeve, all good here. Thanks for stopping.' I hold the door close so she can't come in. She's carrying a dish and her smile slips.

'Brought soup. Chicken and vegetable.' She's looking at me with a maternal tenderness, like she wants to squash me with a hug. I don't want any of it.

'You sure you don't want to stay over at ours tonight, honey?'

'We're grand here, thanks, Maeve.'

'All by yourself?' She moves closer to the door, trying to glance down the passage. 'No boyfriends?'

'No boyfriends. No wild parties. I'm going to have a long soak and then watch something.'

'I'll check in at nine.' Maeve thrusts the soup into my hands.

After my bath, I come downstairs to find the boys eating. The soup smells good, neither of them appear poisoned, but no way am I eating that. Instead, feeling rebellious, I pour a half-glass of Dad's wine.

'We're heading,' Adam slurps.

A car beeps in the drive.

'There's our ride,' Patrick says to Adam.

I walk the boys to the door, reassuring Adam again that I don't mind him staying the night with Patrick.

'Seriously, Adam.' I roll my eyes at him as he grabs his guitar. 'It's not like you're a whole lot stronger than me.'

'Ah,' Patrick says. He's a beautiful, slightly nervous boy. 'I forgot my phone in the kitchen. Back in a sec.'

Outside, the driver of the car gets out. He steps towards me.

'Zara, how you doing?' For a second I can't place him. And then I remember, he's Aisling's boyfriend.

'Simon, right?' I say.

'Yeah.' He smiles. 'Patrick's my cousin. I'm bringing them down to our farm in Gortashee. You want me to drive him back later?'

'Oh.' This bothers me. I hadn't realised that Patrick was connected to Simon. But if I say anything, then Adam won't go and I know he wants to. 'No, that's fine.'

'Got it.' Patrick waves his phone at me.

'You take care now,' Simon says as they slam the car doors shut.

Adam leaves, and I begin to feel unsettled about my parents being away.

It's not the first time they've left us overnight, but it's the first time without Laila. The first time in such an isolated place. The first time after I've just discovered a weird ... what, cult? ... in the village. I watch rooks fly over the gates of the rookery.

I lock the doors. Downing the wine, acidic and not pleasant, I go to the small den at the back of the house and put on the TV.

I cast a glance at my phone, wishing someone would get in touch. Even Ciara. Even David. Especially David.

I'm struggling to follow what's happening on screen. My eyes are heavy and I'm suddenly so tired.

When I wake on the couch in the den, it's almost dark outside. The screensaver on the TV repeats the same photographs of us. Me and Laila. Laila on the village green. Me and Laila and Adam outside our old house. The walls are covered in wavy lines, the shadows cast by the cut-out lampshade. It gives the sensation of being underwater, or inside a basket woven from shadow.

I didn't turn on the lamp.

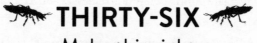

THIRTY-SIX
Make this right

David

I know only fist and muscle. I am all body, all instinct. When Tarc smashes into me again, my skin is slick with his sweat. I hold on to him, to bring him down, to keep me up. He breaks free and we're facing each other, chests heaving, looking for a way in.

Between flaming torches on the lake field, garraíodóirí are gathered to watch. Tonight feels different. The world seems perilous. Unsafe. The watching soldiers take little pleasure in the fight. They're anxious, sensing that unnamed threat gathering speed.

'Water break,' Dad calls, and blows a whistle above the noise of the crowd.

'Push harder, David.' Dad's right there in my face. I haven't had a minute free from him.

I'm fighting to win something I no longer want. I don't want the burden of it. I understand now why Tarc was reluctant to take it on, that he's only doing it now because of the special bond between the War Scythe and the Bláithín.

While I've barely had time to recover from the last fight, Dad's been in his war room. I've watched him plot and plan exactly how he will destroy augurs, kill men, women and children.

And I know it now: we are the monsters they think us.

I'm haunted by the vision of Badb at midsummer. If I win, it will consolidate Dad's authority. That's why he's been pushing me so hard.

'Focus, David.' Dad's face is almost contorted with the strength of his emotion. 'We're almost there. Aim for the back of the thigh, that's where Gallagher is weak. You get it hard enough and he'll go down. And then we win.'

Mamó watches beside Oisín. She's standing there, cool and calm. Unperturbed, like there's no question I'd do anything but what's expected of me. No matter how dirty I have to fight.

And inside me, something screams.

Suddenly it's clear.

I can't do this.

A heaviness cleaves to me, like the sweat and blood on my skin. I can't win. I can't spend the rest of my life doing this. I don't want to fight any more.

'I'm going to make this right,' I tell Dad.

Tarc is better suited to being the protector of the Bláithín. He's a better soldier, a better person, and is connected to Wren in a way that defies reason.

But Dad only hears what he wants.

'Good man.' He clamps a hand on my shoulder. Dad's not entirely bad. There is nothing more important to him than seeing judges thrive; he wants our people to flourish. The problem is his absolute certainty that only he can bring this, and that he is prepared to destroy everything to achieve his vision.

Even after everything he's done, it breaks my heart that he will never be like this with me again. I will never again make him proud or live up to his expectations. After tonight, I will be worse than Oisín. I will be the bigger disappointment. But I will be a little more free.

When the whistle goes again, I stand up. I'm ready.

Ready to lose.

I get in a good few hits first. I don't want it to be obvious, and nor do I want Tarc to get off too easily. If I'm to convince, he must take a beating.

And then, deliberately, I start to flag. I don't avoid a hit I know I can. I soften a blow that I know should be harder. I do it a few more times.

Tarc looks at me quizzically, he knows I'm not doing my best. He goads me into punching harder, but still I hold back. He's tired too and he knows that this has to come to an end soon. I'm not sure if I imagine the nod, the concession that he'll allow me to withdraw. And then I get the punch to my sternum that knocks me to my knees.

'Get up!' Dad yells from the side. 'Get up, you weak bastard.'

I get up.

'Hit him.' Dad is hoarse. 'You know what you need to do.'

I'm so fatigued, I can barely think straight. But I figure, if I aim for the leg and get it wrong, then maybe that will appease Dad. So I pull back and kick, meaning to strike Tarc's uninjured leg front on.

But we're both worn down and I don't anticipate the way he moves. Tarc turns unexpectedly. My boot lands right on his gunshot wound, an arrow to bullseye. Right where Elliot gouged his flesh with a knife not long ago. Tarc howls as he falls. The grass beneath his leg is red with blood. I've reopened the wound.

And his blood stains the ground.

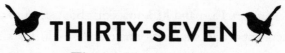

THIRTY-SEVEN
The woven room

Maeve has given me a date for the most exciting night of my life.

LAS

Zara

I sense them before I hear or see them. Maeve is here, she's like candyfloss, sweet and sticky and too much. She must have come by for the nine o'clock check-in. Except it's beginning to darken outside, so it must be much later than nine.

Overkill, I want to say, but I'm losing the battle against sleep. She brushes up alongside the couch and I feel her touch my shoulder.

'Close your eyes.'

Why am I this tired?

And that's when I hear the others behind me. Not just Maeve. I feel a blast of terror. I try to move my hands, but they seem glued together.

I remember Laila and Mom talking about sleep paralysis. It often happened to Laila, where she would be on her bed trying to move but completely unable to. She'd panic, terrified that something was coming for her, but her body would be totally rigid. She'd sense things, people in the room with her, watching her. That has to be what's happening now.

I am rigid from my feet to my neck. My mouth feels tight, like it's been sewn together.

'It's easier if you relax,' Maeve says. A strange noise goes *whir whir whir* like a fan. A clock ticks loudly.

We don't have any ticking clocks in the house.

And then I know. I am not asleep. This is no dream. My mouth isn't sewn together, but covered by a strip of thick tape.

My eyes flutter open again and it doesn't look like the den where we watch TV. I don't see the shelves stacked with books and games. Just the wavy shadows on the wall that seem to slowly circle the room.

'We don't have much time,' Maeve says. 'The boy might decide to come home when he wakes. Simon says he wasn't keen to stay over.'

There's silence for a few moments. I'm fighting my body, forcing my hands to move, my legs to slip down the side of the couch. But I don't budge an inch.

'You sure about this?' The man with the bluest eyes leans

310

over me, looking down at my face. I recognise his voice, this is the man who came into Maeve's house while I hid under the bed. 'A woven room is rather extreme. Seems like we're using a sledgehammer to crack open a nut.'

'You know yourself, we're out of options. The gentle wickering didn't work. Nor did the delve combined with a mildly hostile wickering. She's resisted us all the way. Sibéal embedded an instruction and she even refused that.'

'Sibéal needs to be trained.' The man reminds me of a dentist about to drill into my tooth. 'Before she breaks someone.'

Is this how Laila died? Glued to herself and unable to scream? It's like being buried alive, and I hope her last moments weren't filled with this awful terror.

'Sibéal's talent is fairly new, right?' a girl chips in. 'What is it?' It's like they're having a chat on a Sunday afternoon. While I lie there, immobile.

'Sibéal had no talent right up to her sixteenth birthday,' Maeve replies. 'So I made a plan.'

The dark lines on the wall have grown stronger, and I feel closed inside them. Like I'm in a cage made of shadow.

'How do you plan a talent?' The girl again.

Maeve doesn't answer for a moment.

'Sibéal is a Delver.'

'A Delver?' the girl says. 'I haven't heard of that. And I did a lot of research before I got mine.'

'No one has it any more. Not for two hundred years. Delvers read the patterns inside the mind. At their full strength, they can manipulate minds. Plant thoughts inside a head. Get people to do their bidding. But Sibéal has a ways to go. She's awful clumsy with it.'

I feel a light touch on Laila's bracelet.

'Pretty.' The girl again. 'How did Sibéal get such a powerful, obsolete talent?'

'It didn't come cheap.' Maeve reaches for the bracelet. 'I'll have that.'

I can't move a finger to stop her. Her hand hovers over the crow charm. She pulls it from the bracelet, but she's only just closed it in her fist when she gives a little cry like it's burned her. The charm falls to the ground.

'Now you just lie back and relax.' The man turns his attention back to me like there's nothing weird about this.

I shake my head and try to say no, but it comes out muffled and afraid.

'And we'll take you to the woven room.'

A strobe light is turned on. The people behind the couch, people I can't see, begin to chant words I don't recognise.

'Where is the Eye of Badb?' Maeve's voice comes to me

from a distance. Everything else has subsided, it's just me in the room of woven shadows.

'Smith, her mouth,' Maeve instructs the man, and the tape's yanked off in one searing tear. I let out a muffled yell as fine hairs are ripped out.

'Now, Zara, tell us where Laila hid the Eye.'

'I don't know what that is.' I touch my hand to my stinging skin. 'I've never heard of it.'

'Did you find anything unusual in Laila's belongings?'

I'm not going to play this game. I won't say anything.

'Zara, you're going to have to talk to me, honey.'

The music is creeping up louder, the light strobes faster. It feels like the light is pressing small needles into my skin.

'Just the Wishmaker.' The words must come out. 'But I threw it in the lake.'

'Tell us about the offerings. Did you get any from David?'

'I'm not telling you.'

'We'll take that as a yes. Good girl. You did well. He must really like you.'

'I won't tell you a word of it.'

The man lifts my hand and pulls off Canty's ring with the black stone. 'She's been wearing a protective chant. That would have helped her resist Sibéal.'

'I won't help you.'

'That's what the woven room is for,' Maeve says.

'You can't make me.'

But the words are trying to push to the surface: Entrap, Sever, Truth.

I squash it down, thinking of Mom in Cape Town. I imagine her viewing a new home for us. I picture her walking through it, choosing bedrooms for me and Adam. But not for Laila. Not any more.

I seal my mouth shut. I won't say the words. But then I feel the pull, like the suction created in a vacuum.

'We're going to have to crank things up,' I hear Maeve say before pain shoots through my head. And then everything goes blank.

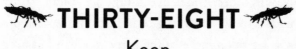

THIRTY-EIGHT
Keep

David

It's nearly midnight and I've been sworn in as the new War Scythe. Dad has declared me the Raker of Garraíodóirí, First Warrior, Protector of the Bláithín. And down the line, when I've earned the badges, First Commander.

I have never been more miserable.

I've escaped the celebrations in the outbuildings behind the Rookery. Down at the lake, I drown my sorrows in a beer. A light drizzle falls but I can't care.

I've won. I can't shake the horror of it.

'Why are you hiding out here?' Dad is behind me.

'Taking a break,' I say.

'People are asking for you.' He hovers too close.

I stand up and sigh. This is my life. Just soldier on. Keep marching until everything falls apart.

'You were brutal tonight.' Dad approves, as we walk. 'You did us proud. Things are on the up for us.'

But why does it feel like things are spiralling towards our end?

I manage ten minutes at the party and then I just can't be there. I can't listen to the cheerful congratulations.

I escape to my room where I take out the cloth hidden beneath my mattress and unfold it.

Only five words.

The strip of leather, a patch of Zara's skirt. The bloodied thorn. A coin and an acorn. I lay them out on the cold wooden floor, trying to find the best arrangement. The leather on top, the patch of skirt beneath. The coin diagonally across. I place the acorn in the left corner, and the bloodied thorn at the heart. I look down at it, trying to think of the clearest phrasing for what I'm seeking.

'Keep.' I test the word, not releasing it.

'Promise.' My voice is getting louder. I'm still not releasing the word into the law. I move the coin to the opposite side. That's better.

'Lucky. Save. Sting.' They're fighting words. Well matched to my needs. It speaks to the mess I'm in.

I say them again and again. I lay my hands over my law: Save us from ruin. From war. From my brother being accused of collusion, being executed for treason. I'm feeling it. Maybe my feeling could be enough.

I pace towards the wardrobe. Back to my words.

I need more. I won't get anywhere with just five words. I don't dare ask for help for Oisín because a botched, weak law could have unintended consequences. Keeping it broad is the only way with such few words.

And then I just do it. Take the leap.

I crouch over the words and form the law.

Let us be OK. It's that vague because my law is weak. Specificity requires strength. But I'll take OK. I say it again and again. *Let us be OK*. Like a child hiding under the covers at night, not the soldier I'm supposed to be.

I'm investing so hard, my eyes are scrunched tight as I wave a hand over the law and release the words. In my head, I see a flash of silver. Wishful thinking. I slump back on my heels, exhausted. I'm looking over the empty husks, thinking they rather remind me of me, when I hear the voice from the doorway.

'What are you doing, David?'

THIRTY-NINE
Never choose you

Sometimes it feels like Maeve isn't completely
honest with me.

LAS

Zara

I wake up alone on the couch. It's a quarter to midnight and there's no one else in the house. The empty glass of wine is on the coffee table beside me. Only Silas scratches in his cage.

It was a dream.

It wasn't a dream.

The house feels changed. It's like the walls still echo the strange chanted music. The striated shadows are faded, but still there.

And I wake up, the words repeating through my mind. Entrap, Sever, Truth.

Somehow, Maeve pulled them out of my head. I feel utterly violated. They gained Mom's trust, engineered that

Adam would be out by having one of their lot befriend him, possibly drugged my glass of wine.

And suddenly, I have to get out of here. The need is urgent. I can't be here alone, not after this.

Before I can talk myself out of it, I decide to see if David's awake. I ring, but his phone is off.

I could go over, see if the lights are on. Pulling a hoodie over my tank, I go out the back and through the hollow.

Through my anger, I try to remember everything Maeve said while I was half conscious. She spoke about a woven room, about Delving.

I can't ignore it any more.

I've stumbled into what Laila dreamed of. I've stumbled into magic. And it's a huge, ugly mess.

I cross the field near the house, moving towards the drive. But again, it's busy, with several black vans parked outside. A buzz of noise comes from the courtyard out back.

I'm at the front door, lost, sad, cross. It was stupid to come here. The lights are on, but so what? It's midnight, I can't ring the doorbell. But I don't want to go back home alone.

Above me a rook screams. It swoops down near my head in a hard, jagged movement. Another comes out of the dark, black wings beating too close to my face. There's another cry as a third rook comes to me at high speed. I run down the front steps, hiding my face. But more birds appear. They don't swipe at me, not yet. They flap above me, screaming and crying. When I step closer to the house, they swoop at me again. One pecks at my hand.

Laila's crow charm is on the floor in the den. Now I understand how it is a key.

'Zara?' I hear the voice through the noise. He lifts a hand and the birds quieten and fly away. And there's Oisín, looking as wretched as I feel. 'Are you all right?'

And I stand there, feeling my face crumple.

'No.'

'What's wrong?' Cautiously, he comes a little closer. 'What happened to you?'

'They came into my house.' My voice catches. 'They ...'

'Who came into your house?' He sounds alarmed. 'What did they do?'

'They got into my head. They stole from me.'

'Where did they take you?' Oisín is frantic.

'We didn't go anywhere. There was a group of them, Maeve, a few others. They said they were taking me to the woven room.'

He flinches as I say the words. And, looking at his quiet distress, I'm finally beginning to understand why Oisín is so wounded. 'They did it to you too.'

'They used those words?' he says. 'The woven room? And you never left your house?'

'Yeah.' I'm scuffing the ground but when I look up, he is pale.

'So it's not an actual place then, but something they conjure up,' he says, like he's finally understanding something. 'I've been looking for a shed, thinking it was a specific place. Like a warped nemeton.'

I don't know what he's talking about, but I'm wired with the need to speak about what happened.

'They use rhythms. Patterns of movement and noise. They did something like it but less brutal before. But tonight –' I shake my head. I am so furious. 'Tonight for an hour, maybe more, they invaded my mind. It's much, much worse than what Sibéal did with her Delving. Is that what they did to you?'

'Ten days.' He gives a dry laugh. 'They beat me up. Chained me. And invaded my head for ten days.'

I'm aghast as I look at him. No one could survive ten days of that.

'I don't want to go home.' I'm reluctant to say it. 'There's no one there.'

'You shouldn't be alone,' he says. 'Not now.' But I know what he's thinking. That it will be difficult for a while yet. That I won't easily get my peace back.

'Is David awake?' I'm nervous to ask. I don't know if Oisín knows that David's been weird with me.

'I last saw him down at the lake, he was trying to escape. The party's in his honour.'

'In his honour?'

Oisín shrugs. 'He'd like an excuse to get away.'

As he turns the handle, I hesitate.

'It's midnight,' I say. 'Your parents wouldn't like it.'

'Don't mind my parents. I'll leave you in David's room while I hunt him down. He'll want to hear what happened.'

'Come in,' he says, then whistles up to the sky.

Inside, Oisín leads me through the hallway towards the stairs. The house is huge, and the doors all look the same. Eventually we stop.

'Go on in there.' Oisín gestures. 'It might take a little while to extract him, but no one will bother you.'

He turns away and I push the door open. A lamp is lit and I've taken a few steps into the room when I see it's not empty.

David is crouched on the floor. There are objects I can't make out arranged beneath him. His face is bruised and there's blood crusted on his eyebrow, streaked on his T-shirt. He's whispering, a fraught chant over the objects: *Let us be OK*. He holds his hands over them, scrunching his eyes tight. Then, still crouching, he slumps, his head hanging down.

'What are you doing, David?' I ask.

His face is like stone as he gathers the things on the floor and folds them into a cloth. He draws himself up to his full height.

'How did you get in here?' He steps towards me and I don't like it. This isn't the David I know.

'Oisín brought me in,' I say. 'He found me outside, the birds were going mad, and he came and they stopped.'

'The birds were going mad?' He sits on his bed and I can see that he is bone weary. 'Suddenly now the birds go mad? Who told you to say that?'

He shakes his head, splaying his hands on the covers beside him.

'Was it Maeve?' he goes on. 'Did she tell you that I'm bad and rotten and deserved to be lied to? Is that how she got you on her side?'

He sounds so hurt.

'You should go, Zara.'

'No.' I stand my ground. He looks at me a long moment before getting to his feet.

There's a darkness that's settled on David. It wants to pull him under. The long fingers of the Inky Black.

'I'm really not interested in what Maeve has to say.' My easy voice is a light salve to his simmering.

'I saw you, Zara,' he breathes out like it hurts. 'I saw you with her. Sibéal kissed you. You hugged Maeve. You were all

323

talking and laughing like you're friends. And you insisted I give you the offering.'

He's close enough now that I can reach for him, steady him with my hands on his shoulders.

'I'm sorry about the offering. The day Sibéal messed with my head she hid an instruction inside me. I didn't remember, but every time I wanted to kiss you, I felt the most awful guilt. And after you told me, I remembered what she'd done. And told her to get lost.'

He looks up at me, afraid to hope.

I put my hands on his cheeks, making him look at me.

'What you saw was Maeve warning me to get in line. I'm not on her side.' I hesitate. 'She knew Laila. She made promises to Laila. I don't know what happened, but I think she tricked my sister.'

David's eyes are wary. He looks at me like he wants so badly to believe what I'm saying. But then I remember.

'They did get the offering from me.' I hate admitting it. 'I didn't want to but they took it.'

'Sibéal?'

'Can we not talk about that right now?'

He catches my hand and holds it.

My reproach is gentle. 'You should have talked to me.'

'I don't ...' he licks his lips. '... trust easily. When I thought you'd betrayed me, I was gutted.'

324

'I didn't betray you.'

He drops my hand and says dully, 'You have the Eye. I know you do.'

'I don't know what the Eye is.' But I'm beginning to think I do.

'It's an ancient warrior disc brooch. Family heirloom. Looks kinda like this.' He lifts a less impressive version of the Wishmaker from the drawer beside the bed. 'This is a replica my grandmother had made.'

'That's your grandmother's brooch?' There's no denying the resemblance between the thing in his hand and the Wishmaker. 'That does not look like a brooch.'

'We really need it back, Zara.'

'OK,' I say, quashing the rebellion I feel inside. 'You'll get it back.'

His eyes flutter shut. 'Thank you.'

'What happened to you?' I touch a finger to his eyebrow, trace it down his jaw.

'I won a competition.'

'A fighting competition?' And I wonder again at his world. 'Is the other guy all right?'

'Gallagher gives as good as he gets.'

'Gallagher?' I say. 'Isn't he your friend? Why would you beat up your friend?'

He doesn't answer, just looks at me for an endless moment.

'Zara,' he says eventually, 'I really should keep away from you.'

He's leaning in to me, his face so close. His hesitation is a question. We still need to talk about what's happened. Not just now though. Now, there's this sad, troubled boy that I really like who's right here and I want to kiss him. Without guilt.

I reach up to him.

The clock ticks in his room, the birds shout outside.

David leans down, one hand snaking to my hair and tugging me gently towards him.

But he hesitates, his brow creasing.

'Maybe this should wait until ...'

I press my lips to his. It feels good, so I go in for more. I grab his shoulders to pull him closer. Sibéal hasn't whispered this inside my head.

I don't know what this is or where it's going. But tonight is tonight. And there's nothing better right now. I kiss him, enjoying the feel of his skin, the slope of muscle and bone. I tug off his T-shirt, to trace my fingers over broken skin, the faded scars and the new bruises.

'You've been hurt,' I say to him, and I don't mean the competition he's just won.

'You've stumbled into a battlefield, Zara.' He pulls me tighter into his arms. 'And it's only getting worse.'

'Who's at war?'

'Do you believe in magic?' It seems like he's holding his breath, waiting for my answer.

'Only when I don't think about it.'

'Then don't think.'

I close my eyes, trying to shut out thought.

'Many years ago, too long to remember,' he whispers in my hair, 'there were people who worked magic. The seers divined through stars and flames, and the lawmakers bonded with nature to understand its laws and then set our own. But they started to fight among each other.'

He's holding on to me so tightly as he speaks, as if he's afraid I'll run away. His words remind me of something, but I can't place it.

'For a long time these people, the draoithe, were well respected, but when the world began to change, their magic was no longer wanted and they were forced underground. They went separate ways, the augurs and the judges. Sealed off from the rest of the world, they changed. Magic spiralled inwards instead of out towards helping others. Going underground made the tension between the two groups worse, like putting a lid on a boiling pot.'

'And you're one of them?'

'If I were, I wouldn't be allowed to tell you that.'

But I hear what he's really saying.

'The rules are very, very strict.' He pulls back to look me in the eye. 'Especially for the judges. The consequences of disobeying are severe.'

This is bigger than anything I'd imagined. Even with what he's told me, I suspect I can't fully grasp it because it's totally outside of my familiar.

'And Laila knew all this?'

'Knowing things can be dangerous.'

'I'm not afraid.' Not any more. Nothing can be worse than what Maeve did to me this evening, and I've survived that.

'You can't breathe a word of this.' His voice is urgent. 'If anyone knows …'

'This is not some godforsaken outpost where everyone has gone all primal,' I bite back. 'Normal society also has rules and these are policed. And people who do bad things get punished. I could take this to the Guards.'

'Law and order are infested with judges.' He gives a small, bitter smile. 'That won't help you.'

'But how do I help you?'

He says nothing, just draws me closer. He lifts me up and then I'm flat on the bed, my hair spread across his covers as he leans over to kiss me. It feels like we lose minutes, hours, days, weeks there. We're so lost in each other that I don't even hear the banging on his door until it opens a crack.

'David,' a voice hisses.

David lifts his head and freezes.

'It's only Oisín,' he whispers. 'I'll see what he wants.'

'I should probably head home.' I watch David as he gets up from the bed, calling for Oisín to hang on.

I pull the covers over my shoulders, suddenly cold.

'Shit's going down,' Oisín says as David cracks open the door. 'Dad was on his way up for you.'

'What's wrong?'

'What isn't?' Oisín's quieter. His voice is muffled, but I can hear enough.

'There's been an attack on warden homes. Three within a ten-mile radius have been vandalised. Dad's going for immediate retaliation.'

David turns to me and grabs his T-shirt. 'I have to get down there.'

'We'll talk tomorrow.'

'Will I stay with Zara?' Oisín pokes his head around the door. 'After what happened?'

David pauses in pulling down his T-shirt. 'What do you mean, after what happened?'

'You didn't tell him?'

'We didn't get to it.'

'Unfortunately, Zara found out the hard way what the woven room is,' Oisín says. 'I'll explain as we walk.'

David looks back at me. He's anxious to hear this.

'We *really* don't want Dad coming up here.' Oisín steers him away and nods to me. 'I'll be back in two.'

With the door shut, I'm out of the bed like Jarlath Creagh is on his way up, breathing smoke out of his nostrils.

I grab my things. And pause. On David's bedside table is the replica brooch. I pick it up, and wonder: What would Horrible Zara do?

Zipping up my hoodie, I see it: the long black beetle on the bed. I lift it, feeling the light touch of it on my skin. And then there's a sharp burn.

'Ouch,' I say, dropping the insect back on to the covers.

'That's good luck.' Oisín has opened the door, and he's actually smiling. A genuine smile that lights up his eyes. Perhaps like the boy he was before. 'It's a really good sign.'

'Being bitten by a beetle?' I'm dubious.

'When you're with my brother, yes.'

I don't understand what he means but he seems happy.

'Sounds pretty busy down there,' I say, inclining my head to the sound of voices downstairs.

'You've no idea.'

'How will I get out?'

'There's another staircase that leads down to the kitchen. C'mon, they're all in the war room. They won't see you.'

'You have a war room?'

He looks at me curiously. 'You still don't know what you're tangled up in, do you?'

'What happens in your war room?'

'That's where Dad schemes and dreams.'

Red the blade, how could I forget?

Oisín is wrong. Getting downstairs isn't a problem, but the kitchen isn't empty. Someone is at the sink, running the tap. What is this house and how are there so many people up and about at nearly three in the morning?

The slim blonde woman turns from the sink. Her eyes widen as she sees me.

'Oisín,' she gasps, and I want the earth to swallow me. I'm wearing pyjamas. I've been messing around with her son in his bed. I smooth my hair but drop my hand when I realise it probably makes things look worse.

'Zara had a break-in at the tenants' house.' I'm grateful for Oisín's detached air. 'So she came over. I'm going to hang there until morning.'

'I didn't realise you were friends.' His mother composes herself.

'Zara is David's friend.' Oisín mimics the way his mother says 'friend' and her water goes down the wrong way, leaving her coughing. Is the idea of me and David enough to make his mother choke? My cheeks are burning hot and I don't know if it's anger or embarrassment.

'Do you want anything before we go?' Oisín is leisurely crossing the kitchen. I wish he'd just get a move on. 'Water? Tea?'

'No, I'm grand,' I mutter. 'It's nice to meet you, Mrs Creagh.'

'Zara, wait,' Mrs Creagh says as I turn away. 'It's Lucia. And I'm sorry about your sister. About Laila. I spoke to her a few times down by the lake and she was a special girl. So passionate.'

I don't know why her words bring a lump to my throat, polite condolences rarely do. But there's something heart-felt in the words and I'm grateful for them.

We cross the fields and head back to the house.

'Don't mind Lucia, she doesn't bite. If she seemed cold, it's because she's surprised. David's never had a girl over. Dad puts a lot of pressure on him. He has ambitions for David.'

'Yeah, I guess.'

'He's trying to find his way,' Oisín says. 'I just hope he chooses to be free.'

We're quiet as we walk back to the house.

At the hollow, I say, 'You don't need to babysit me.'

'I'm not babysitting you, Zara.' He leads the way through the hedge. 'You're my support group. This is the foundation meeting of the woven room survivors' club. Do you have whiskey?'

332

★

When Adam comes home in the morning, Oisín has already left. We'd stayed up in the den playing Assassin's Creed, then dozing off to Netflix. It's unexpected, but Oisín feels like a real friend.

'How well do you know Patrick?' I start grilling Adam as soon as he's inside. He's leaning his guitar against the wall.

'What do you mean?' His cheeks are pink and he's defensive. I follow him into the kitchen.

'I mean –' I need to chill so I don't freak him out – 'what do you know about his family?'

'Nothing to know. They're just ordinary.' He's bristling a little at my interrogation.

I don't know how to ask if they're paid-up members of an ancient magic society and did he drug my wine? So I go with, 'Are they Catholic?'

Hurt flashes in his eyes. 'What's wrong with you? What does his religion matter?'

And Adam is so scarlet that I'm beginning to realise something about my brother that I'd only half processed. About why he spends so much time with Patrick.

'It doesn't,' I try to placate him.

'They don't care that I'm some Muslim-atheist-Christian confusion, so why should you care what they believe?'

'I don't. Sorry, Adam. I just want to know more about him.'

I want to tell him to watch out for Patrick's cousin, to never trust Maeve, when we hear the front door open.

Dad's home.

He looks tired and I don't know if he's just back from a conference or a liaison. I wish I didn't care.

Distracted, he makes coffee. Then he just stands there, lost in thought. He's unlike himself and it's making me nervous.

'Dad,' I say. 'What's wrong?'

'I wasn't at a conference yesterday.' He speaks wearily. 'I wasn't honest with you or your mum.'

'Where were you?' My heart is thumping.

'I had a job interview. In Toronto. I've been offered the post and I'm going to take it. You have to decide whether you want to move with me or live with your mum.'

Both Adam and I are stunned. It should have been clear this was coming and yet we're both taken by surprise.

'Where will Mom live?' Adam says.

'I can't answer that.' Dad lifts the cup to his mouth and hides his face from us. 'You'll have to ask her.'

I can't look at Dad a minute longer. Even though I know he's right, that he and Mom should split up, I need to get out of there. I'm walking out of the kitchen when Dad stops me.

'There's more.' Dad takes another gulp. 'There's a chance

I won't go alone. It's not certain yet, but you should know before you decide. I've met someone else but that's not the reason …'

'I hate you.' My voice is cold and calm. 'I will never choose you.'

'Zara, I know you're upset but you know that your mom and I …'

I leave the kitchen. I won't hear more. I think about how I replaced his shaving oil with the love chant. With everything I've learned since, it probably was a love potion. Did I somehow tip the balance? Force Dad to realise that he really doesn't love Mom any more? Push him into the arms of another Lindy?

I throw myself on my bed. It's so bleak, I can't stop the tears.

Adam opens the door. He takes one look at my face, at the puffy eyes and red nose.

'C'mon.' He holds out a hand to pull me up. 'I know it all really sucks right now. Let's get out of here.'

'Where will we go?'

'To where we buried her.'

Laila's ashes were buried in the woods near the ruined cottage. She'd loved the stories of the tuanacul, of the blonde tree girl who lived in the ruin; it seemed a fitting place for her earthly remains.

'I'd like that.' I hesitate, then grab the silver disc from its hiding place and put it in my backpack. Adam is looking at me with a question in his eyes. 'It's Laila's.'

'Do you think she … lingers?' Adam says it almost shyly. We've been brought up with no religion, no heaven or hell or other conceptions of the afterlife. I can't think of Laila as finished, but I don't think of her as a ghost peering in through the windows either.

'No,' I say honestly. 'But I think being here helps us hold on to her.'

I'm terrified of losing Laila again. Our memories will become weaker. We will begin to lose details of her face, the way she moved. Her voice will fade and our stories will become family myth, replacing true recall.

But not yet. For now, walking through the woods, it's pure memory. I can almost see her running in dappled light, gleeful as she talked of the tree prince who would kiss her and make her one of them. I remember her wild laughter, her pure delight, and my heart is so very, very full.

We stop at the tree where we buried her ashes. A cairn of stones marks the spot. A wish, a fear. In the middle distance is the ruined cottage.

While Adam stands over the stones, I move away and take out the silver knotwork disc.

'Sever is offered,' I whisper to the disc. I think of my father's face when I rejected him.

And now, Entrap. I take out my phone, take a picture of the Eye and send it to Sibéal.

I have the Eye. It's yours, in exchange for the truth of how Laila died. No deal without proof.

She texts back immediately. Where are you?

I don't answer. I want her to stew. I have a few hours before I return the Eye to David. A sharp sense of loss stabs at my heart. I really don't want to give it back. It feels like mine now.

So in our last hours together, I'm going to make the three offerings. Because, and I am fully aware of how nutty this sounds, I feel that the Eye wants me to.

FORTY
The only beneficiary

David

Dad's in the war room, and it sounds like he's arguing. Going inside, I see he has a visitor: Meg, Laney's much older sister. Laney's been allowed a few supervised visits, mostly to bring Cassa books, but Meg is unexpected.

'Meg, everything OK?' Meg's doing a PhD, and I haven't seen her much this year. I don't remember seeing her at midsummer. The tension is thick between them.

But Meg barely looks at me as she storms out of the room.

'What was that?' I say to Dad, who's now steering me to the chart of key augur locations. It feels like he's trying to draw my attention from Meg.

'I ordered three raids early this morning.' He points out each house on the map. A bubble of blood forms at the tip of his finger. 'There were two augur casualties.'

Two augurs dead. Woken by a raid. Killed when they defended their homes.

'You're asking for retaliation.' It's an overreaction to the vandalism and Dad knows it.

It's beginning to stir, this sleeping war, and I don't know how to stop it. Remembering that vision of bloodied bodies strewn in the field, I go to Cassa's room. She always knows what to do.

Outside, Elliot stands guard.

'Open up.'

To my surprise, Elliot steps aside. Guess there are advantages to being War Scythe.

Cassa is at the window, looking out at the trees where nests are hidden in the thick green. There are no plants, no flowers in the room. It's cruel to deprive a judge of her totem like this.

When she turns to me, Cassa seems distressed. I have never seen my aunt this distracted. Worried.

She glances at Elliot, who remains just outside the open door.

'So. You're our new War Scythe.' She studies me carefully. 'I have some books you might find useful.'

Touching a hand to my wrist, she walks me deeper into the room. She gestures for me to sit at the desk, and opens an old, thick book. As she leans towards me, she says in a voice too low for Elliot to hear, 'I need help. Can I count on you?'

I give a brief nod. Elliot looks over at us, uninterested as we both bend our heads over the book.

'Niall of the Waters wrote about the wounded soldier, the soldier that has been broken and remade.' She speaks loud enough for Elliot to hear. 'He believed that the broken soldier would become the War Scythe.'

'What can I do?' My words are barely audible. I realise Cassa is taking a risk. She has little reason to believe I won't repeat all this to Dad.

'It will be wickerlight later.' She's quiet again. 'I must perform the final ritual today. If I don't, the Bláithín will remain unfinished.' The ré órga won't happen. No silver magic.

'To start this and leave it unfinished …' Cassa expels a breath. 'It's dangerous for Wren. It's dangerous for our world.'

'Dad wouldn't stop you.'

Cassa tilts her head slightly towards Elliot, a small warning, and says in a louder voice, 'There were some who believe that the wounded soldier will save us from disaster.'

Elliot gives me a small smile, rolling his eyes at the lecture.

'The silver magic will be channelled through Wren,' Cassa continues quietly. 'Jarlath will use her and destroy her.' Cassa is not exaggerating.

'And he'd be the only beneficiary.'

Cassa nods. 'I have to do the ritual today, in the forest, but your father can't know. We must hide it from him.'

Elliot steps into the room. He's looking at the book, which Cassa snaps shut.

'If you are the wounded soldier,' Cassa says to me as Elliot watches her with suspicion, 'you need to undergo Niall's final song.'

She puts the book in my hand. 'I've always sensed this in you. That you could fulfil the words of Niall of the Waters. Tell your father.'

'Tell Dad?'

'I'm sure Jarlath would agree. What an honour for him, if his son were favoured this way.'

I take the book, wondering where she is going with this. If Lucia or Dad performs the ritual with me, that won't help her at all.

'Of course, you're going to have to find someone who can lead you through Niall's final song, a rare and ancient ritual known only by a handful of people.'

She stands up and moves to the window again. I have to admire how she's manipulated Elliot, who hasn't a clue of what's passed between Cassa and me.

'Fortunately,' Cassa continues, 'I am one of them. It's best performed outside. I would suggest the forest.'

FORTY-ONE
Like attracts like

I hate seeing Zara so miserable.
LAS

Zara

Tell me where you are.

I've been ignoring the string of texts, increasingly irate, from Sibéal. Adam and I sit near Laila's ashes and talk about our sister. And really, we should have done this before. Because talking about Laila here in the woods she loved has brought an unexpected peace. I can finally accept that saving my family means breaking us up. Mom and Dad need to sever their bond for us to heal.

You're going to be sorry.

That was the last text, more than ten minutes ago.

'What's going on with you, Zara?' Adam says. 'Is it the boy next door? David?'

'I like David,' I say. 'His family is pretty messed up.'

'Like attracts like.' Adam is dry. 'Is that what's been bothering you?'

'I think Maeve Lawless knows something about Laila's death,' I confess. 'And Patrick and Simon haven't been upfront with you.'

'What do you mean?' He sounds defensive.

'I'm not sure. I'm trying to find out.'

'How?'

I take out the replica of the Eye. 'I'm setting a trap. There's something Maeve wants. I'm going to give her this, a fake. But only once she's told me what she knows about Laila's death.'

'Are you sure this is a good idea?'

'What could go wrong?'

It's time. I've let Sibéal stew long enough. I'll get her to meet me at the village green for the handover, it seems the appropriate place. And here I will offer Truth. Picking up my phone, I see a new message.

I know where you are.

'Let's go.' I don't want to face Sibéal in the woods. And I don't want Adam involved.

But Adam closes his fist around the replica.

'You can't do this.'

'C'mon, Adam, I want to get out of here.'

343

'I won't let you.'

'Give it back, Adam.' I'm impatient. I glance through the trees. Too easy to sneak up on us here.

'No. What if something goes wrong?'

'Adam, stop.' I try to snatch it, but he holds it out of reach. 'Let's just go. We can talk on the way.'

But Adam backs away from me.

'You're not getting it.'

'Adam,' I yell. He's moving closer to the ruined cottage. I scramble up the slope, trying to coax him to come with me.

He flings the fake Eye into the woods. I track the movement and it lands somewhere just above the cottage.

And then, in the distance, close to where the fake Eye landed, I see her. Sibéal. She's not alone. There's a bunch of them, maybe six or more, and they look wild. Frightening. They're carrying weapons, maces, knives, chains. She walks a few steps and picks up the disc that Adam threw. She closes her hand around it.

There goes that plan.

'What's that?' Adam says suddenly.

I hear the strange sorrowful chanting coming up from the ruined cottage. It's a woman's voice, low and strong.

Sibéal gives a loud piercing whistle. I feel the forest stir. 'Get them.'

FORTY-TWO
First duty

David

Dad sends four garraíodóirí with us, not because he's worried about Cassa doing a runner but as a show of his strength.

There aren't usually a lot of people around this part of the woods because the villagers are superstitious and tend to stay away from the ruined cottage. Even so, we huddle in the most sheltered part of the ruin, where the walls are least destroyed. Cassa positions the garraíodóirí outside the ruin, one at each corner.

'Do you have it?' she says to Tarc. He takes out a paste made from the crushed petals and leaves of the magic peonies. He hands me a tub of ash to draw a circle. There's no time to make a bone fire, so we light candles and sprinkle bonemeal, oakmoss and sage.

Tarc anoints Cassa with the paste, on her forehead and chin, and Cassa smears the rest down her arms and legs. It's a clumsy, fast ritual, but rushed is better than nothing.

345

We can't trust the garraíodóirí who stand guard outside the crumbled walls. Whatever they see, they will report to Dad.

'Niall's final song,' Cassa says as she carves a large five-looped symbol in the soil. 'Lucia already performed that ritual on you.'

She sees my confusion.

'She told you it's a variation on the soldier ritual.' I think of Lucia taking me down to the ring of stones at the lake, of giving me that armour. 'It's a ritual to help you find true bravery. It is not the easiest path, but it's the right one.'

She fixes her eyes on me. 'It could hurt. You could lose a lot. But you will gain things you didn't know were missing.'

Cassa lays herself in the centre of the Bláithín symbol. She spreads her arms as she chants up to the canopy of leaves. Her hair, woven with flowers, is spread out on moss and stone, her dress is stained brown from the dirt. Her body is part buried in the soil. Tarc arranges sprigs all around her, drawing on the full strength of her totem as she chants. The garraíodóirí remain stationed outside the broken walls.

Something doesn't feel right. It feels like we're being watched. A curious villager, perhaps. I whistle, signalling to Ian to take a look.

Tarc retraces the Bláithín mark, drawn around Cassa's body, with a staff. Her hair is matted with muck and flowers, her face crumbed with soil. She's saying the closing words, and I'm relieved. I want to get out of here.

'Attack,' Ian yells in a hoarse voice.

There's a wild scream on the other side of the broken walls. The next seconds are confused, chaotic. Grovers are leaping over the walls of the ruin. Ahead of me is Sibéal; I guess she is a grover then. Behind me, more pour in. They come from all directions, letting out blood-curdling cries. My knife is drawn and I've swiped the blade across skin before I fully realise what's happening.

They're lashing out with knives, hammers, pipes, broken bottles. Something slashes my arm, my blood dripping to the ground. Tarc hands a knife to Cassa and I see her gut a grover without hesitation.

'Behind Cassa,' I yell at Tarc, and he strikes at someone coming at Cassa from behind the broken wall.

There're grovers coming at me, more than I'd like. They've painted symbols on their arms and faces, making them look savage, menacing.

Then I hear something that makes no sense.

'David! Behind you!'

I turn in time to see a man coming at me. I get him in the shoulder and turn back.

She's right there, I didn't imagine it. Zara's there in the woods. Her hands to her face. The horror in her eyes.

'Get out of here,' I yell, and turn to fend off another grover. As I turn, I see Tarc fighting two grovers at the same time.

We were vulnerable, exposed at a time when things are precarious between augurs and judges. When Dad has been agitating the hostility between us. Someone must have seen us heading to the cottage; we should have spotted their spy.

We're holding our ground but it's hard. I see a club with spikes hit a new garraíodóir. Blood spurts and he clutches his hand to his head, howling. I throw my knife at the grover, getting him in the neck. I don't watch him fall.

I'm close to Cassa when it happens. A grover charges, swinging a mace. Tarc has his hands full, fighting off two of them. The grover lets go of the mace and it hurtles through the air, towards me. I roll away, but coming up, I find myself with a knife at my throat.

This is it. I will die here, now.

It lasts seconds, the tip of the blade at my exposed throat, but it feels like a lifetime.

Cassa flings herself at my assailant. It's a foolish move and she's so exposed. She's raised her knife and slashes it across his face. Blood bubbles and he touches a hand

348

to his cheek. I'm still looking at him, the surprise in his eyes when I see Cassa slump to the floor. He must have got the knife to her heart at the same moment she slashed his face.

She took a knife to save me.

She saved me, when it's my duty to protect her.

I'm crawling towards them, shouting, 'No, no, no, no!' Tarc is charging the assailant and I hear him screaming as he lashes out.

Blood seeps through Cassa's dress as she lies on the ground. Tarc is as white as a sheet.

Outside the ruin, Zara shuts her eyes to the horror of what she's just witnessed. And I realise I know this: white T-shirt, green leaves. It's the image frozen on Canty's cracked mirror.

I turn to the grovers. Simon watches Cassa, her face a mask of pain. Her body limp. I catch his eye, and something passes between us.

'Fall back,' Simon yells.

'They're vulnerable,' a woman objects. 'We've got this.'

'Now.' Simon turns away, striding from the cottage and the others follow. His words are nearly lost, but I hear them: 'Let them tend their fallen.'

They peel away. I'm grateful for the reprieve.

'We'll have the best medical team waiting for you at

Liscarron,' Tarc says to Cassa. There's an operating theatre at the army base.

'Promise me –' she clutches Tarc's arm – 'that you'll protect my legacy. Guard Wren, don't let them use her. You too, David.' Cassa is lucid but so very weak.

'With my life,' he says.

'She's my first duty.' The words are right and true.

'My wounded soldier,' she says to me. 'My beloved nephew. I know it hurts. But in breaking, the true strength that's hidden beneath will emerge.'

We have to move fast because the grovers will be back to collect their injured and dead. Around me, garraíodóirí are already gathering our fallen. One of them is calling the nearest Garda station, alerting the judges on the force. They might put up a roadblock, send officers to make sure that villagers don't come near so we have a chance to clean up before anyone sees us.

Other than Zara, who's no longer there. I scan the trees, but can't see her. I don't have time to process what she's seen: an unrestrained battle. Me with blood on my hands. The truth of what I am.

Tarc lifts Cassa and runs through the trees towards his car.

I think it happens while he holds her, the woman who is like a mother to him. That as he runs down the slope, desperate to get the help we need, he loses her. I think it's then that she slips away, her essence withdrawing like a word detaching from an object after a law.

Cassa leaves, and only the husk remains.

I walk behind them. I hear Tarc from beneath the trees. A single, haunted cry.

On the path, I find the white orchid and pick it up.

FORTY-THREE
No

*One thing I regret is having deceived Oisín. I would like to
repair my friendship with him.*

LAS

Zara

There's a terrible sound, and it feels like the forest itself
is waking. Rustling. Pounding and shouting. I stand my
ground, anticipating the worst.

Even more men and women come out from the trees
and rocks. I don't know how many. They brandish their
weapons menacingly.

Adam grabs my hand.

But they pass us, moving towards Sibéal and storming
the ruin. Some have painted symbols on their faces, others
have streaked black across their eyes. A man no more than
ten feet away is carrying a club spiked with nails. I surge
forward with them.

'Zara.' Adam sounds afraid. 'Come away.'

People are fighting, aiming to wound. To kill.

And there he is, right in the middle of the mess. David. He's fending off a man when a woman tears at him from the side. She scrapes a broken bottle across David's arm.

I can't look away. I can't even move away.

Injured, David is even more vicious. He's strong, gracefully brutal. He hurts quickly and without remorse. This is not unfamiliar to him: here is his world and it's ugly. He is also badly outnumbered.

'Don't look, Zara,' Adam says, but I can't not.

Adam is now beside me. I follow his gaze, and he's watching Simon swing a wicked-looking mace towards Gallagher.

I pull Adam back, holding on to his T-shirt like that will stop us from being swept up in the chaos.

Through the crumbling walls, I watch. It's barbaric, loud with screams and cries and grunts. I watch David. He's intent on the two men in front of him, and doesn't seem to hear the woman coming from behind. I step forward, screaming, 'David! Behind you!'

And he turns and blocks the woman as she swipes at him.

Maybe I'm more involved than I'd like to be.

It's carnage in there.

And then above the noise, I hear David howl, 'No no no no no!'

He's crawling across the ruin, his face contorted with

horror. He's looking at something I can't see and there's rage and grief etched into his features.

'Something horrible has happened.' Adam's face is crumpled. Laila's death is still too raw.

'Let's get out of here,' I say.

'We should get help.' Adam sounds so young. 'Call the guards.'

I don't think our police can help here.

'Can you give me a minute?' I say to Adam, still looking at David. 'Wait for me at Laila's grave.'

When he's gone, I take out the Eye and look down at it. My trap failed. I don't know what I was thinking, goading Sibéal. Playing a game when I hadn't a clue of the rules or stakes. I can't help feel that what happened here is my fault.

I'm out. I'll give the Eye back to David. Now, before there's any more damage.

A hand snakes around my waist, another around my mouth, and I'm dragged away from the ruin. I'm trying to yell for David, for Adam, but he's too strong. I struggle against him, and after we've gone a little way, he pulls my arms behind him.

'Stop,' he hisses, searching in his jacket. Then a cloth covers my nose and mouth. He holds it there, and holds it and holds it, and then I don't know any more.

FORTY-FOUR
On the birch

David

There's a dark mood at the Rookery.

Lucia has retreated to her bedroom, locking herself inside. Dad, planning the next retaliation, has gone to HH. I'd warned him the augurs would strike back after this morning's casualties. But this is what he wanted.

The sleeping war is waking.

I take a long shower; I can't face anyone. I keep thinking about how Dad used my words. Looks like he won: he's triumphed over Cassa.

Cassa. The pain is fierce. She was my aunt, my leader. Even though she was hard on me, I admired her. Loved her. She was my true Magistrate.

When I get out of the shower, Cill's in my room.

'The girl next door is a problem.'

'No, she isn't, Cill,' I sigh. I chuck the towel on the floor as I dress. Then I pick it up. Lucia doesn't need me to annoy her today.

'I've seen her with Sibéal,' he argues.

'I know what happened between Zara and Sibéal.'

'She's an outsider, David.'

'And? I can't see her because you say she's an outsider?'

'So you're seeing her now?'

'I like her.'

'She's not one of us.' He's stubborn. 'You can't be with her. We have to protect our ways. Outsiders have no right to our words or laws.'

My room door opens a crack, and I'm relieved to see Tarc.

'Do you have a moment?' He tilts his head, and I follow him to Cassa's room.

Wren has returned. She's standing over Cassa's books on the desk. When she turns, I see it. She's different. Perhaps it's her posture or the cold light that comes from her eyes. It is something so very subtle, but unmissable if you've ever really looked at her.

'I can't believe she's gone.' Wren sounds raw.

I glance at Tarc. Wren seems oblivious to any difference in herself. Looking at Wren is like looking into the heart of some ancient thing. Her skin makes me think of tree bark and her eyes remind of the green at the very top of the trees in the woods. Her hair falls down her shoulders in ropes and I think of tree roots jostling for space around an ancient oak.

And then the light shifts, and she's an ordinary girl again.

Cassa's final ritual has achieved her lifelong dream: Wren has become the Bláithín.

'Stop staring at me, David.' I'm glad to hear her snap at me. It feels normal.

'My dad will want to see you.' I'm still staring. 'You up for talking to him?' Meaning, can you be ordinary Wren for that?

'I'm not afraid of your dad.' Her words fall somewhere between teenage boredom and queenly disdain. She moves to the wardrobe and starts packing Cassa's things.

'Do you see it?' Tarc whispers to me.

'Yes.'

'How do we manage this without Cassa?' He runs a hand down his face.

'My dad.' I lower my voice. 'He'll use her, and he won't care.'

'I know.'

I touch a hand on his shoulder. We're unlikely allies. He's never trusted me, and I guess I've resented him.

'We'll make sure that doesn't happen.'

'Cassa will have notes,' Tarc says. He's terrified that without Cassa to guide her through this, the magic will destroy Wren. 'I need to find them.'

'They must be at HH. I'll get Laney looking. But …'

'But what?'

'I think you need to have an escape plan. Prepare cash, have bags packed. A place to go. Just in case. We might need to get her away from Dad.' And I need to say it, because Tarc has no reason to trust me. 'I'm on your side.'

The words are very soft, as if Dad is lurking in the hallway and can hear me pledge an allegiance that he would not approve. 'I meant my promise to Cassa. My first priority. We'll fix this.'

The scepticism on his face hurts, but I guess I deserve it.

'I swear on the birch,' I say, reaching out my hand, and Tarc is a little dazed. This is the ultimate pledge between brothers in the garden. 'I never thought I would do this with you.'

'I swear on the birch.' He touches his snake tattoo, the mark of the garraíodóir, to mine and just like that, my allegiance is shifted.

FORTY-FIVE
Thief and spy

I love this village. Life has been so intense here.
LAS

Zara

I am kneeling on a white marble floor. My eyes slowly adjust after more than an hour of darkness. The ceilings are high, and the furniture is mostly white, stylish, with sculptures on display and paintings on the wall. I've never been here before.

When I turn around, I see a line of young men. They have their hands at their sides and look straight ahead. I recognise the clothes, the black gear with the five-looped symbol I'd seen David wear.

'Garraíodóirí,' Jarlath barks. 'We've found our thief and spy. The Eye is recovered.' He raises the true Eye, the one that I'd held just moments before Cillian nabbed me in the woods. 'Oisín Creagh's name is cleared. He's no longer accused of collusion.'

Jarlath pulls my phone from his back pocket and scrolls through the text messages. I'm so angry that I start shouting at him, 'What are you doing? Give that back.' I launch at him, like a fly attacking a mountain, but two men in black step forward and hold my arms.

'Sibéal, huh?' he says. 'You need better friends.' He scrolls down, finding an old message from Ciara. He tosses the phone to one of the men. 'The mother is out of town. Send a message to her father. She'll be at Ciara's for the next few days.'

Then he motions for two guards to step forward. They grab my arms.

'Where are you taking me?' I dig in my heels.

'We're going to the cage.' He doesn't bother to look at me.

Did he say cage?

'I didn't steal the Eye. I found it.' I struggle against the guards but their hands are like steel bands clamped around my arms.

I may as well be talking to the wall. The guards lead me down a wide, bright hall. The house is large and elegant. It's filled with flowers. Lilies. Funeral flowers. We received endless bunches of them after Laila died. I hear the distant sound of a woman weeping. This is a house of sorrow, it clings to the walls.

We go down a flight of stairs to a narrow underground passage. It smells of damp and patchouli oil.

Jarlath keys in the code and a heavy door slides open. The room is dark and tiny. There's no bed or chair or anything at all, except the glint of white porcelain on the side.

'Your shoes.' The guard is stationed outside, beside the door.

'I'm not taking off my shoes.' And I'm not going in there.

'Please, your shoes,' the guard says again.

Jarlath grips my arms behind my back while the guard bends to untie my sandal. I twist and squirm and when I'm barefoot, Jarlath releases his hold.

It's too chilly down here for my thin T-shirt and summer skirt and I rub my arms. I turn to give Jarlath a dirty look, but he nods to the room.

And only then I see what I've missed: in the small room, a bed of thin nails push up through the ground.

I look at the guard, my alarm evident on my face. But he can't meet my eye.

'Have a good night, grover lover.' Jarlath pushes me and I'm falling through the door. I land on my knees and hands, the nails breaking skin. I let out a loud cry.

Jarlath shuts the door.

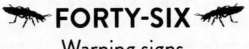

FORTY-SIX
Warning signs

David

I've just stepped outside to ring Canty when I hear my name from the trees down the drive.

'Quick question,' I say as Canty answers. 'What does it mean if I see an image in the mirror before it actually happens?'

'Hmmm. That's new. My guess is it's a warning. Why? What did you see?'

The person who called me is hiding between the trees. Frowning, I move a little closer.

'David,' Canty says on the phone, 'Zara had better not be in trouble.'

'Canty, I have to go. I'll talk to you tomorrow.'

'David.' Canty is not impressed.

'David.'

My name again. I go into the trees, knife ready, when I see him. His face has been kissed, just one peck. He must have come too close to the house.

'Adam?' I say. 'What are you doing here?'

'I can't find Zara.'

'What do you mean?' But the distress on his face tells me what I need to know. 'When did you last see her?'

'She wanted to talk to you at the ruin. I think she had something for you. But she just disappeared. Left me and her backpack behind.'

'That was hours ago.' It's nearly sunset now.

'I'm worried.' He looks terrified.

'We'll find her,' I say. 'You go on home, and if she turns up there, let me know.' I give him my number.

I run down to check Meadowsweet. If Zara needed a safe haven, Laila's shrine is where she would be.

At the derelict house, I climb in through the living-room window.

There's no one in the end room. Not many places to hide either. I check beneath the red silk, just to be sure. Then I see a message laid out between the goddesses.

Zara
I know you are looking for me. I will come soon.
C

The note is handwritten, and I've no idea who C could be. Zara didn't have friends around here, it was one of the things that she'd found so hard. And why do I find this message so creepy?

I put the note in my pocket to give to her later.

I'm going back down the passage when I see the figure waiting for me at the other end.

'Cill.' I'm irritated. 'You keeping some kind of watch on me?'

'Not on you.' He's fiddling with a half-cigarette. 'On your girlfriend, maybe.'

It takes me a second to understand what he means. 'Zara? You've been watching her? Where is she?'

He takes out his Zippo, flicks it on.

'Where is she, Cill?'

He's being deliberately exasperating. He's goading me. And it works. I don't hear her come up behind me. I don't sense the danger because I'm yelling at Cill.

Something hard hits the back of my head and I'm stumbling. I touch my fingers and feel the wet there.

'Sorry, David,' I hear Breanna say before something hits me again.

My hands and legs are bound with rope and tied to the old radiator in the back room near Laila's shrine. A quick job, but it's tight.

I hear the whistling and footsteps approaching. A key turns in the lock. And then he enters, my jailer.

My best friend.

I must be the first War Scythe in history to be captured by his own.

'You wouldn't listen.' He squats down beside me. 'I told you, that girl was trouble.'

'Cill,' I try to interrupt him.

'She had the Eye, Davey. She had the Eye. So many warning signs and still you wouldn't listen.'

'You've got it wrong, Cill.'

'You chose an outsider over your own, Davey. What's wrong with you?'

'Stop, Cill.'

'How could you betray us like that?'

'I didn't betray anyone. Zara found the Eye. She didn't know what it was.'

'And you believe her?'

I exhale. It's futile.

'Why?' I raise my bound hands.

'Jarlath wants you out of the way while he asks her a few questions.'

'What do you mean, a few questions?' Dad did this?

'He just wants to talk to her. See what she knows.'

'Where is she?'

'Jarlath took her to HH.'

'HH? Why all the way out there?'

'Because that's where the cage is.'

'What the fuck, Cill?' I rage at him. 'Zara's not an augur, she's not one of us. She can't spend a night in the cage.'

'Just one night, Davey,' Cill says. 'It's not so bad. You should know.'

FORTY-SEVEN
Follow or you'll be left behind

I watch the ritual on the green with rising dread.

LAS

Zara

They're not exactly nails. More like really sharp spikes. The pain is constant, to the point where hurt becomes my normal and I'm almost numb. And then I shift or doze, only to have the spikes pierce my skin in new, excruciating places.

I remember the scars on David, and while they're too long and too deep to be from these spikes, I wonder what other horrors hide inside this elegant house.

My fingers trace the shape of a beetle that's been carved into the skirting and I find it strangely comforting.

I've been there all night. Light has been entering through the tiny window for a while, so it must be around nine or ten in the morning when Jarlath returns.

'What did you do to my sister?' I say. I don't get up.

'How long have you been working for Maeve?' Jarlath stands at the door.

'Did you bring Laila here?' I fold my arms. 'To this cage?'

'What information have you passed on to them?'

'How did you kill my sister?'

'Did you really think you could turn my son against me? David is loyal to his family. His first priority is his duty as a soldier. As War Scythe. He'll pick that every time.'

Hands in pockets, Jarlath lets out a little sigh. It's like I'm one of many annoying details he needs to take care of in his busy, busy life.

I'm going to waste his time. I'm going annoy him as much as I can.

But then he's yanking me up, pulling me across the spikes. He looks at the blood on my legs, on the spikes.

Back at the door, Jarlath presses a button. Cold water streams through jets in the ceiling.

He's telling me that he can make things much worse.

'You can't just keep me here,' I say, trying not to shiver. But maybe he can. Girls go missing. Girls end up in rivers. I push that out of my head. I'm not without friends here. David will help me.

'We're leaving now.'

He watches me cross the nails, the icy water trailing

down my face, my arms and legs. The water on the floor sluicing down the drain.

The feel of solid ground beneath my feet is a relief.

Jarlath studies me, then says: 'How important is it for you to know what happened to your sister?'

'It means everything.'

He's examining my face. And I study him in return. Set deep in his craggy face are unexpectedly gentle eyes. But the lines around his mouth, on his forehead, make him look hard and mean.

'Give me your hand.'

I hesitate, then stretch it to him. He holds it, palm up, in his.

'I didn't kill your sister.' The intensity in his gaze makes it feel like this is a solemn promise. 'I am in no way responsible for her death.'

I'm still looking at his eyes, and so when the knife slashes the tip of my finger it's shocking.

'I offer Truth.'

Then he drops my bleeding finger and walks away. I recognise the offering.

'Follow or you'll be left behind,' he says.

I scurry after Jarlath, my blood dripping on the marble floor upstairs. We go out a garden door to the black van.

'You've made the offerings? Do you have to use blood?' I say.

369

'All strong magic needs blood.'

'Have you made them all?'

'I have severed, I have entrapped. I'll make the last today.'

'What is the last offering?' I ask.

He opens the back of the van and nods for me to get in.

'Kill.'

FORTY-EIGHT
Invisible battles

David

No one comes until morning. And then it's Dad who opens the door.

'Is this necessary?' I say to him. I want to ask about Zara, but I can't let him see how much I care. I'm really hoping she's just given him the Eye and gone home.

'We're making the fourth offering today.'

'You have the Eye?' My pace quickens.

'David.' Dad sounds disappointed. 'You've been entertaining a spy. You've broken my trust.'

'I'm sorry,' I exhale. 'I'll do better.'

'I know you think I'm ruthless sometimes.'

Sometimes?

'But that's the only way to survive our world. I'm hard on you because I care about you so much. There's always, always a battle on. Some of them are just less visible than others. And the invisible battles are the most deadly.'

I'm not sure that's true.

'You think a quick death during a fight is the worst there is?' Dad lets out a bitter laugh. 'You're young. You'll learn. The most unbearable wounds are those you can't see. When you get these wounds, the invisible wounds that corrode your skin, eat at your heart and leech your vitality, death is your reprieve.'

He's moody. Dad doesn't like going off schedule.

But I'm curious about what he means. I wonder what invisible wounds have begun to form on me.

'What is the fourth offering?'

'Kill.'

I turn from Dad so he doesn't see the distress, the fear on my face.

'You're going to kill someone?'

'I'm not. You are,' Dad says. 'You promised.'

The only way I can carry the burden of being garraíodóir is to hold tight to the Warrior Oath, the vows made on becoming a soldier: that I will only take a life when mine, or someone I protect, is under direct threat.

Killing to trigger magic is something else entirely.

'I never agreed to this.'

'Yes, you did. The night of the ritual of the seed.' I vaguely recall Dad's drunken, pathetic request. *I've a job for you*, he'd said, voice thick from drink. *In a few weeks.* And I'd stupidly promised to do it.

'You're doing this now?' My lips are dry. I could really do with some water. 'Here?'

Dad slices his knife through the ropes.

'Get up.'

I stand, but my legs are unsteady after being trussed up for the night. I push the window open a little, breathing in the fresh air.

Dad's watching. Probably wishing I wouldn't show weakness.

The door opens and Breanna walks in. She's not alone. When I see the blindfolded girl with long dark hair, I'm nearly sick.

But it's not Zara.

It's Sibéal.

I still feel sick.

She's our enemy. She hates us. I'm pretty sure she'd knife me without hesitation if she were in my place.

But I can't. Not like this, not in cold blood.

She's quiet, like she's trying to get her bearings. Suss out the situation. Find out who's in the room.

'I'm not doing this.' I shake my head.

'The War Scythe makes the strongest kill. Now show me how you are loyal to your family and to your people. Kill the grover girl.'

FORTY-NINE
The back room

Grrrrr. I still can't master this infuriating magicky disc thing.

LAS

Zara

I'm pounding at the van door. Screaming for someone to let me out.

And then suddenly the door opens, the sunlight is blinding and I squint at the figure there. He smiles, and I notice for the first time he has dimples.

'Hello, little spy,' Cillian says. He takes my arm and drags me through the wild grass at Meadowsweet, to the open door.

'Let go.' I jerk out of his hold.

'My mistake,' he says pleasantly. 'I thought you'd want to see David.'

'He's here?'

'In the back room.'

'Call him.'

374

'I think you're going to want to see this. See what he's capable of. Who he really is.'

'You don't intimidate me, Cillian.'

Cillian is reaching for me. I know he's going to grab me again and I'm fed up of being manhandled. Feeling the floor with the tip of my sandal, I find a long, sharp shard of glass from a broken window. I crouch to the ground as he comes closer, towering over me.

'But I should intimidate you, Zara.'

I jab the shard deep into his leg.

Cillian shouts at me as he bends over his leg. So much blood.

Now's my chance. I could run away, go home. Be safe.

But David is inside. What if he's in trouble?

I can't leave until I know.

I sneak down the passage, as quietly as I can. There's a key in the door, which I've not seen before. I turn the key, push the door over the warped floor.

Inside the room, near the window, is David. He's sitting on the floor, a knife in front of him.

Sibéal, tied and blindfolded, stands on the other side of the room.

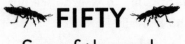

FIFTY
Son of the rook

David

'What's going on?' Zara tries to sound calm, but I can hear the fear in her voice.

I look up at her. Her clothes are wet and crumpled, and there's blood on her skirt.

'Zara,' I say. But I don't know if Dad is listening from the passage, or the next room. He was here just minutes ago, and I can't trust that this isn't some kind of test. If I do the wrong thing, I will put her in more danger. 'Are you hurt?'

'I'm fine. Let's get out of here.'

'Zara, you have to go.'

Behind her, Dad appears in the doorway. He's watching her, his face devoid of expression.

'Come with me, David,' she pleads.

'Go,' I urge her. 'You have to leave. Now.'

She looks at me a long while, and I hate the suspicion I see in her eyes. The fear. She's wondering if I'm lost. Maybe I am.

'David,' Dad speaks up. 'I'm giving you thirty minutes. If you don't act, whatever happens after, the blood will still be on your hands.'

'I thought the War Scythe kill counts more.' The bigger the gesture, the more Dad can ask from Badb.

'It does, but I reckon a completely innocent girl makes for a stronger offering than an unstable augur.'

It's a warning. If he doesn't get his War Scythe kill, Sibéal won't be the victim, Zara will.

Cill comes into the room behind Dad. His leg is bleeding and he's pale. He gives Zara a look of pure loathing.

'It's time, David.' Dad's voice is quiet but firm.

'David, don't do this.' Zara's looking at the blindfolded girl with distress.

'Zara here will be your motivation.' Cill points a knife at Zara's throat. 'Better make a move, Davey. Your clock is ticking.'

Then Dad steps forward and reaches out a hand to me. I don't look at Zara as I take it. He pulls me up to standing, holding out Badb's Eye. I sense her disappointment.

'Red the blade.' Dad places the Eye on my open palm. It feels alive, warm, beating.

'You are a son of the rook.' It's like it's just the two of us in the room.

'I am a son of the rook.'

'You will strike your enemy without mercy.'

'I will strike my enemy without mercy.'

'This is your promise.'

'This is my promise.'

'Do your duty, soldier.'

'As my Cleave commands.'

Touching a hand to my shoulder, Dad leaves.

'Well, this is the most tedious murder I've ever had the misfortune of not watching,' Sibéal says. 'Better hurry, I might just drop dead from boredom.'

'Shut up, Sibéal,' Cill says. She's getting to him, but that's her plan. I can't help but admire her spirit; this girl is wasted on the augurs.

'Or I could provide the entertainment,' Sibéal muses. 'Since I've seen inside all of your tiny little minds. Who first? Maybe Cillian, with his petty jealousies and grim delusions of grandeur. At least David, tosser though he is, had the strength to shut me out.' She thinks for a moment. 'Apart from revealing that he has the raging hots for Zara.'

'And you took advantage of that.' I glower at her.

'Just call me Cupid.' Sheer bravado. I can hear the slight shake in her voice.

'Just fucking kill her already,' Cill grinds. He's backed Zara against the wall, knife pricking her throat.

'And Zara, who's all boohoo about her sister,' Sibéal

continues. 'You want to know what happened to Laila? My mother used her.'

'How?' Zara's face is murderous.

'Maybe I'll take it to my grave?' Sibéal raises her eyebrows. 'But where's the fun in that?'

'How did Laila die?' Zara hisses, oblivious to the knife at her throat.

'Mam told Laila that she'd be gifted with magic and brought into our grove. That she would perform the binding oath between me and Laila, if Laila stole the Eye from the Rookery. But Mam tricked her. Instead of the binding ritual, she performed a sacrifice using the residual energy from Cassa's ritual.'

'The old ways are passed through blood,' Cill says. 'We can't just give it to any random person who comes here.'

'What does it matter?' Sibéal says. 'It didn't happen.'

'It matters.' Zara's face is twisted with grief and fury. 'Laila matters.'

'Oh, I'm grateful to Laila,' Sibéal goes on. 'Thanks to her I've been gifted with a powerful talent that died out centuries ago. I am a Delver, able to glimpse inside your pathetic minds and search through your insignificant thoughts.'

I'd known there was something dark about Sibéal's skill. But resurrecting dead magic through human sacrifice is another thing altogether.

'The plan was that I'd extract the offerings and summon Badb to help us destroy you miserable bastards. But Laila wouldn't hand over the Eye until after the ritual. She told Mam she'd left it in the ruined cottage, and there wasn't time to get it first. But it wasn't in the cottage. Laila had tricked Mam too. She'd hidden it somewhere else.'

'You killed Laila when you didn't have it in hand.' I shake my head. That's cold. 'And you still don't have all the offerings.'

'You pushed me out, and searching Mamó's head is like eating stringy meat. And then she wouldn't leave the Rookery. So we had to innovate. With Zara.'

With Cill distracted by Sibéal, Zara shoves at him, aiming a knee to his groin. He jerks back, taken by surprise, and the knife clatters to the ground. She grabs for the knife, but he twists her arm behind her. The grip is awkward, her body smashed against the wall, and she can't hide the pain.

'Do it, Davey.' He's getting mad. If I don't do something soon, he will hurt her worse. He pulls a razor blade from his pocket.

'Let her go, Cill.' I step towards Sibéal.

'Laila wrote a letter.' Sibéal talks faster, as if that can hold me back. Her hands are behind her back and I see what she's trying to hide: she's been working the rope. The knot

380

is looser, but not enough. 'One that totally incriminates us. She told Mam. I think those may have been her last words.'

'A letter?' Zara says. 'Where is it?'

'I can't tell you that.'

'Don't listen to her, Zara,' I say. 'They don't have the letter. Simon told me.'

Sibéal glares at me. It's time to end this.

There's a buzz close to my ears, and looking up, I see three wasps circling.

Thank the sacred moons. I was beginning to worry.

'I'll do what Dad wants.' I avoid looking at Zara. 'I'll make the kill.'

I've been watching the wasps' nest hanging outside the window since daylight started around four this morning. Without silver magic, I can't command them, but it never hurts to ask nicely.

'Let's have it then, David,' Sibéal taunts me. 'I want you to suffer with burning regret every minute of your miserable life, that you took the life of a completely defenceless sixteen-year-old girl. Go on then. I want to be a ghost. And I'm going to haunt you. My bloodstained corpse will be there first thing in the morning, and every time you fuck up, I'll be there, laughing.'

'You overestimate your value, Sibéal,' I say, moving

381

closer. 'What makes you think I will feel regret at the loss of your life?'

'Enough talk,' Cill says. 'Get it done.'

He's still holding Zara at an awkward angle, but now he's positioned a razor blade just above her eye. One slip, and she could lose it.

'Do you know the damage caused by the attack at the ruined cottage?' I prowl towards Sibéal.

I'm right in front of her now. There've always been two sides of me: the one who lashes out when I'm afraid, when I'm in pain. The monster. And the other one who suffers every consequence of the monster's action. Now, I feel the monster rising. It wants me to lose myself to it.

'We lost Cassa.' That pain is still raw. 'Why would I save you?'

Up close, Sibéal's fear is clear. The disc is warming in my hand, the jagged edges of the carved detail dig into the flesh of my palm.

'David.' Zara's words are tense. 'Please. Don't do this.'

The buzzing is louder. More wasps have come.

I hold the knife out, line it up with Sibéal's chest. I press it against her skin, see her throat work as she swallows.

'Do I get last words?'

'This will destroy you,' Zara says. 'She's not worth it.'

Barely moving, I shift my eyes to Zara: 'But here is

382

revenge. This will break Maeve. You could have a life for a life.'

'No.' Zara shuts her eyes. 'Enough. There's been too much. You are better than this.'

And with Zara's words, I feel Lucia's armour again. My internal shield, a different kind of strength I didn't know I had.

With the wasps buzzing loudly, I leap across the room and fall on Cill, knocking Zara down too. She scrabbles back while Cill and I grapple; he's slashing wildly with the blade. He gets my cheek, and my blood drips on to him. Zara creeps towards the fallen disc.

'Stop, Cill, I don't want to hurt you.' Wasps swarm towards us, aiming for Cill's face.

Zara shouts out in pain. I turn to see that Sibéal's blindfold is off, her hands untied. She's kicked Zara in the stomach, but Zara hits back and the two girls are fighting each other.

The wasps move to Sibéal, forcing her to break her hold. When she lunges for Zara, they descend on her, hanging back only when she does.

But the distraction costs me. Cill knocks my knife out of my hand and he's now above me on the floor. He punches my face, once, twice, three times. Picking up my knife, he raises it high. I don't flinch. If there has to be a death this afternoon, it must be mine.

I'd rather be dead than a shell.

I would rather die than destroy myself by being my dad's obedient little soldier. The wasps will help Zara escape. She will be OK.

'Run, Zara,' I cry as my best friend brings down his hand to plunge the knife into my heart. But suddenly he slumps on top of me. Zara holds the iron cailleach statue in her hands.

Cill lies motionless. Blood seeps from his head.

Zara drops the statue.

'I thought he was going to kill you.' Her eyes are wide with shock.

'He was going to kill me.' Rolling Cill gently, I get to my feet.

'We need to call an ambulance.' She's trembling.

I'm not sure an ambulance can help him now.

'We've a medical unit at the military base.' But neither of us have phones. I'm reaching for Cill's in his jeans pocket, when the door begins to open slowly.

'Oh no, my girl.' An old lady stands in the doorway and scolds Sibéal. 'Put that right down.'

The wasps have left. Sibéal is holding the Eye, and had been sneaking to the door. She smirks. But her expression quickly changes to pain and she drops the disc as if it burned her.

'Leave,' the woman says, and Sibéal, nettled, obeys.

'Callie,' Zara calls. 'You came. I was worried.'

She throws herself into the old woman's arms.

Her silvery hair is loose around her shoulders, and she wears a simple black summer dress. Her face is deeply lined with wrinkles, she must be even older than Mamó. As she comes closer, I realise I know this woman. I've seen her somewhere before. Her eyes are fierce but kind, the lines in her skin map a life lived.

And then I know.

'David.' The woman nods.

Zara, hunched and sad, is tucked into the arm of the fucking Crow-Mother. Like she's being comforted by a long-lost friend.

'You called me,' Badb says to Zara. 'Many times. And now, with four true offerings, you may ask me whatever you want.'

Zara uncovers her face. She opens her mouth and shuts it again.

'Four offerings? To you?' She processes a moment. 'Wait, did I actually complete them?'

'You did.'

'My Truth was rubbish, my Entrapment failed.'

'Your Truth was sincere. Your Sever untethered you. That cage, your Entrapment, rebirthed you.'

'I didn't use blood.'

'You used heart.'

'But the fourth.' Zara looks at Cill, and she is so heart-broken. 'I did that.'

'You did what you had to.' The Badb Catha, goddess of war and destruction, takes her hands. 'Death was in this room today. There was no escaping it.'

Cill is on the ground, his blood on the floorboards. His still form breaks something inside me. My breath catches for the boy who ran beside me, who shared my dens, who played football better than I did. The boy who was never content, who always wanted more. We've shared so many comfortable silences, Cill and I. But this one, this final silence, is difficult, uncomfortable, guilty. His life for mine.

I won't hide the tears that fall as I bend over his body.

'But why me?' Zara says. 'What about Jarlath?'

'You both sang to me. I came to the one whose song I liked more. Now, what will it be? I can punish the augurs who hurt you and your family. I can bring Maeve to justice.'

Zara shakes her head. 'None of that. No death, no chaos, no destruction.'

Badb smiles. 'You've been listening to my stories. An old woman gets weary of darkness, even when that darkness is stitched into her marrow. What will it be then?'

'I want what Laila wanted. I want a life of magic,' Zara says.

Nothing could have surprised me more. I would have thought this is the last thing Zara would want after witnessing how entirely dysfunctional we are.

'Words will flow to you.' Badb touches Zara's mouth, then moves her hand to her heart. 'You will be gifted with a strong affinity and totem, and your bond with your guide will be touched with silver.'

'Just like that?'

'Magic works through ritual,' Badb says. She smiles at Zara and then looks at me. 'Even with my gift, you must make the binding oath.'

'How do I do that?' Zara says.

'Becoming draoithe happens through a bond with another person, whether it's a parent or husband or a friend. A spirit connection that lasts until death.'

'I don't want to get married. Definitely not now.' Her face is grim. I think of her parents. 'Maybe not ever.'

'If you'll have me, I'll do it,' I say to her. 'Without asking anything of you in return.'

'You would?'

'You saved my life, Zara.'

She glances at Laila's shrine, at her goddesses.

'The bond is for life,' I warn her. 'Even if in ten years,

you're with someone else and living halfway across the world, we'll still be connected. You'll get to know me like you've never known anyone else. Everything good, all the boring, down to the horrible.'

'David.' She holds out a hand and I close it in mine.

We stand before Laila's shrine while Badb performs a binding ceremony to bring Zara into the Rose.

Before our blood touches, I whisper, 'Last chance to change your mind.'

She presses her hand to mine. 'This feels right.'

The ancient woman covers our joined hands with her dry, papery palms. She whispers the words in Old Irish. I've never seen a binding oath performed, and I don't know if they all have this same intensity.

She guides us through the promises and when they're made, I put my arms around Zara. I'm surprised to feel her body racked with sobs.

'He's dead,' she whispers.

'And if he wasn't, I would be.'

The sound of flapping wings grows until it fills the room. Breaking apart, I turn and see a hundred hooded crows swirling around Cill. They form a thick, moving veil for a few seconds, then fly out of the window, screaming into the blue afternoon sky.

Zara and I are alone in the room. Badb has left, and Cill's

body is no longer there. No blood marks the spot, only the cailleach statue lies on the floor.

'That can't be used for another hundred years,' I say to Zara as she picks up the Eye.

'Your dad is going to be furious.'

'He will.'

'You made a promise to him.'

'Sometimes we have to break things to find release.' I'll never forget Cassa's last words to me.

'He'll be livid.'

'He won't forgive me.' I try to keep my voice neutral, but she hears the despair. He may be difficult, but he's my dad. And I have ended our relationship.

'Oh, David.' She squeezes my hand.

'Why didn't you get away when you could?' I say.

'I wanted to save you.'

'You did.'

'Why didn't you run?' She puts the same question to me.

I look at the rope and blindfold Sibéal dropped on the floor. Running wouldn't have stopped Dad from hurting Sibéal or Zara. Running wouldn't have stopped Dad from hurting me.

'Because in a different way, I needed to save myself.'

As we leave Meadowsweet, I think of what is salvaged: Oisín is no longer under suspicion. Zara is no longer exposed and vulnerable, she has the unconditional support of the War Scythe in facing both augurs and judges. Dad can't touch her now.

Zara and I walk towards Dad's Rover, which has just pulled up.

Dad can't call on Badb, and without the red button, he won't pursue his war. When we don't retaliate for the ruin attack, the augurs will hold back. That thirst for blood will eventually dissipate. People will live. For now.

We will be OK.

I look my father in the eye.

FIFTY-ONE
Where Laila was

*If my parents would just accept the inevitable, we could be
happy here.*
LAS

Zara

A few days have passed and Mom's home. She's different.
Calmer, more at peace. Dad's moved out and the house feels
less tense, like it's been cleared out. A deep scouring that's
removed layers of dirt.

'I don't want to live somewhere else,' I tell her as she
brings my hot lemon and sits beside me on the velvet
sofa. I'm staring out of the window, thinking about
that night spent on a bed of nails. That same magpie is
out there.

'I don't either.'

I look at her, startled. 'But you went to Cape Town to
check things out.'

'Being there made me realise, going back was an excuse

rather than a real answer. I wanted to reclaim something that was long gone.'

'You've been miserable here.'

'I've been so miserable here with your dad. I couldn't do the one obvious thing I needed to do.'

I take a small sip of lemon water.

'So what now?'

'Well, what would you like?'

'We want to be here.' I don't hesitate. 'Where Laila was. And where we've settled these last months even though it's been horrible.'

And Horrible. Which has been necessary. Which has been my awakening.

I'm still struggling with my anger towards Maeve. At how much I need her to account for what she did to Laila. But I don't want the kind of justice David's dad would mete out. Or Badb, for that matter.

I still can't get over that I've been having casual morning chats with the goddess of battle over the last weeks. While I knew she was steely and strong, she was also gentle. Wearied. I guess we bring out our darkness when it's necessary. It doesn't mean it should define us.

'Dr Kelly will retire completely by the end of the year,' Mom says. 'He wants me to take over the practice.'

'Will you?'

'If we're all agreed,' she says. 'I like working there. I like this funny little village. If you and Adam are happy to stay here, then I am too.'

For the first time in ages, I want to fling my arms around my mother. I feel such relief, no longer worrying if the rug will be yanked out from beneath us.

Mom brings her cup up to her lips. Both hands are wrapped around it and I notice she isn't wearing her rings.

'What will you do today?' I don't want her sitting around and missing Dad.

'Adam wants to go for a hike,' she says. 'He's been low since Patrick went off grid.'

We haven't seen Patrick since before the fight. Just a short message about how he's gone to stay with cousins in the west, and nothing more. Mom's making a project of Adam's broken heart. I think they will help each other.

'I worry about you with David.' Her face clouds over. 'A bad relationship can poison you slowly from within, I should know.'

'I'm seventeen, Mom.' I nudge her shoulder with mine. 'We're not getting married in the morning. And he's really not like that.'

I won't mention the bonding thing. Because that's different; I might fancy the pants off him, but that has nothing to do with what we did at Laila's altar. Rather, our attachment feels grounded in how we've both discovered ourselves in ways we hadn't before.

'I like him. He wants to do the right thing. His home life is complicated, and his dad is hard on him. Romantic relationships aren't the only ones that can be toxic.'

She's looking at me with sadness and I realise she feels bad for letting us down. For being absent in her grief, for not being brave enough to end things with Dad earlier.

'There's something different about you.' She speaks hesitantly.

'I've changed.' She's more part of me than ever now, Horrible Zara. In the cage, as I bled, I imagined my skin growing a chitinous layer. I imagined it encasing my heart, protecting me.

In that cage, I awoke to myself.

How different everything has become. How my world of school and camogie and my old friends are now a pale echo.

The new real, with its beating intensity, is this world I've stumbled upon. Through her death, I found what Laila wanted. I am so deeply part of this world of impossible things. My attachment to David is armour against its many dangers.

'Zara?' Mom's staring at me, worried.

'Give David a chance,' I say, and she squeezes my hand and nods.

There's a tap on the door and Mom rolls her eyes. 'Speak of the devil.'

'Mom,' I warn.

'All right, all right.'

Mom lets him in while I finish my lemon water. She doesn't hide that she is examining him with her doctor eye. But she's polite, she smiles and I guess it's a work in progress.

'I've some news,' he says. 'You're getting new neighbours.'

'Really?' Mom is happy. 'Who?'

'Oisín and I decided it's time we set up by ourselves. It's for the best, the way things are with Dad. We'll still be close to Lucia.'

'Oh.' Mom is less happy. 'Where are you two off to so early anyway?'

'Going for a walk down the fields.' David threads his fingers through mine. I feel it, that synchronicity between us, and it makes me smile. 'Then my grandmother wants Zara for brunch.'

I wish he hadn't put it like that.

But David's very attached to his grandmother, and I'm relieved that she hasn't outright refused to see me, as Jarlath has.

'Will you leave me David and his mother's numbers?' Mom says. I guess she's always going to feel protective of us.

'Sure, Mom.' I pick up my phone.

'You play WordSpat?' David sees the app on the screen.

'Yeah.' I smirk. I'll beat his sorry ass any day. 'I played with Laila.'

'You can play me. If you want.'

'If you dare,' I say.

I open the app, which I haven't done since Laila died. The last game she started is still saved, awaiting my move.

Boot. It's a shitty word. Laila's first words were always much better than that. Why would she play such a weak opening?

'Oh my God.' I'm in the garage as fast as I can get there.

I open the boot to her car and there's nothing. Just spare swimming gear in a musty gym bag.

It's so slight, it's barely noticeable, but the floor isn't sitting evenly. I lift up the flap and pull out the spare tyre. Beneath is a slim notebook. Laila's diary.

I pick it up. Her words. I am so elated to have found a way to understand what she was thinking and feeling in those last months. I look at the front page, and two letters fall out.

396

The first is short:

20 March
I am going to the village green tonight. Maeve Lawless has a drug similar to devil's weed that she's been pushing me to try. I don't want to experiment with devil's weed again, or anything like it, but Maeve is relentless. I think she wants me to test it before she sells it to the kids in the nearby villages. She keeps on about it, even though I've told her no many times. I'll try a small bit tonight. Just once, to get her off my back.

'What's that, Zara?' Mom comes into the garage. I hand the page to her, not sure if she'll buy it. She knows the results of Laila's post-mortem, so she'll have to believe that this unnamed drug is somehow untraceable or hadn't been tested.

But Mom wants to believe. She's weeping big ugly tears. This is what she was searching for in all her sorting, it's the proof she was always looking for.

Clever girl, Laila. She's made sure that Mom has a way to get Maeve to account for that night. While Maeve can keep her secrets of magic sacrifices, she'll have to answer for providing a mind-altering substance that resulted in the death of an eighteen-year-old girl.

The second letter is addressed to me. I hide it in my pocket when Mom isn't looking.

A little later, David and I go through the hollow at the back. A magpie lifts from a tree, a second following close behind. They fly towards me, flapping their wings as they wait. Reaching out a hand, one lands on it, briefly, then they lift up and fly away.

'I think your guide has chosen you.' David smiles. He seems relieved that even though it's of the crow family, it's not a rook.

I think of that night when I first went through to the Rookery. I think of Laila finding her way through the hollow, stepping into these fields and into a world of magic.

David leans down to pick a blade of grass, squeezing it for a moment.

'Free,' he says, and pulls a cloth from his jacket pocket, where he wraps it up. Then, his arm around my waist, we walk to the Rookery.

AFTER THE END

20 March

My dearest Zara,

If you're finding this letter, then things haven't worked out as I wanted.

Tonight I will go beneath the wickerlight, the time when the veil between this world and the other realm is thin.

A few weeks ago I stole an antique brooch called Badb's Eye from the Rookery. Maeve arranged for me to get a key by introducing me to a man called John Canty. She gave me the code to the safe. In return for the brooch, she would grant me my greatest wish: to bring me into her grove. In the end, I didn't need the code, because Oisín is such a sweetheart. I slipped it into my pocket when he was distracted. Tell him I'm sorry that I did that to him when he's been nothing but a friend.

But then I realised, if Maeve wants this brooch so badly, it must be very powerful. And if it's magic I'm looking for then why give it up when it's in my hands? Maybe I can get it to work for me. So I held it back, tried a few things, but I can't crack it. So tonight I'll give it to Maeve once the ritual is successful. For now, I've hidden it in your old smelly parka, the one you vomited on at the fair and never wear, even though I've told Maeve that I've left it in the ruined cottage until after the ritual.

But I can't shake the feeling that something is wrong.

I've come to the green earlier than we arranged. And there's a blonde woman here, surrounded by boys. It's unlike anything I've ever seen: these boys are half naked, dancing and drumming and marked with black swirling lines. This is real magic. A ritual is under way, but it's not me that's at the heart of it.

I've rung Maeve, who says to hang on, she'll be here any minute and my turn is next. I don't know, I've got a bad feeling. I've rung you, but you must be busy. So I'm writing this down for you instead.

Zara, if you find this, then something's awry. Maybe the transformation only half took, and I've become something else. Or maybe they've wiped my memory to erase the secrets I've learned. It's hard to know with Maeve.

But this letter is the truth of tonight. And if it has

gone wrong, even if I'm now only a shell of a girl, or turned into meadowsweet or a toad, then know that the big adventure is all I've ever wanted. Life is nothing without risk. Hold your tears, because I've found magic. I wish you can too.

All my love,
Your bigger (more beautiful) sister,
Laila

 **GLOSSARY**

Augur
Druid faction made up of seers whose magic lies in their ability to perceive and manipulate patterns.

Badb (said: Bive)
Irish goddess of war and death, often appearing as an old woman or as a crow. On the battlefield, the Badb would manipulate the minds of the enemy and confuse them. She may appear to foreshadow death.

Bards
The third group of draoithe, the poets, who are believed to have died out in the early twentieth century.

Bláithín (said: Blah-een)
Translates as 'little flower'. In draoithe lore, the Bláithín is an augur girl who fell in love with a judge boy. After he was fatally injured in battle, she made a deal with the forest to save his life and was changed into a meadowsweet bush. Some judges believe a new Bláithín will bring on the golden age of magic.

Brithemain
The historical name for the judges, derived from the Brehons, the lawmakers in early Irish history.

Cailleach (said: Kal-yagh)
The Irish word for hag or old crone. It is linked to an ancient, mysterious figure, the Cailleach, a mother goddess and winter queen, who has strong connections to the land.

Camogie
Camogie is a women's Irish sport very similar to hurling. It is played with a long stick with a flattened end (hurley) and a leather ball (sliotar).

Cleave
The Cleave is the leader of a gairdín. The First Cleave is the highest authority in a country and may also be the Grand Magistrate, the leader of all judges.

Delve
An exceptionally strong, potentially destructive talent that has died out. It allows an augur to read and manipulate the patterns of the mind.

Draoi [pl. draoithe] (said: dree/dree-huh)
Druid(s).

Gairdín (said: gore-deen)
Garden. Used as the collective noun for judges. It refers to the smaller communities to which a judge may belong. They're usually organised by geography, except for the Rose, the First Cleave's gairdín, where membership is determined by family status.

Garda
An Garda Síochána, the guardians of the peace, is the police force in Ireland. Both gardaí (pl.) and guards are commonly used.

Garraíodóir [pl. garraíodóirí] (said: gar-eea-dor/-ey)
Gardener(s). The military unit of the judges, who pride themselves on their skill and art in fighting.

Grove
Collective noun for augurs. As with gairdíní, they are smaller communities of augurs and perform rituals together.

Judge
Druid faction made up of lawmakers believed to descend from the Brehons, the lawmakers in ancient Ireland. Judges are a hierarchical society with a strong connection to nature. They can be found in both Ireland and the US.

Knot

Knot magic is a complex form of draoithe magic. It usually involves a knotwork design, for example a triquetra, triskele, spiral or cross. The knot may be a precious object, but could also be made by hand. Knots require action: there will be words or offerings attached to a knot and these must be performed in order to make magic.

Nemeta

Threshold space. Nemeta are sacred sites where the veil between the real and the magical is thin. They are the source of all draoithe magic, and without them draoithe have no access to magic. Nemeta must be bonded to a grove or gairdín.

Offering

An action required in order make Knot magic. Draoithe must complete the offerings in order to release the magic of the Knot.

Ogham (said: Ohme or Ogam)

Early Irish alphabet made up of strokes across a line.

Raker

See **War Scythe**

Ré órga (said: ray oarga)
Golden age. The judges recognise two ré órgas in their history which brought them military prowess and wealth. They anticipate a third, which many believe will be triggered by the third Bláithín, bringing abundant silver magic.

Talent
Before they turn sixteen, augurs receive a talent. While augurs have a generally enhanced sense of pattern, their talent is their particular strength. Many augurs can use their talents to divine the past and present.

Totem
Judges have an affinity for natural elements (for example plant or animal) which is narrowed down to their totems (tree, flower, bird) and then their specific guides (oak, peony, magpie).

Tuanacul (said: tua na cwyll)
Kilshamble folklore warns of the people of the forest, the Tuatha Na Coille, who seduce their victims and extract their vitality.

Sunder
A historical moment where draoithe succumbed to internal division and fighting. During Sunder, draoithe split to form separate communities of judges, augurs and bards.

War Scythe
First Warrior. The contest for this title is open to young garraíodóiri, with the right family history, at the onset of manhood. The title is for life, though there are ways in which a Raker may be challenged and usurped.

Wickering
Augur form of mental manipulation using rhythm and patterns.

Wickerlight
Threshold time. A period of time when the unexpected may occur.

 ACKNOWLEDGEMENTS

When I was a young teenager, my best friend died in a car accident. Writing this book, inhabiting Zara's grief, made that time feel immediate again. She was a beautiful soul: bubbly, kind, full of fun, thoughtful, popular and so very loved. Her name was Marsha Trimmel and, decades later, I still feel that loss.

As usual, there are many people who helped create this book and prepare it for the world. I am fortunate to work with a brilliant editor, sharp eyes, sharp mind, who really gets stuck in with the revisions – Ellen Holgate, thank you. I am grateful to the wonderful people at Bloomsbury, both past and present, and especially Cal Kenny, Emily Marples, Emily Moran, Jessica Bellman and Hali Baumstein. I know there are more, and I am deeply appreciative of the work you all do. Thank you also to Emma Young and Jessica White. In South Africa, thank you Jennifer Ball and Verushka Louw.

Claire Wilson, iron hand in a velvet glove, I am endlessly grateful to have you, with your wisdom and humour, in my corner. And also at RCW, thank you Miriam Tobin.

Emma van der Vliet, my partner-in-crime from before times, thank you for reading, for identifying my particular brand as the '*vrot* Ophelia' – you get me. Thank you Catherine Creaven for the beautiful artwork you've drawn for my fictional world, but also for letting me drag you into the woods, to ruins, to post offices, or wherever, and always laughing.

Thank you David Joyce for talking torture with me. I learned so much.

Thank you Cathal, most excellent of men, for reading and for all your support, practical and emotional. But mostly, I'm really happy that you're not like the dads in this book.

LOOK OUT FOR

THE WREN HUNT

A SPELLBINDING THRILLER
AVAILABLE NOW

ONE
With honey

You catch more flies with honey.

Maeve's words chased through my head as I walked towards the village, her flowery bag slung over my shoulder. Good girl gone looking for trouble.

It was quiet in the main street. It always was the day after Christmas. In other towns the wren hunt was a happy occasion with dancing and music. Wrenboys in costumes with loud banging drums. Delighted crowds looking on. But things were a little more bloody in Kilshamble. That's how it goes in a village built around an open-air slaughterhouse.

The Spar was shut, the handwritten sign at the Gargoyle turned to '*closed*'. The twinkling lights outside the pub only emphasised the quiet: no laughter, no music spilled from inside. I paused, scanning the village green. They liked to hide around there. They'd fold out of the shadows, from the church's stone façade, from the thick hedge.

I passed the butcher's, the hotel, until I came to the ghost estate on the outskirts: semi-detached houses that had been hastily assembled in the boom years and now stood empty, running to ruin. No one wanted to move out here. Not if they didn't have to.

This wasn't how it was supposed to work. The boys usually came looking for me, not the other way round. But earlier that afternoon, Maeve had found me in the kitchen, where I'd been staring at burned toast.

'You catch more flies with honey,' she'd said, handing me the flowery bag, the one she used at the Spar for bread, cheese and a naggin of Powers. She stepped closer, conspiratorially.

In the bag was a bottle of whiskey and a loaf of Maeve's apple bread.

'I think you should talk to them,' Maeve had said. Backlit by the window, her fuzzy hair was framed by the dark clouds and their silver linings. 'Reason with them. They're older now. The game has run its course.'

'Smith said to stay home.'

'Smith also says that facing up to problems,' Maeve looked at the burned toast in my hand, 'is better than hiding from them.'

Hiding seemed pretty appealing to me. But if I didn't go out today, they'd wait. They'd come to the cottage tonight, throw stones at my window, signalling the beginning of the hunt. And the anticipation of when they would finish, maybe on my way home from the shop tomorrow or out at the weekend, was worse.

She frowned, and standing there in her dress with its crazy flowers Maeve looked strangely dangerous.

'I'll go.' Before Smith woke from his nap.

'This ends today,' Maeve had said. She spoke so fiercely it seemed like it was possible. That I would give them gifts and it would stop.

Taking my face in both hands, Maeve kissed my forehead. I had to dip to let her. Her roots were showing grey again.

'This ends today,' she repeated. But it lacked the fervour of the first time.

Dropping the toast in the slop bucket, I searched the junk drawer for the letter opener I'd stashed there. Then Maeve hustled me out, jacket in hand.

She sent me into the dark day to catch some flies.

And there I was, alone in the ghost estate, feeling the creeping cold. I ran my eyes over the houses, wishing I wasn't the stand-in bird in this warped version of the hunt. It struck me as odd that I'd never seen a real wren hunt, except on TV, and there the masked wrenboys parading the streets with the plastic bird made it look like such a merry, rousing thing. Not like this, this secret hunt that none of the villagers seemed to notice, this chase that was so dark and unhappy. On TV, the masks and music were mysterious and thrilling, but here they felt sinister.

'David.' I cupped my hands around my mouth. My voice echoed through the untended square. The houses stared back with empty eyes.

No trace of the boys. Just an old Coke can in the middle of the road.

It was always the thrill of the chase for them. Those final exhilarating minutes when they closed the distance between us. It didn't happen often, but there'd been years when I won. When I got away, gasping for breath as I ran through the cottage gate while David watched from the trees.

But most of the time, they caught me. Tracked me through the village, the forest, even down by the lake. And they'd make me sit with them while they drank beer and decided on their trophy.

A dull, echoing scrabble that might have been boots against loose stone came from the other side of the rubble heap. My immediate reaction, deeply ingrained, was to run. I held my body rigid and refused to turn away.

'David.' My voice was loud and angry.

The sound of high-pitched male laughter echoed through the empty space. I moved towards the running footsteps. By the time I climbed the rubble heap, they were gone.

Not for the first time, I cursed my name.

Wren.

Might as well stick a sign on my back saying, '*Please hassle me on Stephen's Day.*' It was the only thing my mother had given me before she ran off with a man from God knows where when I was a few days old. Fallen in with a bad crowd, her judgement had been clouded by an addiction to heroin. She'd taken money and jewellery and left me behind.

I jumped down from the rubble and kicked the Coke can, watching it rattle away. Walking on, I heard deliberate noises from just beyond: scuffling, some rustling. But when I turned and called out, no one was there. Purple clouds hung low, making the near darkness tighter.

Talk to them, Maeve had said. When I left the cottage, flowery bag in hand, I was sure I would find the boys, hand over whiskey and cake, and reason with them. But that was before the darkness started settling in. That was before they started playing hide-and-seek.

A distant noise broke the silence. It could have been an echo of laughter or a cry from somewhere in the woods. A fox, I hoped.

The faint smell of cigarette smoke wafted over, and then it was gone.

In the village, they said that the woods weren't friendly after sundown. They said that bad things lurked in the forest, hidden behind the dank, fallen boughs. The good people of Kilshamble liked nothing more than blood and gore. We were fed gruesome stories with mother's milk.

We loved best the stories of the bloodthirsty tuanacul, the people of the forest, who would crush you in their embrace. Beautiful, strong tree men with roped muscles, who kissed you until you withered. Women with lips of petal, who lured you close and wrapped vine-like arms around you, choking the life out of you.

I believed these stories as much as I believed in aliens and ghosts, so barely at all. Except on those days when the light was violet and the wind blew wild and the forest and fields felt restless.

'Wran.'

He said my name the way they did in the old song.

My tormentor.

While I was fixed on imaginary dangers, the real trouble had nestled in close. He spoke my name as gentle as a caress.

Wran.

He almost sighed it.

I felt a hand on my shoulder.

'David.' Maybe I could pretend that this was a normal chat between neighbours. 'You have a good Christmas?'

He reached out his other hand and steered me to face him.

'Sure.' He leaned in, smiling. 'But I prefer Stephen's Day.'

He was good-looking, tall, with the back and shoulders of a rower. For the last three years, he'd attended a posh boarding school overseas. He had that easy confidence that came from wealth. From being told that he deserved the best and no one else mattered. But it was more than his rich-boy arrogance that made me despise him.

He was one of *them*.

If it wasn't so awful, it might almost be funny, David's instinct to target me. That somehow, blindly, in playing this game, he'd stumbled upon his true enemy. I was the Capulet to his Montague, the hot to his cold, the white queen to his black knight. I was the oil to his water, the bleach to his ammonia, the salt to his wound. We were everything that was anathema to the other.

I was augur to his judge.

We would never be friends.

David didn't know what I was, yet he sensed something was amiss. Something about me vexed him. Something he couldn't quite put his finger on. He didn't know that from that very first chase years ago he'd unwittingly recognised me. This game was blueprinted in hundreds of years of hostility between judges and augurs.

'About that,' I said. 'About the *game*.' I said the word carefully, hoping he couldn't read my fear. 'It's been enough.'

'Enough?'

'Yes. No more. This ends today.' Maeve's words sounded weak and watery when I said them.

'Yeah?' David seemed to have come closer without having moved at all. 'What are you going to do about it?' He took a drag of his cigarette before crushing it under his shoe. 'Run?'

'Nothing to chase if I'm not running.' If only it were that simple. Better to be a hunted wren than a sitting duck.

I pulled the whiskey from the flowery bag. But looking at David, something seemed different. He was cooler than usual. Smirkier. Behind stood his toadies, Brian and Ryan. All muscle and no brain.

'I'm calling a truce, David.' I handed over the whiskey.

David smiled, then examined the bottle.

'I'm after passing my exams,' he said. 'In the mood for a little celebration.'

He twisted the cap open.

'I'm getting a new tattoo to mark the occasion. Maybe a wren?' He paused as he held the bottle to his lips. 'In a cage. What do you think?'

He took a slug, and slowly screwed the cap back on. He held out his hand to shake mine. Reluctant, I placed a tentative hand in his large, rough one. He closed on my fingers and pulled me towards him, whispering in my ear with whiskey-flavoured breath, 'You better fly, little bird.'

Pulling away, I stood my ground, holding myself stiff so that my legs wouldn't just run, run, run, as everything inside was braced to do.

'Game over,' I said.

'Little Wren, the game is just beginning.' And there it was again, that cool assurance, which made me think that the stakes were somehow raised this year.

I searched his face to see if he'd finally figured out why he hated me so much. As I stared, I saw a flicker of distaste, his sense that something about me was just plain wrong.

But he didn't know.

He came closer. I didn't move. This close, I could feel the heat from his chest. He reached out a hand to clamp my wrist.

'Maybe we should see if your friend wants to play. What's her name again? The pretty blonde one?'

Nearly dropping the flowery bag, I pulled away. But damn it if I was going to let him bring Aisling into his crazy game. Even as a child playing in the woods or quarry, Aisling had never liked to run. No way would anyone do this to her.

I turned on my heel and fled.

'I'll give you to fifty,' David called after me.

I was out of reach by three. I could hear him counting slowly, as if we really were playing hide-and-seek and he was being especially patient.

It would be quicker to cut through the woods. But I wasn't the idiot girl in the movies who hurled herself into the arms of the axe-wielding maniac by going into dark places.

David and the others were right behind. They were gaining on me fast. Night would fall within the hour. I picked up my pace.

Turning the bend, I saw the boy standing in the road. Waiting. His clothes were dark and the way he stood, still and slightly hunched, made me think of the tuanacul. He was like a tree come to life, sorrowful and ancient. He turned his head, and it was Cillian, wearing a mummer's mask. The surprised, painted eyes stared at me. Of the four bullies, he was the one most likely to become a finger-severing psychopath once he graduated from terrorising girls. That boy put the kill into Cillian.

He began the slow whistling of the song I had come to hate: *The wran, the wran, the king of all birds.*

Of course they had split up. That's why David had given me such a generous start. Cillian was ahead, waiting. To the right was the McNally farm, Cillian's family. I couldn't go there. Behind me, the other boys were getting closer. I could hear their answering call, fast and raucous: '*Up with the kettle and down with the pan. Give us a penny to bury the wran.*'

So, like the idiot girl in the movies, the one who ends up hacked to bits, I ran into the woods.

MARY WATSON is from Cape Town and now lives on the West Coast of Ireland with her husband and three children. Highlights of her adult writing career include being awarded the Caine Prize for African Writing in Oxford in 2006, and being included on the Hay Festival's 2014 Africa39 list of influential writers from sub-Saharan Africa. *The Wickerlight* is her second book for young adults, following *The Wren Hunt.*